KNIGHT MOVE

Jennifer Landsbert

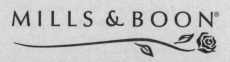

MILLS & BOON®

First published in Great Britain 2000
Harlequin Mills & Boon Limited,
Eton House, 18-24 Paradise Road, Richmond, Surrey TW9 1SR

© Jennifer Landsbert 2000

ISBN 0 263 82321 0

Set in Times Roman 10½ on 12¼ pt.
04-1000-74104

Printed and bound in Spain
by Litografia Rosés S.A., Barcelona

'*You* are the lady Hester?' he demanded.

'How dare you come here?' Hester retorted. 'Isn't it enough that you have insulted me on my own land, without coming into my house to insult me here too? Your very presence is intolerable to me, sir.'

'But, my lady—' Maud tried to interrupt.

'No, Maud. I will not have this miscreant or his accomplices in my house. There is no hospitality here for such as he.'

'But he is—' Maud tried to continue.

'I wouldn't care if he were the king himself,' Hester interrupted. 'After the way he treated me this afternoon, only an imbecile or an oaf would expect me to offer him hospitality. Which, sir, are you?'

His eyes locked with hers and seemed to pierce into her, but she was determined to see him off. The whole courtyard seemed to hold its breath as the stranger opened his lips to reply.

'I am Guy, Lord of Abbascombe,' he said. 'And you are my wife.'

Jennifer Landsbert lives in Brussels with her husband and their two young sons. She worked as a journalist before becoming a mother, and is now well-used to writing to the accompaniment of *Teletubbies*. She has always loved literature and history, so writing historical fiction is the perfect combination of the two, as well as the fulfilment of a lifelong ambition. Jennifer and her family enjoy exploring the Belgian countryside in search of settings for new novels.

Chapter One

'Hey, you! YOU! Get off my land NOW!' Hester yelled at the galloping horsemen, but the sharp March wind snatched at her words and carried them away, over the clifftops and out to sea.

The riders continued their game of chase, their huge hound leaping and cavorting, barking gleefully at the fun, as they tore across Hester's freshly ploughed field.

'Ruining everything,' she raged as she marched towards them, her clogs sticking in the mud as she stomped through the thick, wet soil. Suddenly, one of them, a large, muscular man on a black steed, swooped round towards her, his thick, dark hair swept out behind him by the speed of his horse.

'Get out of the way, woman,' he shouted, as he thundered past her, his horse's great hooves throwing up a cloud of muck, showering Hester from head to foot.

'*Ugh!*' she spat, furiously wiping the mud from her eyes. The outrage! This scruffy devil, an intruder on her land, destroying the weeks of hard labour she and her men had put into preparing the soil, and he was treating her as if she were the trespasser.

'Who do you think you are?' she yelled back.

This time he heard her. He reined in his horse hard, and turned to stare at her.

Hester saw the scar first, its deep, crescent shape puckering the skin from eyebrow to cheekbone. Then she noticed the black, menacing eyes glaring at her through the tousled locks of hair, which the wind had swept across his forehead. His lips, surrounded by thick stubble, sneered down at her.

'You stupid wench!' he shouted, as he approached. 'You could have been trampled to death. If I hadn't seen you in time, you'd be lying senseless in the mud by now. What the devil did you think you were doing?'

'Trying to save the crop from your idiot games, you fool.' The bold words tumbled from her mouth in spite of his terrifying appearance. Everything about him was dark: his horse, his hair, his eyes, even the leather of his coat and breeches. And no doubt his heart too, thought Hester. He'd kill me as soon as look at me.

But she refused to let fear master her. She was determined to get this wretch off her land and away from her people. Somehow she could always find the courage to face danger for their sakes.

Holding her head high, she fixed her eyes on him and felt the force of his glare burning into her. She delved deep into her reserves of courage and found the words: 'I want you off this land before I—' but her command was interrupted by the arrival of the other five riders.

'Friend of yours?' one of them called out with an insinuating smirk.

'Hardly,' returned the dark rider. 'She seems to be ordering me off the land.'

There was a chorus of laughter around her as the six mounted men closed in.

'Ordering you off the land? That's rich,' said another in an ugly tone and with a face as repellent as his friend's.

Hester could see the swords hanging in scabbards by their sides, their handles glinting against the leather of their tunics, a warning in the thin, spring sunshine. But she must not let them see her fear. The more they tried to scare her, the braver she must appear.

She flung back the mud-spattered blonde curls which had escaped from her plaits. 'Yes, I was ordering you off this land,' she pronounced majestically, her turquoise eyes flashing. 'You will leave Abbascombe immediately, without causing any further damage to the crops.'

But instead of obedience, her commands were met with howls of derisory laughter. How dared they? How dared they treat her, the Lady of Abbascombe, with such disrespect? Hester felt herself blushing crimson with fury, her face burning with indignation, and heard the men laughing even louder as they sat high on their steeds, looking down on her as if she were an entertainment.

'You must forgive my friends' mirth, my dear lady,' the dark one said, his words heavy with scorn. 'We have returned to England after many years overseas and the latest fashions are new to us, particularly this fashion among fine ladies for adorning their garments with mud.'

His friends threw their heads back, guffawing raucously at her expense. Of course, he was right that she was covered with mud—mostly his fault, she thought angrily. But she had to admit to herself that, with her hair awry, her workaday woollen skirts hitched up to allow her freedom of movement and wooden clogs on her feet, she wasn't looking her most ladylike. Still, that was no excuse for his appalling rudeness.

'At least this mud will wash off,' Hester flung at him. 'But no amount of cleaning would wash away your ill breeding, sir.'

His eyebrows arched with surprise, elongating the scar, which tugged threateningly at the corner of his eye. Time seemed to freeze as Hester waited for his reaction, regretting that her angry quip had been unwise. There was no laughter now; the only sound was the wind whipping off the sea. Suddenly she felt how vulnerable she was; alone here in the field with six armed strangers; rough-looking men, perhaps desperate outlaws who might do anything. She longed to look around, to scan the horizon for a friendly form, to gauge exactly how far from help she was, but did not dare show such a sign of weakness.

His eyes locked into her and Hester steeled herself to meet his fearsome gaze, clenching her fingernails into the palms of her hands to stop herself from shaking.

'The vixen knows how to scratch,' he said, addressing his friends, but glaring straight at her. The depth of his voice filled her with dread. Then he glanced round at his cronies, his dark eyebrows arched as if he were seeking their opinions. They looked at each other for a moment, Hester's heart pounding with suspense. Then suddenly all six of them dissolved into laughter.

She stared at them. Being laughed at was almost worse than being scared. How dared they treat her with such insolence? How dared they not take her seriously?

'Yes, I do know how to scratch,' she shouted above their mirth, determined to gain the upper hand. 'And if you don't leave immediately, you'll feel the pain of it.' Hester was used to being obeyed and expected her words to command respect at the least. But instead this impudent rogue and his henchmen just laughed all the more. Hester stared at them, fuming with rage. She almost wished he had attacked her rather than laughing at her. At least then she could have defended herself with dignity, instead of standing here humiliated, the object of their scornful jokes.

'I'm so scared,' he mocked, fixing her again with his dark eyes, but this time they were twinkling with mirth. Beneath his tangled hair, his skin was dark too, tanned by long days in fierce sun, and his lips, twitching with amusement, showed a sensuous pleasure in teasing her. He was enjoying this, insulting her in front of his loutish companions. It was absolutely intolerable that a bunch of dirty, scruffy outlaws should speak to her in this way—and on her own land too.

'Now, look here,' Hester began, pulling herself up to her full height. 'I will not stand for this—'

At that moment the huge hound came speeding up to the group, its long limbs moving so swiftly that,

before Hester had seen it, it had already launched itself at her. She felt the shock of pain as a great thud
on her chest knocked all the wind from her lungs and
sent her flying backwards. The ground seemed to rise
up and smash against the whole length of her helpless
body, surrounding her in a blinding shower of mud
and muck. She lay, too dazed to speak, the hound's
paws on her chest forbidding all movement, as it
arched over her, growling menacingly, baring its
fangs at her terrified face, saliva dribbling from its
snarling jaws.

'Get this hell-hound off me,' she managed to wail.
But the dark rider was already off his horse, his tall,
powerful body striding towards her.

'Amir!' he called in a masterful tone. 'Amir!
Leave!' Instantly the dog was off her and instead he
was there, leaning over her, his broad chest blocking
out the sky as he extended his hand to help her. She
reached out to grasp it and realised she was trembling.

'How dare you—how dare you—' she stammered,
sitting up quickly and doing her best to pull her heavy
skirts free of the cloying mud.

'My lady, allow me to help you to your feet,' he
said with infuriating mock gentility.

'That blasted dog is dangerous,' Hester scolded, in
an attempt to regain her shattered dignity.

'My dog is trained to protect me. She obviously
saw you as a threat. Your manners are very aggressive
for a woman.'

'A lady,' Hester snapped back, correcting him, as
she placed her hand in his.

'Oh, yes, of course, a lady. Please forgive me,' he
replied, as if humouring her. She saw amusement

flicker across his mouth as he tried to suppress a smirk. 'Now, what was it you were saying? That you wouldn't stand for something?'

The arrogant wretch! Still making fun of her for the amusement of his cronies.

'You're too kind,' Hester replied with a deceptive smile, curling her fingers around his hand. She was determined to make him regret having mocked her and now she saw the way to teach him a lesson, the only sort of lesson an ill-bred wretch like this would understand. She gripped his hand tightly as if to accept his offer of help, then with one swift movement she yanked her arm back with all her might, pulling his heavily muscled body off balance.

'Serves you right!' she shouted as he swayed towards the ground. But in his struggle to regain a foothold, he struck out with his strong arms, catching her on the shoulder and sending her slamming back into the mud a split second before he toppled after her.

Hester gasped, fighting for breath, trapped between the cold, squelching mud and his hot, heavy body, pressing against the full length of her, hard and muscular, pinning her to the ground. 'Get off me, you brute.'

'Brute, am I?' he snarled in her ear, his breath sending shivers down her spine. She could feel the firm power of his muscles as his chest pressed against her breasts, and the musky scent of his body filled her senses, leaving her weak beneath him, her blood pulsing through her veins so violently, she was sure he must feel it too. 'I came to help you up and you thank me with a mud-bath. And you call *me* ill bred,' he rasped into her ear, the stubble of his chin and cheeks scratching painfully against her soft skin. 'You have a lot to learn about manners, woman.'

'Have you no idea how to treat a lady?' she protested, fighting to free herself from his strong arms, which were locked around her like a cage.

'I know all about treating women,' he breathed against her cheek, the warmth of his lips seeming to burn into her as he whispered against her skin. 'Would you like me to treat you?'

Her outrage brought sudden strength to Hester and in an instant she had pulled her arm free and lashed out at him, but he caught her hand just as it was about to strike his face. His grip was like iron as he shot a look down into her face.

'Wildcat!' he exclaimed. 'Is this how you treat a returning hero?'

'Hero?' she spat back. Who did he think he was, this ill-mannered lout? 'Behave like a gentleman and let go of my hand.'

'Only if you promise not to use it against me,' he said, heaving himself out of the mud and on to his feet.

'I'll use it against anyone who insults me.'

'See what a gentleman I am?' he asked, ignoring her remark and surprising Hester by offering his hand once again to help her up. She was beached in the mud, her skirts weighed down by clods of muck, but there was no way she would touch his loathsome hand again.

'I'd rather lie all day in the mud,' she scowled up at him as she struggled on to her hands and knees.

'You're obviously more used to it than I,' he sneered.

Hester, speechless with indignation, could only watch as he whistled for his horse. The lithe creature trotted over immediately and stood completely still as his master sprang athletically into the saddle. However disgusting he was as a person, there was no denying he was a very fine rider, so at ease in the saddle that he and his horse seemed to move as one.

'For the entertainment you have afforded us,' he said without looking at her, flinging a handful of coins into the mud beside her. 'Farewell, my lady wench,' he shouted behind him as he sped away, followed by the other five, the hound bounding at his side.

'How dare you insult me with your money? How dare you call me ''wench''? How dare you insult the Lady of Abbascombe?' she yelled after him, finding her voice again at last, but he was already far away. 'Wretched, damned lout,' she cursed to herself, venting her rage and frustration on the cold sea-wind. 'He'd better not show his face here ever again. I'll set every man in Abbascombe on to him if he does.'

As she struggled to her feet, trying to flick some of the mud off her skirt, Hester caught sight of William, her loyal farm bailiff, and a group of villagers running towards her. They were racing across the fields, eager to help; too late to be of use, but, alas, not too late to see their lady covered from head to foot in mud, as if she were a hog in its sty.

Hester would have preferred to be left to slink home in dirty but dignified solitude, but now there was no choice. She shook her skirts energetically and wiped at her face, although she suspected her efforts were covering her skin in more smears instead of cleaning it. Then she stood up straight to face her people, determined to behave nobly, however ignoble she might look.

'My lady, are you all right? Did those men hurt you?' asked William, all concern for her as ever.

'I'm not hurt at all, just very muddy,' Hester reassured him, putting her hand up to pat her plaits into place and finding a great lump of muck sticking to her hair.

'We saw them from Clifftop Field and came as fast as we could.'

'It's all right, they've gone now. Never to return, I hope.'

'They looked like crusaders, my lady,' said Guthrum, a giant of a man, the largest and strongest in the village, who worked regularly in her fields, as well as cultivating his own plot of land.

'You could well be right, Guthrum. They were certainly brutish enough.'

Crusaders returning from the Holy Land—yes, of course. The dark one had said they had been abroad for years. Now that the war was over and there were no more Saracens to kill, the adventurers were back. A group had passed through the village last year, demanding food and shelter. One had tried to seduce one of the village girls and there had been trouble. And now six more of them were riding roughshod over her land, destroying everything in their path. She'd had bitter experience of their type in the past— a long time ago, when the war began ten years earlier—but she hadn't forgotten, could never forget the way that brute had treated her when he left for the war.

Suddenly all the old memories came flooding back,

memories of that other crusader, long lost, thank God, no doubt dead and buried in some Saracen land years ago and good riddance. But the wound still throbbed with pain when memories touched it.

'Right,' she said to the men, shaking her head to try to clear the unwelcome thoughts and trying to ignore the muddy flecks which flew from her hair. 'Let's forget about them and finish off the sowing. A little more mud will make no difference to me. Eadric,' she said, calling to Guthrum's son, a trustworthy boy who was working with the men for the first time this year, sufficiently strong now to help with the heavy work of guiding the oxen and plough. 'Eadric, those men dropped some coins. Why don't you gather them up and share them amongst the children who are scaring the crows? Keep one for yourself.'

'Oh, yes, my lady,' said Eadric as he dashed off, his round face alight with the glee of being entrusted with an important task. Hester wouldn't touch the money herself, but her people would be glad of a little extra.

These days there was a feeling of optimism in the village and on the smallholdings of Abbascombe, but the bad days were not so long ago that anyone could feel complacent. And some of those days had been very bad. They'd had hard years, which had tested them all, but they'd pulled through—well, most of them had. Wet summers and harsh winters, poor harvests and high taxes—taxes to pay for those blasted crusades, of course. War games for the lords, while the ladies stayed at home and struggled to keep body and soul together on the land.

Hester followed her workmen back up to Clifftop Field. This was the furthest field of Abbascombe Manor, on the very edge of the cliffs. It was Hester's favourite, with the sea crashing on to the rocks hundreds of feet below, the waves beating a constant rhythm even on the balmiest of summer days.

While the men had been gone, the women and children had been doing good work scaring away the birds, throwing stones or whooping every time a crow or a gull swooped down to peck at the freshly sown corn.

'Right, William, how are we getting on?' Hester asked, businesslike now, though her cheek was still stinging from the scratches of that miscreant's bristles, and her hands were not quite steady yet.

'Not too bad, my lady. We'll have to work late, but I reckon we'll be able to finish tonight.'

'We'll have to. If Breda is right, the rains will start tomorrow and there'll be no more ploughing after that.' Breda, the wise woman, could almost always be trusted to predict the weather. On sleepless nights, Hester had sometimes watched unseen as the mysterious old woman limped out of the village before dawn to judge the formation of the clouds, the scent in the air, the way the frogs were swimming... Whatever it was she relied on for her information, it seemed to work.

According to Breda, the next week was to be filled with rain. Hester thought of the six riders and hoped they had a long journey ahead of them...a long, wet journey, very wet and cold, with no one foolish enough to offer them shelter, not even in a barn.

'Good to get a bit of water on the new-sown corn

though,' William was saying as Hester's thoughts veered back to the present.

She nodded her agreement. She and William always agreed. They had been working closely together ever since the old lord had died. She'd had her doubts about Benoc, the previous bailiff, who'd always had a tendency to callousness when dealing with the labourers. As soon as she had become sole mistress of Abbascombe, she had begun to watch him carefully and when she caught him selling her grain to corn factors in Wareham and pocketing the proceeds, she had given him his marching orders and appointed William.

Young and keen, William was a local boy who knew the manor inside out. He knew exactly which crop would grow best in which corner of the soil, the tiny variations from field to field, the way the sweep of the wind differed from one clifftop to another. Most importantly, she knew he loved Abbascombe almost as much as she did and that she could always trust him to do what was best for the manor.

Hester looked around at her beloved land, at the men guiding the plough through the ground behind the great, plodding oxen; at the furrows in their wake, like little waves on a fresh day at sea; at the seagulls soaring overhead. To her left, the women were sifting the grain, ready to start sowing on the freshly turned earth.

'My lady, my lady,' called Nona, one of Eadric's little sisters, her whole body suffused with excitement, her brown plaits bouncing on her shoulders as she ran up to Hester. 'I've got the corn dolly. Look! Here she is.'

'Are you looking after her?' asked Hester, stooping to greet the tiny bright-eyed child, whose clothes and clogs were caked with almost as much mud as her own. No one here minds my muddiness, Hester thought as she examined the corn dolly with Nona. I'm not ashamed of being covered in the soil of Abbascombe or of working in the fields with my people. Anyone who thinks that makes me less of a lady is a fool.

'Do you know the story of the corn dolly?' Hester asked.

Nona beamed a gap-toothed smile, 'She goes to sleep in the winter, then she wakes up when we plant the corn.'

'That's right. Every summer we make a dolly from the last handful of corn that we cut, so that the spirit of the corn can rest all winter whilst it's too cold out in the fields. Then in the spring we put the dolly back in Clifftop Field so that she can enjoy the good weather and make the corn grow, so that we can eat bread. Are you going to put her back in the earth?'

Nona nodded enthusiastically. 'Let's go and find a good place to put her,' said Hester, taking the little girl's hand and leading her across the field to the sowers.

No one knew how many corn dollies had been woven from Abbascombe corn, but it must have been a great number, Hester thought. And she would do all she could to ensure that there would be a great many more, so that Nona and her children, and her children's children, could go on living and loving on this beautiful land.

* * *

All through that fine afternoon Hester worked alongside the villagers, helping to sift and sow, and scare the birds, even helping to lift the plough when it stuck on a boulder beneath the surface of the soil. This was her land and these were her people and there was nothing she would not do for them.

For them she would be brave and bold, though deep inside her, well hidden from view, there still shivered the tiny, timid twelve-year-old girl who had first set eyes on Abbascombe a decade ago. Her mind flitted back to that cold, winter's day when she had first seen the manor, covered in snow. She saw again the old lord, who had seemed so frosty at first, but who, in the pinch of his own sorrows, had warmed to her, almost stilling that sharp, throbbing pain left by the death of her parents.

'Right! That's it!' William shouted triumphantly as the last grain of corn slipped into the earth and the corn dolly was tucked into her warm, soil bed by Nona. 'Well done, everyone. That was a hard day's work well done.'

'And now you can all come back for a good meal,' Hester added.

They tramped towards the house, weary but pleased, with the night closing in quickly around them. They had worked a long day, urged on by the prediction of rain, so that by the time they reached the gates it was almost dark.

As soon as she entered the courtyard, Hester realised something was wrong. Something in the air sent warning signals shooting through her brain. Her eyes sped rapidly from wall to wall, her senses sharpened by some instinct deep inside her which whispered danger.

Two of the stable-lads emerged from the darkness, carrying torches, which they stuck into brackets on the wall to light their way. Their flames sent flickering orange light dancing through the shadows all around the courtyard. It was then that Hester saw the horses standing at the trough. Strange horses. Six of them. And then she saw him, his broad, strong back, dark like a shadow, turned towards her, his black, matted hair trailing onto his shoulders.

Just the sight of his back sent her heart leaping into her mouth and all the rage and fury of the afternoon filled every vein in her body, blotting out all around her as she stared at him through the half-light. His leather-clad shoulders looked even broader and more threatening than they had in the field. And he had an infuriatingly arrogant air as he stood there, oblivious to her, without so much as a by-your-leave, his long, leather-clad legs astride, his boots firmly planted in her courtyard, with such nonchalance they seemed to suggest that the very ground belonged to him.

Somewhere, as if from a long way off, she could hear her old maid, Maud, calling to her, 'My lady! My lady!' Hester dragged her eyes away from the intruder and saw that Maud was trotting towards her across the courtyard, as fast as her fat, old body would move. 'My lady Hester!'

At the sound of her name, the dark rider wheeled round with a speed and agility which signalled the power of his body. Once again she was looking into his loathsome, churlish face. In the shadowy gloom, he appeared darker and craggier than before, the stubble of his beard seeming to veil his face in darkness.

His eyes flashed out of the shadows, and Hester felt herself flinch as they stirred in her some deep, best-forgotten memory. In an instant it was gone, as those eyes skimmed over her without pausing for recognition, as he scanned the group of workers returning from the field, passing from face to face, as if he were searching for someone in particular, for a set of familiar features.

'Oh, my lady, you'll never guess!' Maud was panting as she reached Hester and began tugging at her sleeve. But at that moment Hester's eyes locked with the eyes of the dark rider as he fixed her with a stare of disbelief, his lips parted and his face ablaze.

'You!' he breathed. The word was meant for himself. But time suddenly seemed to have stopped in the courtyard, as if everyone there sensed the tension between the two of them, and his deep whisper echoed in the silence.

Hester stared back, hostility furrowing her brow. She had nothing to fear now, surrounded by her own people in the courtyard of her own manor house. Now he would be taught to regret having treated the Lady of Abbascombe with such disrespect. All around her she could feel the stillness, as if every person there were waiting for her to give the order to attack.

She held the caitiff in her sight, meaning to give him a sense of her power this time.

'*You* are the lady Hester?' he demanded, splitting the silence with his commanding voice, his eyes searching her up and down in a most insulting manner.

'How dare you come here?' Hester retorted. 'Isn't it enough that you have insulted me on my own land, without coming into my house to insult me here too? Your very presence is intolerable to me, sir.'

'But, my lady—' Maud tried to interrupt.

'No, Maud. I will not have this miscreant or his accomplices in my house. There is no hospitality here for such as he.'

'But he is—' Maud tried to continue.

'I wouldn't care if he were the king himself,' Hester interrupted. 'After the way he treated me this afternoon, only an imbecile or an oaf would expect me to offer him hospitality. Which, sir, are you?'

His eyes locked with hers and seemed to pierce into her, but she was determined to see him off.

'Well, sir?'

The whole courtyard seemed to hold its breath as the stranger opened his lips to reply.

'I am Guy, Lord of Abbascombe,' he said. 'And you are my wife.'

Chapter Two

For a moment the world was frozen as they stared at each other. Behind her, Hester could feel the stunned silence of William and the men.

'My husband's dead,' she managed to say at last, her words falling like stones into the stillness of the courtyard.

'Who told you that?' he challenged, fixing her with his dark stare.

Hester hesitated, her eyes mesmerised by his face, scanning its contours for clues, searching for some resemblance between this dirty, scarred stranger and the handsome youth who had stood beside her ten years earlier, making his vows to the priest. 'I—no one. I thought…' she trailed off.

'You hoped,' he said, finishing her sentence for her. He tossed back his hair with a sardonic, humourless smile that shaped his lips but did not touch the rest of his face. 'I've been away protecting the Holy Land from the Saracen and you've been wishing me dead.'

Hester tried to measure him with her eyes. Was he her husband? All those years ago she had spent only

minutes in his presence, and even then, timid and bewildered, she had hardly dared to look her bridegroom in the face. He had seemed so tall, so fine, so
grown-up, but she had been only a small, frightened
girl, newly orphaned, who had been passed from pil-
lar to post for the sake of the fortune she had inherited.

The memories of those terrible days came storming
back. The fever which had killed her parents within
two days of each other. The arrival of the king's men
to wrench her away from everything she knew. The
news that the king had accepted the Lord of
Abbascombe's offer to stake finances for the crusades
in return for Lady Hester Rainald, whose fortune
made her a fitting bride for his son, even though
Hester was only twelve and his son, Guy, was twenty.
The memories charged through her head until she
thought it would explode.

'How do I know you're who you say you are?'
Hester said out loud, her voice bold and challenging,
hoping to break the spell of the past. Maybe he was
just a chancer trying his luck, a vagabond who had
happened to hear the story of the missing lord of
Abbascombe. Perhaps he would have no proof at all.

'Don't you know your own husband, lady?' leered
one of the five cronies, who had gathered in the
gloom behind the dark rider. 'My God, you have been
away a long time, Guy.'

The name shot through her. Guy. But, of course,
his accomplice would call him that. It was just part
of the plot. It proved nothing.

'Prove that you're Guy Beauvoisin,' she demanded.

'Prove it!' he repeated, fixing her with a menacing

glint. 'I come back to my own home, my land, and you ask me to prove that I am Guy Beauvoisin. You take an awful lot upon yourself, my lady.'

'I've had to,' Hester snapped. 'There's been no one else to do it.'

He glared back at her. His eyes, full of anger, flashed at her like daggers and stirred another memory in Hester's breast. Suddenly she was back ten years ago, standing in the hall, watching as her new husband confronted his father. Both men with their broad shoulders flung back and their eyes ablaze, the father heavier and a little shorter, the son fired by rage, rebellious indignation spilling from his lips as he cursed the marriage which had just been solemnised. 'I've carried out your will to the letter, sire,' he was saying. 'I have married this pathetic, orphaned child. I have done what you required to save your precious Abbascombe from ruin. And now I consider myself free to do as I choose. I intend to leave with the crusade immediately. I will not remain here to continue this mockery of a marriage.'

The painful scene played itself in her memory. Hester tried to blot it out, attempting to concentrate all her attention on the here and now. She must keep her wits about her, watch this man's every move in case he gave himself away as an impostor. He was hesitating now.

'Go on,' she prompted, pushing her advantage.

'You're serious?' he questioned. 'You really don't recognise me?' Hester shook her head. He sighed and Hester tried to read his thoughts, but his face was inscrutable. 'I am Guy Beauvoisin,' he began, 'direct descendent of Guy the Harrier, who fought with

William the Conqueror and was given Abbascombe
for his services to the king.'

'Anyone could have found that out,' she scoffed,
then fixed him with a challenging stare. 'Continue, if
you still wish to try.'

He took up the gauntlet. 'You are the Lady Hester,
only child of Sir Richard Rainald. You were a twelve-
year-old orphan, a ward of the king, when my father
chose you to be my wife.'

'That is widely known. You've still proved nothing.'

'You want something that only you and your husband could know?' he asked, his voice carrying a hint
of danger which made Hester clench her fists involuntarily, until she felt her fingernails grazing into the
flesh of her hands.

'Of course,' she breathed, feigning insouciance, but
feeling herself cornered. Her heart pounded with the
rhythm of the doubts in her mind. Was he her husband? Don't let it be him, she wished. Please let him
be dead.

Suddenly he was advancing towards her, his long,
muscular legs covering the ground in an instant.
Hester shied back instinctively. The air between them
seemed to crackle with his presence.

'You want me to tell you?' he demanded and the
question sounded like a threat.

At that moment there was nothing she wanted more
than to keep him at a distance, as far from her as
possible. The memory of his closeness that afternoon
sent those same shivers coursing up and down her
spine. She searched her mind desperately for a way
to avoid his proximity, but before she could find one,

he was there at her side, his hand gripping her elbow
so tightly it made her flinch, as he bent his lips to her
ear. He was so close she felt again the tips of his
bristles grazing her cheek as he rasped, 'After our
vows, when we were truly man and wife, I looked
deep into your eyes and said, ''Don't look so scared,
little girl, I shall never force you to fill the office of
a wife. You may go back to your dolls.'' '

A dart of pain shot through Hester at the memory
of those words of rejection. Suddenly she was back
ten years ago, that frightened girl, fighting back the
tears when she realised that this new husband felt only
contempt for her. It had been exactly as he said, the
same words, the same voice. She pulled away from
him and again found herself looking into those eyes.
They were the same too, in spite of the way the scar
pulled at his brow, in spite of the changes the years
had wrought on the rest of his face. She had to admit
to herself now that she recognised his eyes.

But she was no longer the terrified little girl whom
he could buffet with his scorn. She was strong now,
strong enough for the whole of Abbascombe, and she
would not be bullied. Hester summoned up her
strength and fixed him hard with her eyes. As she
glared at him, she thought she detected some effort
in his face as he returned her stare.

'My lord,' she said, curtsying low, her muddy skirts
sweeping the cobbled floor of the courtyard. 'You are
welcome to Abbascombe. We have long awaited your
return. Speak your will and it shall be done. Your
humble wife asks your bidding.' The words came out
somehow, however unwilling she was to speak them.

There was a clamour all around her as the specta-

tors, who had held their peace for so long, suddenly
spoke all at once. Hester felt rather than heard their
voices. All her attention was fixed on him, the so-
called husband she had never expected to see again
as long as she lived. He was back and she knew he
was trouble.

As the villagers swarmed around him, eager for a
good look at their fabled missing lord, greeting him
with cheers and questions, Hester stepped back and
took a long, hard look at him. Yes, she could see the
resemblance now, even though he was smiling as he
shook hands and returned good wishes. It was a
broad, warm smile, taking the place of the scowls,
fury and mockery which were the only expressions
she had ever seen on his face until now.

Hester could not share in this joyful scene. She felt
numb and terribly alone. Mechanically, she turned
away and allowed her feet to lead her towards the
house. Suddenly she felt like a stranger in her own
home, superfluous, unwanted. The unfairness of it all
stabbed at her chest. After all, he was the one who
had deserted them. She was the one who had kept
Abbascombe alive during the long years of the crusade. How could they welcome him back after the
way he had betrayed them all?

In a daze she wandered into the kitchen. She often
came here first after a cold day out of doors. The
warmth and delicious smells suffusing the little stone
outbuilding, separated from the main house for fear
of fire, always seemed so cheering and welcoming.
Today, though, the normal busyness had become a
frenzy of activity. Fritha, the cook, had been expecting to be feeding a hall full of hungry labourers after

their day's work in the fields—and suddenly she was faced with the return of her long-lost lord. Normally level-headed, it was no wonder she was a little flustered by the news.

'Oh, isn't it wonderful, my lady? Maud says he's just like his father was at that age.'

'Does she? Of course, I can't judge.'

'Oh, my lady. And to think we all believed he might be dead, begging your ladyship's pardon. But after all those years and not a word.'

'That's quite all right, Fritha, many crusaders will never return from the Holy Land. It was always possible that my lord might have been one of them.'

Oh, why, why did he have to come back and spoil everything she'd worked for? Just when the worst was over and she could start to enjoy life at Abbascombe, her Abbascombe. No, not hers anymore. His Abbascombe. She'd have to get used to that. By law, everything belonged to him. Even she herself belonged to him, Hester thought with a shudder.

How could anyone call that justice? He didn't care for her or for the manor. He'd made that clear when he deserted them both. He had left her behind to struggle and strive, to dirty her hands with the Abbascombe soil, to cover them with blisters and chilblains from hard work out of doors in all weathers. She had earned Abbascombe. By rights it was hers. And if he thought she would give it up easily, he had a lesson to learn.

No doubt he intended to lock her up indoors with tapestry work and harp-playing, while he strutted about the fields—her fields. Of course, he'd be sure to make a mess of everything again. He would leave misery and destruction in his wake as he had ten years before.

'My lady? Which would you like, my lady?' Fritha was asking, looking into Hester's face with a frown.

'Which?' Hester repeated absent-mindedly.

'The venison or the beef?' Fritha suggested, her tone making it clear this wasn't the first time of asking. Hester looked blank.

'For my lord's dinner tonight. Of course, it will mean dinner will have to be served later than usual. If only he had arrived earlier in the day, I could have prepared something really special.' Fritha had obviously been running through all the options, while Hester's mind had been churning.

'But we're saving those meats for Easter, aren't we?' Hester returned.

'But, my lady—'

'No, no, don't break into the stores, Fritha. That bruet we had last night was perfectly good. Haven't we got any of that left?'

'There's plenty left, my lady, that's what I'm giving all the villagers. But you can't give that to his lordship on his homecoming. It's not good enough for him.'

'We looked on rabbit bruet as a great treat three years ago, have you forgotten?'

'I know, my lady, but—'

'If it's good enough for all of us, it's good enough for him. The bruet will be fine, Fritha.'

'But—'

'I will not break into our stores for him and his uncouth friends,' Hester snapped, her sharp, angry words making Fritha jump. 'Rabbit bruet is more than they deserve.' As soon as the words were out of her mouth, she knew she shouldn't have said them, but she couldn't help herself.

Feeling Fritha's surprise heavy in the air, Hester turned her back and strode out of the kitchen, giving the cook no more chances to cajole or argue. She paused for a moment in the covered walkway which linked the kitchen to the hall. There was the hiss-hiss of whispering, which had begun as soon as they believed her to be out of earshot.

She couldn't make out the words, but she guessed the purport. What's wrong with her? Not pleased? Didn't she want her husband back? A man other women would do anything to please—and no doubt many had. But she wouldn't step an inch out of her way to please him. He could go back to his paramours in the Holy Land for all she cared. In fact, she wished he would.

Hester continued on, along the passageway, through the buttery and into the great hall. She paused at the entrance, glancing up at the timber beams arching high above. The hall was deserted, but soon the dark rider would be here, presiding over his homecoming feast. Hester marched purposefully across the rush-strewn floor. As her feet fell on the soft rushes the scent of herbs wafted up. As she had ordered the day before, new rushes had been laid with sweet-smelling herbs from the garden. He would find nothing slovenly in her housekeeping. A thought flitted across her mind: she hoped he would not think the new rushes had been laid in his honour.

Of course, the perfect lady would have ordered the best of everything and hidden her feelings, Hester thought as she strode up the stone staircase, which rose at one end of the hall, leading up to her solar and the other chambers on the first floor. She knew full well that she wasn't anyone's idea of the perfect courtly lady—these years of coping alone had seen to that. Why should she pretend to be one of those soft, pliant creatures, when the world had forced her to become as hard as the Abbascombe rocks in order to survive the buffets of the stormy years?

What did she care if everyone knew the truth? Why should she pretend to be something she wasn't? And why should she pretend to care for him after the way he had treated her?

Hester needed to be alone and the only place was her solar. With its sparse furnishings and magnificent view down over the fields to the sea, it was the only refuge now from all the flurry and excitement of this hollow homecoming.

As she reached the solar, though, she stopped short on the landing outside. The door was open and inside two of the girls were hurriedly changing the bedlinen, while two more were attempting to attach to the wall a moth-eaten old tapestry which she'd banished years before. It was a picture called *The Betrothal* and showed a knight kneeling to a lady in a garden of roses. Its sentimentality annoyed Hester intensely. In the middle of all this activity, Maud was behaving like a whirlwind, pulling old gowns from the chest, holding them up for examination, then discarding them on the floor.

'What on earth is going on?' Hester demanded, flinging back her plaits with a toss of the head, which reminded her that her hair was still caked with dried mud.

'Oh!' Maud jumped, turning to see her mistress. 'We're just doing a little housework, my lady—'

'Was this your idea?' Hester interrupted, nodding at the tapestry, which was now hanging limply by one corner since the girls had let it go in their shock at seeing their mistress. It was obvious that Maud had intended to do all this without her knowledge and to present her with a *fait accompli*.

There was a nervous silence. 'Well?' Hester prompted.

'I thought it would make the room a bit prettier,' Maud suggested, her head on one side. 'A bit of colour. And I'm just trying to find a pretty gown for you to wear tonight. And the girls…' she petered out, seeing the rage on her mistress's face.

'The girls are changing the bedclothes,' Hester finished for her.

'Well, yes, my lady.' Maud smirked. 'They're putting on the bridal linen. See how beautiful it is. See the embroidery and the fine stitching. It was worked by his lordship's mother years ago, but it's still beautiful. I've kept it wrapped with lavender and…'

Hester felt herself blush red hot. One of the girls giggled, but Hester didn't trust herself to look her in the face and scold her. All she could do was stare at the bed. Her bed. And now everyone was expecting her to share it with him. That rude, dirty stranger who'd come to steal everything she loved in the world, the very things closest to her heart. And, as if that weren't enough, he would take her body too.

Body and soul. Body and soul. The words pulsed through her mind. He owns me body and soul.

'Get out…and take that stupid thing with you,' she commanded, flinging her arm towards the tapestry.

'But, my lady—' Maud began.

'But, my lady, but, my lady! That's all I hear from everyone. Don't torture me by talking your rubbish.'

'But it's such a great day, God be praised. Our lord is back. Your husband…'

'Leave me,' Hester insisted and held the door wide for the girls and Maud to exit, then slammed it behind the old woman and surveyed the room. The tapestry still hung there limply.

The whole place had gone mad—and for what? For the return of a man who had deserted them all when they had needed him most. They were simpletons to welcome him back. Didn't they realise he would be off again in a trice whenever it suited him?

She spun around to the tiny window slit in the wall. A little moonshine glowed through it, an invitation to her eyes. There were her fields, lying beneath the vast night sky, stars twinkling above them, and the sea beyond, huge and dark. She could hear it crashing relentlessly against the cliffs. Hester stared out into the inky gloom and felt emotion pricking at the backs of her eyes.

'I won't cry,' she whispered to herself. 'No matter what he does to me, what he takes from me, I won't cry.'

It was the vow she had repeated to herself for the past ten years, ever since the fever had taken her parents. Ever since then, however dire life had been, sheer willpower had prevented her from shedding a single tear.

She felt as alone now as she had done then, coming to this strange place, full of strange faces. She knew them all now, but none of them understood her feelings, none could understand her horror of this thief-husband come to wrench away from her all she valued.

But moping wasn't the answer—that would solve nothing. What she needed was action, a plan. Hester scratched at her head, trying to stimulate her thoughts. No plans jumped to mind, but she did realise that she was still covered with mud, now dried and flaking. In fact, it was making her scalp itch and her clothes stiff. She definitely needed to change her clothes and have a really good wash, and, yes, Maud had thought of everything. As well as a fire blazing in the hearth, there was a large bowl of hot water in the corner behind the screen.

Glad to be doing something, Hester pulled off her clothes quickly, dropping them in a muddy heap on the floor. The water was warm and smelled of lavender. There was something calming about standing in her warm bedroom washing herself after the shocks and humiliations of the day.

She picked up the cake of soap. It was one of the few luxuries she allowed herself, quite different from the caustic soap they boiled up in the kitchen using lard, which stank to high heaven as it bubbled away. This soap was fine and hard, pale brown in colour, made in Spain using oil of olives and smelling pleasantly of that distant land. Hester had bought a stock of it at last year's fair in Wareham on Maud's strict orders, else the price would definitely have deterred her. 'It's what my lady Adela always used and you could do worse than emulate the old mistress's ways,' Maud had scolded time and again when she saw the dirt which always seemed to be ingrained in Hester's hands.

As Hester scrubbed at her arms with the soapy flannel, her mind grew numb, which seemed a blessing after the way it had been racing a few minutes before.

She dipped the cloth into the water and rubbed it more gently over her skin, trying to wash away all the tension and uncertainty which that man—her husband—had brought with him. She unplaited her fair hair and fluffed it out before dipping her head into the bowl. The water soothed her aching head as she massaged her scalp. Looking down, she almost smiled as she saw the contents of the bowl turning brown with mud. How often Maud had berated her for her unladylike ability to attract dirt.

Tipping the dirty water into the slop bucket and refilling the bowl from the warm jug, Hester began to rinse herself clean. Across the room, the door clicked as it opened and shut again. So, Maud had soon recovered from her scolding and was returning to help her dress.

'Pass me a towel, will you?' Hester called out, as she stood dripping behind the screen, squeezing the water from her long hair.

'Towel, please, Maud,' she called again. Maud was being slow, perhaps still sulking from her telling-off. Hester rubbed the flannel over her face one last time in case any mud lingered. Some soap dripped into her eyes and stung so sharply that she stood there blink-

ing and wincing, unable to see anything as her eyes
watered with pain.

'Ouch, I've got soap in my eyes. Where's that
towel?' she demanded, sticking out her hand until the
towel was thrust into it. 'Thank you,' she said, dab-
bing at her sore eyes. They were smarting less now
as she raised her head and found herself looking not
at the plump, familiar face of Maud, but into the hard,
rugged features of her husband.

'You!' she cried. 'I thought it was Maud.'

'No, it's definitely not Maud,' he replied, his eyes
lingering on her naked curves.

'What do you think you're doing?' she demanded,
trying to cover herself with the towel. 'How dare you
enter my room without my permission? How dare you
pretend to be my maid? Have you no honour? You
despicable…' Hester realised there were no words to
describe the outrage he had perpetrated.

'Don't be ridiculous, woman, I didn't pretend,' he
protested heatedly. 'You heard me come in, you asked
me to pass you a towel. I fetched you one. I don't
need permission to enter my own house.'

So this was how it was to be. He intended to tram-
ple all over her, allow her no rights, no privacy…

'You despicable rat,' she snapped.

'Holy blood, woman, is there no reason in you? I
didn't even know this was your chamber. I haven't
set foot in this house for ten years, remember?'

'How could I forget?' Hester shot back.

'If you must know, this was my mother's room,'
he continued reluctantly, clearly not at ease giving his
explanation. 'I have happy memories of it. I wanted
to see it again. When I entered I thought it was empty.

Then you asked for a towel. I supplied it. I did not follow you here to prey upon you and claim conjugal duties, as you obviously expect,' he said forthrightly, but Hester could see his eyes travelling over her body again and felt herself blushing red-hot under his gaze.

She tried to pull the towel further around her, but was painfully aware of its inadequacy. 'Prove you're telling me the truth by not looking at me in that way,' she ordered.

He laughed, a deep, rich chuckle. 'My wife seems to require many proofs from me,' he rejoined, 'but I will avert my eyes if you wish. Ah,' he said as the door clicked open once more, 'perhaps this is Maud now.'

'Oh!' squealed the maid, seeing them together. 'Oh, forgive me,' she said and turned in a fluster to leave.

'Maud, come back immediately,' Hester cried.

'Oh, are you sure? I'm sorry, my lord, I... My, my, what a joy to see you two getting on so well. Who'd have thought it after ten years apart?'

Hester's blush of embarrassment merged with one of rage as Guy grinned in the most infuriating manner.

'Who would have thought it, indeed?' he echoed, raising his eyebrows and aiming a sardonic look at Hester.

'And how much you've changed, my lord,' Maud continued, oblivious to her lady's discomfort.

'So has the lady Hester,' he remarked, looking her up and down. She tugged again at the towel, and took a step backwards, trying to retreat into the shadows. 'I must say, Lady Hester,' he continued, 'you have certainly grown beyond all recognition. I had not expected that such a skinny little girl could have grown so well.'

The cheek of the man! Hester felt as if her blushes would never fade as he grinned at her, his eyes lingering on the curve of her hips and breasts, which, she was only too aware, the towel did little to hide. And it was all made worse by his obvious enjoyment of her embarrassment. How could she live in the same house as this objectionable, uncouth lout?

'Well, much as I would like to stay and assist with lady Hester's toilette, I must go and wash myself. I look forward to seeing more of you at dinner,' he grinned, throwing a last insolent look in her direction, as he turned on his heels and left the room, closing the door behind him.

'Not a word, Maud,' Hester ordered grimly as the old woman turned to her, her mouth open and drawing breath, ready for much chatter.

Hester dressed hurriedly, pulling on a woollen dress of deep green which had been washed and darned since she had last seen it. Maud's skill had made it look fairly respectable once more, far more so than when she had last discarded it, when the hem had been stiff with mud and the threadbare patch on the elbows had finally worn through. Glancing down at herself, she saw the way it clung to her hips, then flared out towards her ankles.

'And now, my lady,' Maud suggested tentatively, but with a look of cautious determination, 'I think this would look well with the green.' She was holding out a fine girdle, woven in gleaming, amber-coloured silk, with threads of gold running through it.

'Where did that come from?' Hester asked, her eyes fascinated by the way the cloth was gleaming in the firelight.

''Twas my lady Adela's. I'm sure she would have liked you to wear it. She would have been fond of you.'

''Tis too fine, Maud,' Hester said, turning away in search of her usual, workaday girdle.

'You can't wear that,' Maud expostulated, following her eyes to where the woollen girdle lay, trailing amongst the heap of clothes on the floor. ''Tis covered in mud, my lady. All these things must be washed immediately to soak out the soil.'

'What about my other one, the brown one?'

'That one is still airing after yesterday's wash,' Maud replied firmly. 'You can't go down without a girdle. You'll have to wear this one,' she concluded, as she gathered up the muddy pile of clothes and headed for the door with an air of finality. The shabby old brown girdle had long since dried, but she wasn't going to let on about that. She had also decided not to tell Hester that the silken girdle had been worn by Lady Adela on the day of her marriage to the old lord, Sir Guy's father. She knew her wilful young mistress would have thrown it aside, and Maud was determined to have a little wedding-day finery in evidence for the return of the young lord to his bride.

Hester tentatively fastened the girdle round her hips. Its silken weight hung perfectly, the long tie falling down the centre of her skirt, transforming the faded wool of her dress into a fitting background to show off its amber and gold magnificence. She had not worn anything so fine for years. She only hoped her new-found husband would not assume this finery was in his honour. The last thing she wished to do was to flatter his vanity.

By the time she reached the hall, all the others were seated at the long trestle tables, ready to receive their meal. Sir Guy and the other five were on the dais, already tucking into the wine. As lady of the house, it was her place to serve the guests on the top table. She strode over to the door where the serving girls were appearing with the great bowls of bruet.

'I'll take that one for the visitors,' she said to one of the girls.

As Hester slopped out the stew of meat and vegetables on to the huge, round chunks of bread which sat on the table in front of each of the diners, one of the knights demanded, 'What meat is this, lady?'

''Tis an Abbascombe speciality, a delicacy hereabouts,' Hester told him.

After an exploratory mouthful, he spluttered, 'Rabbit! Beauvoisin, she's serving us rabbit. An Abbascombe delicacy indeed! Is this how you are welcomed home?'

'My lady was not expecting us, Sir Edward. You must make allowances,' Guy replied, then he looked towards her and beckoned her over, indicating the empty seat beside him. She sat down silently and picked up her spoon.

'I'll tell you what, I wouldn't stand for it,' Sir Edward continued. 'You should show her who's master, start as you mean to go on, just like training that hound of yours there,' he said, nodding at Amir, who lay quietly beneath the table at Guy's feet, waiting patiently to be fed titbits from his hand.

'Do you compare my wife to my dog?' Guy asked, amused, glancing at Hester's furious face.

'I do indeed. Too many of you young fellows make the mistake of showing injudicious leniency. A wife must be trained to obey her master exactly as a dog unless you wish to store up trouble for yourself later on.'

'I suspect ten years' absence has stored up enough trouble already, sir.'

'All the more reason to act now. Let her feel the strength of your hand tonight.'

'After ten years away, Sir Edward, I believe Beauvoisin will have better things to do tonight than to beat his wife,' one of the other crusaders interjected with a leer and they all laughed, except Guy. Hester felt his eyes on her but didn't dare raise hers to return his gaze. She felt herself flushing with a burning *mélange* of embarrassment, indignation and trepidation.

The villagers were having a merry time of it at the other tables, knocking back their mugs of ale and toasting the return of their lord. Hester looked at them enviously. She would have much preferred to have been sitting with them, instead of with these offensive, opinionated louts. In fact, she thought, she would have preferred to have been one of them, then at least she could have chosen not to marry. She stole a furtive look at Guy as he drained his goblet of wine. He had said he was going to wash, but it had made little difference to his appearance. He was still scruffy and ill-kempt and his clothes smelled of long days in the saddle. He was eating his stew, while Sir Edward continued his lecture on the advantages of wife-beating.

'I'll tell you what,' the old boar was saying. '*My* lady will not dare to serve me with rabbit bruet when I reach home. Now, look at that obedient hound of yours...' This was too much for Hester. Didn't the offensive old fool know when to stop?

'If men treat their wives no better than their dogs,' she retorted loudly, 'they will behave like dogs and bite their husbands when they have the chance.' The table hushed and six pairs of male eyes fell upon her. She felt their hostility, but wouldn't back down now.

Sir Edward spluttered indignantly, the juices of the stew running down his chin. 'I'd like to see my wife dare,' he returned sharply.

'You'll never see it, Sir Edward, for she will be too afraid of being struck to do it openly. She'll creep up behind your back when you're not looking and then she'll bite you hard.'

Sir Edward was turning red with apoplectic rage. He began hammering on the table with his fist, his eyes popping as he exclaimed, 'Never heard anything like it, Beauvoisin. This damned wife of yours needs some discipline...'

'Sir Edward,' Guy addressed him sharply, 'You have been away from the company of ladies for a long time. You are unused to the courtesy which is their due, else I am sure you would not have damned my wife.' Hester shuddered at that final word, but longed to hear Sir Edward's reply.

'No, indeed. 'Twas not my intention to offend,' the older man said sheepishly. 'But such words from a

woman, Beauvoisin, surely you must understand…'
he ended, casting a look of appeal at Guy.

Hester felt ready to whoop with victory, until she
saw that Guy was nodding as if in agreement. She
opened her mouth with a rejoinder on her lips, but
suddenly Guy's hand was gripping her arm. He
leaned across to her, hissing in her ear, 'That's
enough baiting of Sir Edward, my lady. No matter
how you dislike him, he is a guest at your table.' She
swung round at him. 'And I'll have no more tongue-
lashings from you either,' he rasped without giving
her a chance to speak. 'Else I shall be tempted to
follow his advice and try to beat some respect into
you.'

'That's it, Beauvoisin, you give her what for,' Sir
Edward was cheering.

Hester slumped back dejectedly in her seat. Her
whole world had turned upside down. Here were
these uncouth louts at her table, giving her orders,
saying that she should be beaten. She, who had ruled
here as absolute governor for the last four years since
the old lord's death. It was intolerable, it was disgusting, it was disgraceful—and yet there was nothing
she could do to evict them from the domain which
had been hers until this afternoon, when this devil of
a husband had returned to shatter her kingdom.

'My lady, not eating?' asked Maud as she brought
another flagon of wine to the table.

'I'm not hungry,' Hester replied flatly.

'Oh, you must eat,' Maud cajoled gently, then
whispered, 'Don't worry, my lady, it's natural to be
nervous. After all, it's just like a wedding night for
you, but don't be too anxious, it won't be that bad.'

Hester pulled away from her confiding whisper. Maud meant only to be kind, but Hester couldn't help scowling so fiercely that the old woman went scuttling away out of sight.

More courses followed. Fritha had managed well in spite of the lack of warning, determined to impress her lord even in the face of Hester's strictures. For the top table there were whole eggs fried in batter with mint custard, shellfish in a vinegar sauce, and an elderflower cheese tart, while humbler dishes and plentiful ale flowed freely for the villagers.

At last the dinner was over and the villagers rose to leave, many rather unsteady on their feet. In past years this had been a merry night for Hester, celebrating the end of sowing, but tonight she could hardly muster a smile in return for their wishes of 'Good night, my lady'.

'Ah,' exclaimed Sir Edward, 'at last we can have some civilised entertainment. I was beginning to think those yokels would never leave. If I were you, Beauvoisin, I wouldn't give my hall over to them so readily. You don't want people like that getting the wrong idea.'

Guy bowed his head politely and made no reply, but Hester could stand it no longer.

'Sir, those people you refer to so disparagingly have worked ceaselessly on behalf of the lord of Abbascombe all these years he's been away. Thanks are in order, not...'

'Well,' Sir Edward continued, addressing Guy, ignoring Hester as if she were beneath contempt, 'you see, she's been completely spoilt by having her own way. That's the one fault with the wars—too many women left masterless. And this is the result. You're going to have your work cut out with her.'

'I do believe you're right, Sir Edward,' Guy replied. 'And you advise beating how often? Daily? Or perhaps twice daily in such a bad case as this?' Hester felt her ears burning with outrage as she heard the words. What sort of monster was this so-called husband? What sort of hell was he bringing to Abbascombe?

'Can't beat a woman like that too often, in my opinion.'

'My thoughts precisely. And when should I begin?' There was a devilish glint in his eye as he stole a look at her. Hester met his eyes fiercely, fury ablaze in her face.

'Oh, no time like the present. Start tonight. Don't delay.'

When her husband turned to regard her once again, there was a broad grin on his face, not a cruel grimace, but a look of amusement. Then, to her astonishment, he winked at her before turning back to Sir Edward. 'But a game of chess first, I think,' Guy said, rising from the table.

He went to one of the side-tables and returned with a magnificent silver board and an intricately carved wooden box. He set these down on a low wooden chest close to the fire and he and his friends settled down in a huddle. Hester had intended to leave them at the first opportunity, but these intriguing objects held her spellbound. She had never seen anything like them and her curiosity led her to the fireplace as if it pulled her on a string.

The board was a silver square, richly decorated

with swirling patterns inside the criss-crossing squares. From the box, Guy took many beautiful little figures, fashioned delicately in ebony and ivory, and placed them in rows on the squares of the board. Hester stood watching, entranced by their loveliness. She had never seen anything so perfectly crafted. She even forgot to sulk as they began to play, bewitched by the gorgeous little figures, the weird creatures and strangely attired people they represented.

'Is it from the East?' she asked at last, unable to contain her curiosity.

Guy moved one of the smallest pieces forward to the next square. 'It is,' he replied, meeting her eyes and seeming to welcome her interest. 'It is very popular amongst the Saracens.'

'How strange that you should want to bring back their things when you went there to kill them,' Hester found herself remarking.

'Damned barbarians deserved to keep their chess no more than they deserved to keep the Holy Land,' scoffed Sir Edward.

Guy glanced at him with a barely hidden expression of scorn. Hester realised in an instant that he shared none of Sir Edward's views. But, instead of disagreeing openly, he merely replied, 'It is a clever, strategic game, good for exercising the brain.'

'And so beautiful. I have never seen such fine carvings.' Hester could not restrain her exuberance. Her husband looked up at her in surprise.

'Yes, I think so too,' he replied quietly, looking into her eyes. 'Perhaps you would allow me to teach you to play, my lady,' he offered.

'You'd be wasting your time, Beauvoisin,' Sir

Edward cut in. 'Women can't understand chess. It's beyond them. Too much thinking involved.'

'Perhaps the Lady Hester could prove you wrong, Sir Edward. I believe she may have the necessary skills for chess,' Guy replied in a level voice, his dark eyes still fixed on Hester.

'Pah!' spat his opponent.

'I should like to learn,' Hester ventured.

'Then come, my lady,' Guy said, patting the wood of the settle on which he was sitting. 'Come and sit beside me and watch the game. 'Tis the best way to learn.' Hester hesitated. She longed to watch and learn, but she also wished to keep her distance. Then he raised his eyebrows as if to repeat the invitation, and she found she could hold back no more. In a moment she had crossed the short distance between them and was sitting by his side.

As he moved the dark carvings he told her their names. 'This is the *pedo*, the foot soldier…and this is the elephant, or *al-fil*, as that creature is called in the Saracen tongue.'

'You speak their language?' Hester gasped in amazement. Guy nodded.

'What's that, Beauvoisin?' Sir Edward broke in. 'Not using those damned Saracen words again? I've told you about that before.'

'So you have, sir,' Guy replied mildly, casting another surreptitious wink at Hester.

She did not know what to think. Suddenly it was as if they were allies against the ghastly Sir Edward. But Guy wasn't her ally, he was her enemy, her thief-husband, who had stolen himself away and had now returned to steal Abbascombe away from her too. And yet, there was something about his presence which drew her.

He leaned forward to move the little horseman and, as he did so, his knee brushed against hers. She felt herself flinch. He must have felt it too, for he moved away from her slightly, allowing her a little more space on the settle. He continued to explain the game as if nothing had happened. 'We call this piece the knight. He is the heroic warrior riding into battle, rather like your husband.' There was a note of bitterness in his voice and his smile, as she looked up, was a sardonic one.

'You said earlier that you were a hero,' Hester ventured.

'So I did,' Guy murmured, just loud enough for her ears only. 'But I do not always mean everything I say.' He paused. 'I said some other things to you earlier which I would prefer unsaid, if 'twere possible.'

Sir Edward was moving the intricately-carved chariot.

'That piece is the *rukhkh*, or chariot in our own language,' Guy explained. He paused for a moment, then his hand went straight to his knight, swooping down upon his opponent's king. 'And that, Sir Edward, is shah mat; meaning, my lady, that the king is without resource, nothing can save him and therefore the game is over.'

'You've won!' Hester exclaimed.

'There's no fooling you, is there?' Sir Edward spluttered, draining his goblet once more. 'I say, I didn't expect that. How did you manage it? Oh, I see. Well, Beauvoisin, damned good play.'

One of the girls brought yet another flagon of wine

and there was a clamour as goblets were thrust forward for her to fill. Guy and Sir Edward stood aside, allowing the other knights to cluster around the board and begin a new game, rather more fuddled and wine-sodden than the last.

Hester took her chance to move away and went to stand in a shadowy nook beyond the great fireplace, where she thought she might observe her guests unnoticed. After a few moments, though, Guy was beside her once more.

'So, my lady, would you still like to learn chess?'

Hester nodded silently. The game still fascinated her, but she was wary of allowing him to draw her into private conversation. Instead, she continued to stare towards the chessboard as if studying every move, though heaven knew her thoughts were dominated by the man beside her.

He allowed the silence to last a few moments longer. The fire crackled and spat as it caught a new log. The knights' goblets clinked and chinked as they drank.

'What had you planted in that field?' he asked then, his voice low and serious. 'The one where we...' he hesitated, searching for the right word '...where we met this afternoon.'

'Barley,' Hester replied tersely, her annoyance returning with the memory of those heavy horses on her crop, and of the indignities she had suffered at his hands.

'We were in high spirits, having reached our destination,' he said, a note of apology in his voice, as he drained the wine from his goblet and set it down on the settle with a clatter.

Hester nodded, but said nothing.

'It has been a long absence and a lengthy journey home,' he continued.

'My lord has no need to explain. It is your own crop to do with as you choose. I did not know then who you were,' Hester answered in as level a voice as she could muster.

'And I did not know… should perhaps have realised, but…'

'You still call Abbascombe "home", then?' Hester interrupted, unwilling to hear his explanations.

'Of course. There has not been a day these ten years when I did not think of it, and of those I had left here.' There was an openness in his words which surprised her.

'I had not thought you would ever return,' she replied matter-of-factly, determined to keep all hint of emotion out of her own voice.

'There were times when I shared your doubt, but I always meant to return, always wished for a homecoming. And now I am here,' he said, looking around the hall. 'I am luckier than many who will never see home again.'

'Is it as you remembered?'

'Some things are the same,' he nodded. 'But others are greatly changed.'

As Hester stared intently ahead of her, pretending to watch the chess, she suddenly felt his hand reaching for hers. As his strong fingers closed around hers, she tried to pull her hand away, but he tightened his grip. She was frozen to the spot, caught between a wish to flee and a strange longing to remain.

'You, my lady, for instance. The passage of ten

years has done much to change you,' he continued, his voice a deep whisper in the shadows.

'I was a child when you left.'

'That is the picture I have kept in my memories.'

'You thought of me?' Hester demanded, leaping on the idea. It had never seemed likely that she would have featured in his thoughts. The gawky girl foisted on him in marriage, the last thing he could have wanted. Why ever should he think of her when he had run away to escape the doom of being married to her against his will?

'Yes, of course I thought of you,' he replied, a breathless urgency in his voice. 'I thought of you very often. I wondered…' He hesitated.

'What had become of me?' Hester supplied, as lightly as she could manage.

'Not only that. I wondered what we might have become together…' and as his words evaporated, he was lifting her hand to his lips. Hester expected the usual kiss on the back of her hand, but, as he lifted her hand upwards, he turned it lightly in his fingers, so that his lips fell upon her palm and lingered there. She felt the roughness of his bristled skin, but also the softness of his lips in a gesture so intimate that the rest of the world seemed to disappear. Suddenly she and he seemed to be alone in a sensual world, in which the sensation of his lips against her skin was all that mattered. She could feel it taking hold of her, taking control.

'Oh, yes, I have thought of you,' he whispered, his breath tingling against the soft skin of her arm. Hester could feel herself sinking into his words, into the depths of that voice, its velvety darkness enveloping her.

She felt his other arm close around her waist and realised he was pulling her towards him. The scent of the wine on his breath filled her nostrils as he lowered his head towards hers and she knew in an instant that he intended to kiss her. As if a bolt of lightning had illuminated the night, she suddenly saw again all his faults and wrongdoings, which somehow he had managed to conjure out of her mind.

So, he thought he could return after ten years, ten years in which there had been no word to say whether he was dead or alive. Ten years through which she had striven to bear the humiliation of his absence; years through which she had struggled to keep Abbascombe alive. He thought he could come back now, the returning hero, to take what he wished from the demesne and from her.

In a flash Hester saw again the bridal linen which Maud had laid on her bed, smelt its lavender scent, felt its smooth freshness against her bare skin, felt his hot flesh against hers, and she knew she could not bear it. Could not bear to give in to him, could not bear to allow him his rights after all he had done. The years of desertion, the pain, the emptiness. She could not give herself up to him, to be torn apart again by his callous disregard. He might want her now, at the end of his journey, a homely possession to be reclaimed. But what of tomorrow or the day after? What would he want then?

With dazzling clarity, she knew that she must escape him if she were to save herself from obliteration in his arms. His proximity seemed to have sapped the strength from her limbs, but the gathering terror in her mind concentrated all the energy back into them. With one swift movement she pulled herself out of his grasp, her hands braced against his broad chest. Her eyes met his for an instant, looked into those dark pools, as he murmured, 'Hester?'

She hesitated an instant. Then she summoned the final ounce of strength necessary for her escape. She stepped away from him and, as she left his touch, the spell was broken. She turned her back on him and she was away, running across the hall and up the staircase, not daring to look back now in case he followed her.

She was sure she could hear footsteps close behind. She must reach her solar in time to slam the door in her pursuer's face and shoot the bolt home. Her feet were on the landing, she had reached this far without feeling those powerful hands pulling her back. And now she was at her door. She darted inside, slamming the door behind her and shooting the huge bolt home across the thick, solid oak.

She pressed her ear to the wood, listening for the footsteps, but all she could hear was her own laboured breath panting with exertion and fear while the blood seethed in her head.

She waited, every nerve and muscle in her body tense with anticipation as she held her breath, trying to hear what was happening outside. There seemed to be silence. Was he creeping up on her? The element of surprise? It didn't matter, she told herself, there was no way he could get through this great, heavy door. She pushed at the bolt once more to make sure it really was secure. Yes, it was absolutely fast. She had nothing to fear.

She slumped on her bed, her nerves quivering and her ears still listening for tell-tale sounds. Then, as exhaustion washed over her, it submerged her fear, and swept her into a dark, troubled sleep.

Chapter Three

Hester woke early the next morning. She always woke early, but this morning she felt weary and heavy after her troubled night.

Guy had loomed in her confused dreams, chasing her down dark tunnels and across wintry landscapes, hissing that he had come to take what was his by rights. She had seemed to be running all night, always only one step ahead of him, so that whenever she looked over her shoulder, his face was there, close behind, dark and nightmarish, with that scar tugging eerily at his eye.

Hester shuddered at the thought of it as she flung back the bedclothes. She needed to get out into the open, where the fresh sea breeze could blow away these morbid thoughts.

She hastily pulled on the green woollen dress she had discarded the night before and hurriedly fastened the laces of the bodice. Over this she tied her work-aday brown girdle, fresh from the wash, and hitched her long skirts up into it, allowing her to move as freely as the women from the village who wore their dresses in exactly the same way.

Of course, it wasn't the done thing for the lady of the manor to emulate their example, but Hester didn't care about that. Practicality was all important. She wasn't some doll to sit at home and look pretty, nor would she be turned into one, no matter what her husband might wish.

Her husband… Hester knew she would be expected to stay in the house and see to breakfast for him and his friends. But after last night she knew she couldn't bear to look at him again so soon. She needed to gather her strength before facing him.

Gently, she slid back the bolt on her door and crept out of her room. No one seemed to be about. Hester hesitated for a moment, listening, then tiptoed down the stairs in her stockinged feet, clutching her clogs in her hands.

At the door, she slipped her feet into the heavy wooden shoes; then she was out, clomping across the courtyard, secure in the belief that none of her un-welcome 'guests' were yet awake. Well, she couldn't hang around waiting for them all day, she reasoned to herself. If they couldn't be bothered to get up at a sensible hour, they would have to manage without her. After all, she had a farm to run. She couldn't lie around in bed all day in the luxurious manner of a knight.

Hester knew William was planning to start work on the vines now that the corn was sown. She began to make her way to the vineyard, then stopped in her tracks and turned back. No. First, she must tell the bees.

It was the custom, an important one, always to tell the bees when something happened. If the keeper omitted to tell them of a birth or a death, so the folklore went, they would all fly away, leaving their hives empty and taking their precious honeymaking skills with them. Hester had been looking after the bees almost since her arrival at Abbascombe. The old lord had considered it a good task to give his new daughter-in-law, hoping to reawaken her interest in life after the traumatic turmoil which had brought her to his demesne. He had been right. She had learnt the beekeeping skills quickly and easily, and had grown to love the work. And the bees had thrived in her care, producing more honey than ever before, and multiplying their numbers so that now she had eight hives, where before there had been only five.

Every now and then over the past years, the possibility had flitted through her mind that one day she would have to inform them of Guy's death. If word had ever arrived of him, she would have whispered it into their hives. But no word had ever come. And now, instead, he was back at Abbascombe, his presence larger and darker than before.

As she reached the orchard, she saw the dew still glistening on the leaves of the trees, a mist rising off the hills beyond. The early mornings were still chilly and the bees were too sluggish to be about their business out of doors. As she bent over the first hive, she could hear the familiar, reassuring buzzing inside.

'He's back,' she tried to say, but her voice came out a dry, tight whisper. She cleared her throat, determined to announce the news properly. 'He's back. Not dead after all. Guy Beauvoisin is returned to

Abbascombe as lord…and I…I hardly know what this means for me. Four years of playing at being lord, of believing that Abbascombe was mine, and now what?' The question seemed to hang in the air like the mist. 'Last night I fled from him,' she confessed. 'Part of me longed to stay, but the rest of me knew 'twould be madness to trust such a one as he. Don't you agree, bees?' She paused, as if they might reply. The bees buzzed on soporifically. Then Hester turned on her heels and headed back towards the vineyard. An occupation was what she needed. An occupation and William's cheery chat.

She found her bailiff alone in the vineyard, pruning the wiry stems.

'Morning, my lady,' he called, beaming at her in surprise. 'I didn't expect to see you this morning.'

'I wanted to have a look at the vines. Where's everyone else?' she asked, looking round the lonely plot.

'It's early yet,' William replied good-naturedly. 'And I think most of them will have headaches after last night. A lot of toasts were made to his lordship's return.' He chuckled.

'Oh.' Hester felt too annoyed to say more. The last thing they needed was to fall behind on the land because of Guy's return. He'd created quite enough mayhem without debilitating her workforce too. 'Well, let's get on. Why don't you show me what needs doing?'

'The best thing would be if you hold the vines steady whilst I cut them. If you just hold the stem here while I…' His words petered out with the effort

of cutting the tough old growth as William sawed
away at it with a knife so sharp it made Hester wince.

The vines produced plentifully in good years,
standing in a sheltered lee of the land where the sun
baked down in the summer. Hester and William
worked their way around from vine to vine, with
William cutting and pruning judiciously. Engrossed
in the work, the morning passed quickly, and Hester
was almost able to rid her mind of unpleasant
thoughts of her long-lost husband.

'What do you make of this?' William asked, calling
her attention to a woody lump on the bark of one of
the vines.

'I'm not sure,' Hester said, peering at it closely.

'Should I cut it out? What do you think?' They
were standing beside each other, their faces close in
consultation as they considered this problem, when
they heard the sound of horses' hooves nearby.
Looking up, Hester saw the person she least wanted
to meet. There he was, her husband, sitting majestically on his horse and leading another horse behind
him…her horse. At his side ambled the hell-hound.
It barked threateningly at the sight of her, still eager
to protect its devilish master from the supposed threat
of her presence. Guy quieted the dog with a single
word, 'Amir!'

'Morning, my lord,' William greeted him cheerily,
oblivious to the weight that had descended on
Hester's heart. 'We were so busy examining this vine,
we didn't see you coming.'

'Evidently,' Guy replied, his face expressionless.
'Good morning.'

Hester tried to return the greeting but the words

dried in her mouth. She steeled herself to look up at him, managing to train her eyes on his face, hoping she had masked the difficulty which the effort cost her.

As her eyes focused on him, a bolt of surprise shot through her for he looked quite different. The thick bristles were gone, replaced by a strong, broad cleft chin. His hair was no longer a matted mess on his shoulders, but short and luxuriant, a deep, rich brown instead of dirty black. He no longer looked like a filthy ne'er-do-well, but actually like a lord, a person to be respected. But appearances can be deceptive, Hester thought to herself, as she weighed him with her eyes.

He seemed to sense that she was examining his new looks and said, 'My bags have arrived this morning by pack horse, so I am able to attire myself rather more fittingly.' Then he added with a mischievous glint in his eye, 'I find I have woken with a slight ache of the head. Perhaps it is due to the quality of your wine, my lady.'

Was this to be his manner to her after last night? Teasing and flippant? In his mind had nothing of significance occurred when she had pulled away from his embrace in the hall? Was he so indifferent to her after all?

'My wine is of the finest quality,' she snapped back, though she knew it wasn't true. Her wine was adequate and quaffable, but no one would have called it the finest.

He grinned back at her, barely containing a laugh, amusement all over his face, and she realised she had risen foolishly easily to his bait, just as he had expected. She felt like kicking herself in punishment for being so predictable.

'Well, however the ache settled in my head,' he continued, 'I thought a ride in the fresh air would clear it.'

He paused, glancing at her horse, obviously expecting her to offer to accompany him. Hester did not reply, determined not to make life any easier for him than she had to. There was an awkward silence. William coughed and tried to look very concerned about the vines.

'I hoped you would ride with me,' Guy added at last. 'I had an idea of riding over the Abbascombe land with you as my guide.'

'Surely you haven't forgotten your way, even after ten years,' Hester said curtly, determined to remind him of his scandalous absence at every opportunity.

'I dare say not, but I would like to hear what's been happening in my absence.'

'I am needed here to help with pruning the vines,' she returned, confident of having found a good excuse.

But William immediately spoke up. 'Oh, no, my lady, don't worry about that. I can manage without you. I'm sure you'd enjoy riding over the demesne.'

Hester glared back at him, wishing for once that he wouldn't always be so obliging. If only he could have read her thoughts, or at least been quicker on the uptake, he would have realised that the last thing she wanted to do was to spend the morning alone with her husband. But William just beamed back at her, reiterating, 'Don't you worry about me. The others will be along soon. You're always working, my lady, why don't you have a day off for a change?' Then, before she could protest further, William was standing by her horse, offering to lift her up into the saddle while Guy held its bridle.

It seemed as if she had no choice, but Hester wanted to make it clear to Guy that she would have much preferred to stay with the bailiff working on the vines, so she flashed an extra-warm smile at William in thanks, then lingered for several minutes discussing the work for the day.

Leaning down from her saddle, she chatted and laughed with William, while surreptitiously keeping one eye on Guy. He was glowering, a thunderous look on his face now that he thought no one was watching him. So, he was not quite so cool as he liked to pretend. A feeling of satisfaction crept over her. No wonder he felt out of place, she thought, as she and William chatted about the vineyard. He knows next to nothing about the vines, and William and I know everything. What good is he to Abbascombe? He may be the owner by law, but what does he really know about this land or any of its crops? With any luck he'll realise how useless he is here, useless and unwanted. Better he should give up and go off back to some war—the further away the better. Just leave us in peace, she thought as she turned to face him.

'So,' she said out loud, with as little grace as possible. 'Where do you require that I should go with you?'

'Why, lady, I require that you should accompany me on a tour of the Beauvoisin land,' he replied stiffly, as he motioned to his horse to move off. Hester nodded her assent and followed as he led the way.

'I should have thought that you would have preferred to spend the day with your comrades in arms,'
she commented after a few moments.

'Yes, no doubt, but they have already left to continue their journeys homewards, otherwise I am sure
they would have been glad to spend this time with
me.'

So he admitted he would rather be with his loutish
friends than with her. Hester felt a sudden irrational
twinge of pain at the admission. She stamped it down.
After all, she didn't want him here. If he preferred
their company, why didn't he go with them instead
of staying here to plague her?

'How unfortunate for you to be without them,' she
commented wryly.

'Yes—and for you, of course. Had I been occupied
with them, you could have spent the whole day with
your bailiff as you wished,' he said sharply, looking
away from her towards the grey horizon.

Great banks of cloud were looming there, threatening to bring the rain which the wise woman had
predicted. If only they would speed their way across
the sky, their rain might call a halt to this detestable
task of accompanying him around Abbascombe.

They traversed the fields in silence, deliberately
looking at anything except each other, while Amir
bounded off, running great circles around them, covering ten times the distance of their more sedate journey.

Hester knew Guy wanted her to make conversation,
to tell him what had happened in this field over the
past few years, which crops they'd planted here,
which had been most successful, the problems they'd

had. As they rode on, the information buzzed in her head. This is where we found blighted leaves on the turnips, but William pulled out the affected plants and burned them and the disease spread no further. We counted ourselves very lucky for that. And this is where the plough broke three years ago. And here is where William tried planting leaf beet for the first time and it grew beautifully. Why should she share it all with him, these precious, happy memories? Especially if he wanted to know?

As these thoughts were buzzing through her mind, Guy slowed his horse to walk alongside hers. Hester glanced sidelong at him, trying to measure his mood. Then he spoke.

'My lady, I wish to learn about the land, and I believe there is much you can tell me,' he declared, as if he had read her thoughts. Hester looked back at him and again felt the weight of his dark eyes upon her.

'You do not wish to share your knowledge with me?' he asked with alarming directness. 'Why would that be?'

Hester glared back at him. How could he ask such a question? After ten years' absence…after last night…how could he dare to ask?

'I am not a fool, my lady. I can understand how little you may have wished for your husband's return, and how unwelcome that return may be to you. But I am here now and I mean to stay.'

'How long for?' Hester tossed back at him, feeling the meanness of her words even as she uttered them, yet saying them nonetheless. After all, he deserved to hear them.

'For good,' Guy replied evenly, still watching her face. 'I am here to stay and I mean to be a good keeper of the land.' He paused and looked into the distance, then continued, "Twould be best if we could work together as a team. I can see how much you know of Abbascombe and what it means to you. But if you cannot bear to work with me, then I will rule the demesne without your help and I will seek advice elsewhere.'

A gasp caught in Hester's throat as she felt the force of his words. Of course, that was what he would do. She had not really expected anything else. But, as well as a threat, he had issued an invitation. He had offered to work with her.

'When you say "work together as a team", what exactly do you mean?' she asked, trying to sound her most businesslike, allowing no hint of emotion to escape in her words. It was the same voice she used when negotiating prices with the corn factors, a voice which hid her true feelings like a verbal mask.

'I know nothing of farming or of the land, but I want to learn. You can tell me what I need to know. And instead of continuing to manage Abbascombe alone, as you have in the past, we can carry the load together.'

Hester hesitated and looked at him. His gaze seemed to be open and honest, yet she felt troubled by his suggestion.

'It is a disgrace that you know so little of your own land.' She could not help it, the words slipped out before she could prevent them. She expected anger in return, but Guy's face remained impassive.

He nodded, paused, then spoke. 'My education fitted me for fighting. It taught me nothing of farming.'

'But you could have learned if you'd wished.'

'Perhaps I could. No doubt I should have done. But I did not know how much I desired it until I was far away from Abbascombe, living in the hot sand of the desert. And my childhood was taken up with learning how to be a knight, far away from here.'

'In Devonshire at the house of Lord Perigord.'

'You know of it?' Guy replied in surprise. 'Then you know too that I was absent from Abbascombe from the age of seven to seventeen.'

'Seven?' Hester repeated. 'I had not known you were only seven when you left.' She thought of how she had been wrenched away from her own home at the age of twelve, how painful that had been. But, at seven, how much worse?

'Yes, seven,' Guy continued, oblivious to the sympathy that was suddenly welling up inside her. 'My mother died the following year. By the time I returned I was too full of knightly endeavours to settle to farming.' He laughed, a hollow, sad laugh. Hester met his eyes. Something in their depths stirred a chord within her. Why not accept his offer? Why not try working with him? At least then she would still have some control over Abbascombe. The alternative was to be completely ousted.

'Very well,' she told him carefully. 'Let us try working as a team.' And then she began to talk of the land as they rode across it, the crops, the soil, the people. The words flowed easily once she had started and Guy listened attentively, seeming to absorb what she said, remaining silent mostly, but asking sensible

questions every now and then, questions which suggested he was serious in his desire to learn. Inevitably,
William's name cropped up again and again in their
talk.

'You and William get on very well together,' Guy
commented one time.

'Of course. William is my great friend. We work
together every day. My burden would have been
heavy indeed without him. He is an excellent farmer,
knowledgeable and sensible, and also on good terms
with all the tenantry. Everyone likes William,' Hester
enthused, ready with praise for her bailiff.

'Especially you,' Guy interrupted.

'Yes. I have leaned on him these four years, and
he has never let me down. I could not value anyone
more highly than I prize William.'

'And you appointed him? He was your choice?'

Hester nodded. 'The old bailiff, Benoc, was dishonest,' she explained.

'Dishonest? Benoc? My father never detected him
in any dishonesty, I think.'

'Maybe not, my lord, but in the last few years of
his life, your father was weakened by—by—' A blow
hovered on her lips. She bit back the words 'by your
desertion, by the appalling, callous way you treated
him'. She did not quite have the nerve to utter them.
Instead she continued, 'By circumstances. His health
became worn and he could not keep so careful a
watch on his affairs as he might otherwise have done.'

'I see. And you blame me for that, do you?' In
spite of her careful choice of words, he had heard the
accusation in her voice.

Hester hesitated. What was the point of pretending?

After all, he hadn't tried to make things any easier for her all those years ago. He had made no attempt to soften the blow, so why should she spare his feelings now?

'Yes, I have been used to blame you,' she said boldly. Guy's face clouded over and Hester feared what his response might be, but instead of lashing back at her, he said nothing and they rode on in silence.

All at once she felt a pang of sympathy for him and felt a little guilty for having been so blunt. Had it really been that simple? His father had been old, after all—and even old lords had to die some time. But, then again, the old man had been devastated by Guy's disappearance. And why should she make excuses for this man who had also deserted her? If he wanted the benefit of her knowledge, he must take it as it came.

'I did not learn of his death until I reached England. I had expected to find him still here,' Guy said quietly, his voice breaking in upon her thoughts.

'Oh.' Hester bit her lip, realising how fresh the news was to him and feeling a sudden pang of sympathy. 'I did not know.'

''Tis no matter. Maud told me he fell from his horse.'

'Yes, we believe he suffered a seizure while out riding alone. His health had been slipping for some time. He hardly complained, but I know he had been suffering from pains in his chest. Guthrum found him with his horse grazing nearby. He looked peaceful,' Hester said, remembering the old lord's face when

Guthrum and the others had carried his lifeless body up to the house.

Guy nodded. 'He died on Abbascombe soil as he would have wished. He loved this land above all else,' he commented. 'And you, my lady, you love it too. But was there no one who could have relieved you of the burden of its daily care?'

'Whom do you mean?' Hester asked quickly, her hackles rising.

'No guardian to guide you?'

'You forget I am a married woman, my lord. Married women generally turn to their husbands for support,' Hester retaliated.

'But in my absence, did my father not appoint a guardian for you?'

'He did not expect to die, my lord,' Hester said sharply. 'But he did expect your return. I believe he thought daily to see you riding into the courtyard.'

Guy looked away from her, saying nothing, but turned back a moment later, 'Was there no one in your own family to help you?'

'My family all died of fever before I came here. There is a cousin of my father who inherited the estate, but I never met him. In any case, I preferred to manage things myself. I had already learned a great deal about the demesne, and if you think I was alone you mistake the case for I had help and support from everyone here. William, in particular, has been my rock.'

'William. Of course.' Guy merely nodded and said no more.

They rode on in silence until they reached the village. Here, he began again to take a keen interest in his surroundings, slowing his horse to a walk while he looked all about. Hester let her horse trail close behind, watching him as he surveyed the dwellings. Just ahead, she could see Judith working on the plot of land beside her father's cottage, turning the soil ready for planting. The tall, skinny girl, who was no more than sixteen, had been bothering her recently to let her leave the manor to marry a man from Wareham. Hester couldn't understand why anyone would want to do such a thing and kept putting Judith off in the belief that she would grow out of so preposterous an idea.

It was ridiculous, of course. Hester couldn't understand why she should choose to get married at all— but if she were really determined there were plenty of young men in the village who would have done very well. The idea of anyone wanting to leave the place where they had grown up, particularly when it was as beautiful as Abbascombe, to marry a virtual stranger filled Hester with incredulity.

Judith looked up at the sound of their approach, and began to move towards them with a look of cautious determination on her face. Hester could guess what was coming next. She had been through the arguments so many times with the girl and really couldn't be bothered to discuss it all again. Her answer was still 'no'. Why couldn't Judith see that it was for her own good and give up? Didn't she realise by now that there was no way Hester would give her permission? And to leave the manor without permission was impossible: to do so would make her an outlaw, constantly running the risk of capture, severe punishment and forcible return.

Judith opened her mouth to speak and Hester braced herself for more pathetic pleadings about love and happiness. But instead Judith said, 'My lord, please may I beg a word with you? I have a petition I wish to make. A very important request.'

Hester bit her lip. She had forgotten that she was no longer the ultimate power of Abbascombe and now this came like a slap in the face. Suddenly it was as if she didn't exist. Now they would all go to him with their requests and grumbles. She felt a stab of pain at the thought of being supplanted, a stab which made her bark, 'Not now, Judith, this is neither the time nor the place.'

As soon as the words had left her lips, she knew it had been a mistake to speak in his place. Judith dropped back, stung into submission.

'Judith,' Guy replied, seizing the opportunity. The skinny girl smiled up at him. 'Why don't you tell me your petition?' he prompted with a friendliness which left Hester feeling spare and unwanted as he looked down at the girl with warmth in his eyes.

'Oh my lord, thank you. I—I wish—I wish to marry,' Judith faltered nervously, hesitating to find the words and twisting at the pinafore she wore over her dress.

'Well, that's very good,' he said, encouragingly. 'Who is the lucky man?'

Yes, wait until you hear that he lives in Wareham, Hester thought. You won't look so pleased then.

'He is a wheelwright…in Wareham, my lord. His name is Collen.'

'I see. How did you meet a man from outside the manor?'

'My father goes to market in Wareham, my lord, and sometimes he takes me with him.'

'And what does your father think of this match?'

'He says he would be sorry to lose me, my lord, but that Collen is a good man. He works hard. And...and we love each other very much, my lord,' she brought out the words bravely, blushing fiercely.

Hester turned her eyes heavenwards. She'd heard all this rubbish before and was astonished that the girl hadn't seen sense yet in spite of everything she had told her about the foolishness of even considering such a match.

Of course Guy would deny her request. He would not want to lose a capable pair of hands from the estate. And it wasn't just Judith they would be losing. If she left, they would also lose the children she would have—that had to be considered too. No sensible landowner would want to deplete his workforce. Hester watched as Guy considered his reply.

'Well, I'm sure no one in Abbascombe would want to lose you, Judith, but nor would I want to stand in the way of love.' He smiled.

Hester felt her mouth drop open in surprise. What was he talking about? Love? What about Abbascombe's workforce? Judith's skills and potential? Abbascombe couldn't afford to lose its workers to Wareham.

'Why don't you and your young man come and see me together? And I'll need to speak to your father too. All right?'

'Oh, my lord, thank you. Thank you so much,' Judith said, beaming up at him with a look of such beatific happiness and gratitude, it seemed to light up the whole village. Hester had never seen anything like it before and stared in wonder at the girl's simplicity.

'Not at all. I look forward to meeting Collen,' replied Guy. Then he pressed his horse onwards and they continued through the village and beyond, down towards the beach.

As soon as they reached the sand dunes, Amir gave a yelp of delight and went tearing down to the water, plunging into the cold waves, sending up a shower of spray which glistened in the sunlight.

'I used to love riding across the sand when I was a boy,' Guy said, breaking the silence between them. 'The beach is one of the places I have missed most. I used to think of its cool waves lapping at my feet, especially in the heat of the day when we were camped in the desert.' Hester rode silently by his side, frowning with censure. She longed to hear more of the Holy Land, its deserts and scorching sands, but she was determined not to join in his attempts to make conversation as the horses picked their way carefully over the shifting sand.

'Do you know, I think I remember Judith as a little girl? I'm sure I used to see her playing in the sand,' he said as he tried again to provoke some response from Hester. 'So, my lady, you do not approve of this match,' he said at last, raising his eyebrows, leaving her no option but to reply. They had reached the firm sand at the water's edge and the wind coming off the sea was lifting his hair as she looked across at him.

'Of course I don't,' Hester replied tersely. 'And frankly I am astonished that you are willing to encourage her. It would be far kinder to make it clear from the outset that it is impossible, than to raise her hopes falsely.'

'But I don't intend her hopes to be raised falsely.'

'You surely don't mean to let her leave Abbascombe?' Hester demanded, wide-eyed.

'I don't want to keep her here against her will. Her heart is elsewhere. The girl's in love. Surely you can see that.'

'Love!' exclaimed Hester.

'What do you mean?' he demanded, turning to face her.

'I mean that it is ridiculous for you to talk of love when you ought to be considering the good of Abbascombe.'

'You sound just like my father,' he said, glowering as if it were a reprimand. 'But I would rather consider Judith's happiness than always be thinking about some piece of land.'

'No doubt, my lord, but then you haven't been slaving on this land, doing your utmost to hold the demesne together in spite of everything.'

'I am well aware that you have worked hard here, my lady, but surely you can sympathise with a girl who's in love? Surely you would not keep her here to be wretched and lovelorn?'

'She will grow out of it.'

'How can you be so sure?'

'Of course she will,' Hester returned harshly. How dared he talk of love after the way he had treated her and his father? What did he know of feelings? Now that he was clean-shaven, she could see the features of her bridegroom in this older man's face. Recognition brought the painful memories storming back into her mind and Hester felt her pulse begin to race with anger.

'And I thought women were supposed to be the soft sex,' Guy mused aloud.

'Soft? Women can't afford to be soft when they're left to do everything. If you let Judith marry this man, we'll be losing a worker from our land, a valuable, skilled pair of hands, not to mention all the children she'll have. Don't forget we'd lose them too.'

'What a harsh view of life you have,' he said, looking down at her with wondering eyes that seemed to bore into her.

'Just practical,' Hester retorted defensively. 'Someone has to worry and plan ahead so that there's something to eat when the frosts of January freeze the ground. Being in love won't feed anyone.'

'But when a husband and wife are in love, maybe they will take care to feed each other,' Guy suggested, watching Hester closely.

'Pah!' she snorted, throwing her head back. 'In love! He just knows a good bargain when he sees one. Judith's a useful girl, who has learned her skills here, I might add. I used to think she was clever as well as useful, but obviously I was wrong, otherwise she wouldn't be so keen to throw herself away on some outsider who'll take her away from all her friends and probably beat her when she has no one to turn to for help.'

'That is not really your view of life.' Guy checked, his dark eyes staring into her face.

'I judge by my experience,' she lashed back at him, all her fury and fear at his return spilling out into her voice.

'Surely the world has not treated you so very badly…' he began, then faltered and looked down at his horse's bridle.

Hester glared at him, then looked away in disgust. How could he say so? After the way he had deserted her, knowing that she was an orphan in a strange place, far from home and missing all those who had ever cared for her. How could he? She wouldn't even sink to naming her grievances. He knew them well enough.

Why was it he could be so understanding to Judith, so sympathetic to all her foolish passions, but feel nothing for Hester, for his wife? She tried to force the question away, to push it to the back of her mind, as she had been used to doing all these years whenever she had thought of him. Those old, bitter doubts: how could he have rejected her so publicly, so hurtfully? Why couldn't he have cared for her? What had it been about the sight of her? Why had she so revolted him that he preferred to flee thousands of miles to war, to likely death, rather than live in the same house with her?

All the old pain stormed through her, leaving her body feeling tense and brittle. Her emotions were churning too violently to allow her to speak. She looked up at him and found him watching her. He reached out his strong arm and caught at the bridle of her horse, holding it tightly so that the creature was instantaneously still. He fixed her with those dark eyes that seemed to look right into her soul and Hester felt herself trembling not exactly with fear but with a kind of dreadful anticipation, holding her breath, not knowing what he might do next.

'My words were not meant to upset you. They were said lightly. I can't undo the past, but shall we at least try to be friends?' he murmured at last, his grimace cracking into an apologetic smile.

Hester had no wish to be his friend. She couldn't think of anyone less trustworthy as a friend. She tossed back her plaits and looked past him out to sea.

'When I left all those years ago, I thought it was the best thing to do. I did not think you would have wanted a husband.'

'Nor did I want one,' Hester snapped back. 'No more than you wanted me as a wife.' Guy nodded his agreement, and perversely she felt as if he had rejected her all over again.

'You were very young,' he continued.

'I was a child,' she interrupted bitterly.

'Exactly so. I did not approve of the way my father had sought your fortune. I felt he had made use of both of us.'

'He, at least, cared for me,' Hester retorted, not wishing to hear a bad word said about the old lord.

'I have no doubt that he loved you as the daughter he never had. 'Twould have been difficult not to.'

Hester stared back at him. What did he mean by that? 'If you mean to win me by flattery, sir, you will find it harder than fighting the Saracen,' she replied.

'I know,' he nodded, and a smile hovered on his lips. 'The Saracen were hard opponents, but even they showed a little mercy sometimes. Could you not find it in your heart to make allowances for a scarred old warrior, my lady?' He was casting that spell again; Hester could feel its force hanging in the air between them.

'I have buried my heart,' she replied flatly, but felt no conviction in her words, for at that moment her heart was pounding as she looked at him.

'I am sorry for it,' he said slowly. 'If that is so, I wish that it may be buried in fertile ground. Then perhaps there would be a chance...'

Hester said nothing. She could not look into his eyes any longer with safety. Instead, she managed to drag her gaze away, turning to face the waves, where Amir was leaping with passionate excitement.

Guy followed her gaze. 'Do you think, my lady, that there may be a chance?' he pursued.

Hester froze in her saddle at his question. It demanded a response, but what reply could she give? She did not want him here; she hated his very presence; she longed for his departure...and yet...and yet... Her heart was still pounding with the intimacy of this conversation, with the thrill of possibilities behind his words. But to tell him so would be to expose herself once more to his cruelty. How could she take that risk?

At that moment, Amir bounded back up the beach. As she reached Hester's side she halted to shake the water from her coat. A torrent of icy droplets deluged Hester, showering her gown.

It was the escape she had sought. No need to answer that question, no need to show her true feelings. Instead she turned back to Guy with a passable display of anger on her face.

'Are you completely incapable of controlling your blasted dog?' she demanded, doing her best to sound annoyed, while secretly thanking heaven for this distraction.

'I'm sorry,' he began, but his words dissolved into that deep chuckle she had heard the day before. 'Are you very wet?' he asked, stretching out an uninvited hand to touch her sleeve. As his fingers brushed against her arm she shivered involuntarily.

'You are cold,' he assumed wrongly. 'Here, wear this,' he offered, shrugging off his leather jerkin and throwing it around her shoulders. It carried his scent with it.

'Amir, come here,' he ordered. But Amir was no longer gambolling playfully. She was utterly still, her powerful body tense, her ears pricked, her nose twitching in the air, pointing in the direction of the cliffs which loomed at the end of the beach, their rocks rising jaggedly into the sky.

'What's the matter with the animal now?' Hester asked. Amir had started to whine.

'She can hear something,' Guy said, straining to hear whatever it was that had alerted the dog.

Hester listened too. A gust of wind stung her cheeks. As it died away the thin cry of a distant voice reached her ears.

'What was that?'

She scanned the beach and cliffs. She could see no one, then suddenly her eyes rested on a small dark figure clinging to the rocks of the cove, the surging waves of the incoming tide crashing only a few feet beneath.

'Look!' she cried, pointing to the spot. Guy followed her gesture. In an instant he had dropped her horse's bridle and urged his horse onward, speeding along the beach, followed closely by Hester.

The sand petered out where it met the rocks of the

cove and here the waves were already crashing
fiercely. At low tide it was possible to walk right into
the cove from the beach, if you didn't mind wading
through cold water. But, once the tide had turned, this
route was very quickly cut off and the shallow pools
became deep and treacherous, covered by fierce, surging waves.

Guy reined in his horse as he reached the end of
the beach.

'Looks like a boy,' he said.

'It's Eadric,' Hester cried, recognising the small
form, horror-stricken to see her favourite in such
grave danger. 'Eadric!' she called. 'Climb higher! The
tide's coming in.'

She wasn't sure whether the boy had heard her or
not, but he scrambled at the rocks and managed to
pull himself a couple of feet higher. As he found a
new foothold, the rock beneath him gave way and
went crashing down into the foaming water below.
Eadric managed to cling, terrified, to the rock face,
his limbs frozen with fear. Hester could only watch,
numb with horror, her mind blank to everything but
the boy's awful plight. But Guy was leaping down
from his horse. She jumped down on to the sand behind him.

'What are you going to do?' she demanded.

'I'm going to fetch him,' he said, as if it were obvious. Then he was clambering over the rocks, fast
and agile, seeming to find his way instinctively over
the sharp crags. Hester watched, hardly able to
breathe, as Guy picked his way from rock to rock, his
feet confident even on the treacherous patches of sea-
weed.

Amir tried to follow him, but the rocks were too steep for her and she came slipping back onto the sand. She yelped and whined, running back and forth along the shore, her eyes fixed on Guy's back as he climbed further and further away from her, further and further into a danger where she could not guard him.

He was moving so quickly, with the skill of an animal, feeling rather than thinking his way. Then suddenly his feet slipped from under him and he was left hanging by his fingers from the rock face, seeming to hover in the air, about to plunge into the angry water beneath. Hester gasped and made a dash towards the rocks before she realised she was a useless onlooker, unable to reach him in time, unable to do anything. Perhaps she should leap on to her horse and race to the village for help? Her mind panicked, unable to form a cogent plan, as Guy clung with those strong arms, his feet scrabbling to find a hold on the rock. The next moment, he had found it and was off again, inching his way towards Eadric. The boy was still frozen, hugging the same patch of rock, too scared to move anything but his eyes, and they were on Guy, willing him ever closer.

Hester's heart was beating in her mouth as she watched. 'But why?' she demanded under her breath. What do I care? Wouldn't it be the best thing if he plunged to his death? Haven't I believed him dead all these years without grieving for him? It's just for Eadric's sake that I care, she told herself. Guy only has to survive long enough to save Eadric.

At that moment another horse galloped up and William was beside her.

'Oh, no, heaven help them!' he exclaimed, following her gaze and seeing Guy inching his way around the cliff face to where the terrified boy was clinging. 'This was what I feared.'

'How did you know?'

'Nona told me he'd gone looking for seagulls' eggs. So I thought I'd better ride down and check he was all right. If only there were something I could do,' he said, jumping off his horse.

Hester hugged Guy's jerkin around her. It was still warm from his body. She buried her nose in the leather collar, catching that hint of his scent, an aroma of masculinity. She realised she felt strangely comforted by its faint, musky smell. She wished she could hide her face inside it too, but her eyes were painfully drawn to the terrifying prospect of the boy's stranded figure out there on the cliffs.

'Look, he's almost there. He's going to do it,' William cried excitedly.

'They've got to get back before they're safe,' Hester reminded him, still trembling with fear, not just for Eadric, she realised at the back of her mind, but for both of them.

'They're going to be all right,' William reassured her. He put his arm around her. It was fraternal and comforting, and seemed to give her hope as he spoke. 'His lordship knows what he's doing. He's a skilled climber, look at the way he moves, always holding and feeling for the next hold. He won't fall and he won't let Eadric fall either. Eadric will be fine now he's got his lordship there to guide him.'

Hester prayed that William was right. But what if Guy misjudged, or if the rock gave way, or if Eadric slipped? How could she watch as they plunged into the water, certain to be dashed against the rocks? The suspense seemed to last forever as they inched their way round the cove, even slower together than Guy had been on his own. This time Guy was being careful, taking no risks, and there were no more missed footholds, or cascades of stones beneath his weight.

As they came nearer, Hester could see that he was talking constantly to Eadric, encouraging him, telling him where to tread, taking no chances with his young charge. At last they were within reach of the beach. Guy jumped down, sending up a shower of sand, then held out his arms to catch Eadric.

As he turned to look at Hester, she shrugged off William's arm and dashed over to where he stood beside the pale and shivering boy. Amir was leaping up at Guy, trying to lick his face, delighted by his safe return.

'Eadric, how could you be so stupid?' Hester scolded, her fear turning to anger now that he was safe.

'I was looking for seagulls' eggs,' the boy muttered sheepishly. 'I didn't realise the tide was coming in so quickly. I'm sorry, my lady.' Then he turned to Guy. 'Can I really be your squire, my lord?'

'Of course. I promised, didn't I?' Guy replied. Hester stared at him.

'Your squire?' she repeated.

'When we were on the rocks, I couldn't move but his lordship said that if I climbed back with him I could be his squire,' Eadric explained.

'Yes, I said I needed a brave young man to help me. I promised Eadric that I would choose him if he proved himself to be sufficiently brave.' Guy was speaking without looking at her, his eyes anywhere but meeting hers.

'We had planned on having Eadric's help on the land this year. He's strong enough to do a man's work now alongside his father,' Hester told him, trying to force him to look at her. A voice inside her wanted to tell him how brave he had been, how courageously he had acted in saving the boy's life, but instead she found herself talking about the farm, while he wouldn't even meet her gaze.

'I'm sure you can spare him,' Guy said, looking towards William.

'No one would want to stand in his way, my lord,' said William, nodding his acquiescence. 'Becoming your squire is a great opportunity for a lad.'

'That's settled then.'

Guy was wet from the spray of the waves, his shirt flattened against his chest, showing the curls of his black hair against his dark skin, his sleeves clinging to the powerful muscles of his arms. Hester shrugged off his jacket and held it out to him.

'Here, don't catch cold,' she said, more gently than she had ever yet spoken to him. He reached out and took the garment from her hand without a word. Finally he looked into her face, but it wasn't the look she had expected. He fixed her with a black stare that made her shudder. Then, instead of draping it around himself, he flung the jerkin over Eadric's shoulders.

'That was magnificent climbing, my lord,' William was saying, apparently unaware of the tension in the air.

'I'm sure you would have done the same if you'd

arrived a few minutes earlier,' Guy snapped back dismissively. Then, pausing, he lifted his eyes to William and said more slowly, 'It's funny: you two always seem to know where to find each other, don't you?' and he glanced from William to Hester and back again.

William laughed good-naturedly. 'I suppose that comes of working together so much. But I didn't come looking for the lady Hester, my lord.' Guy raised his eyebrows and William continued, 'No, I came looking for Eadric. I knew he'd be getting up to some mischief.'

'Really?' Guy queried, as he lifted Eadric up onto his horse and swung himself up into the saddle behind him. Then he pressed his heels into the horse's flanks and sped away over the sand, with Amir bounding and barking at his side.

Hester watched him go.

When he was out of her sight, he slowed his horse and rode more gently along the sand.

'I dare say you've no need of a scolding, Eadric, for you'll not do that again in a hurry.'

'No, my lord,' the boy replied sheepishly.

'You and I can be good partners, I do believe. I can teach you the work of a squire, and you can teach me the ways of Abbascombe. What do you think?'

'Why, yes, my lord,' Eadric exclaimed with enthusiasm. 'As long as the lady Hester and William will not mind doing without me.'

'They will bear it. Their names fit comfortably together, do they not?'

'Oh, yes, my lord, they are always together.'

'In the house as well as in the field?'

'Often as not, my lord. My father says they have much to chaw on…I mean, to talk about.'

'To chaw on will do, Eadric. I took your meaning. And I am sure you are right. Indeed, 'tis as I suspected. They have much to chaw on,' he repeated pensively. 'And a third person, especially when that person is a long-lost husband, is not likely to be a welcome participant in such a conversation. Is that not so, Eadric?'

'No, my lord. I mean, yes, my lord,' Eadric responded, eager to please, but unsure what his reply should be since the significance of his lordship's words had flown over his head.

'And why should it be otherwise? What right had I to expect anything of her? She believed me dead. She was lonely. Of course she would have found companionship elsewhere. Even a lord can be a fool sometimes, Eadric. Don't you forget that.'

'No, my lord,' Eadric nodded, hoping this was the correct response.

Guy merely nodded to himself and rode on towards the village.

Chapter Four

Hester flung open the door of the estate room. There he was, as she had suspected, sitting at the rent table. Checking up on her behind her back. His lean, athletic form in *her* chair, with the rent roll and the accounts spread out before him, his hound at his feet. The animal had been lying with her head resting patiently on her paws, but Hester's entrance brought Amir to her feet in an instant, letting out a bark of warning, followed by a menacing growl.

'Call off your dog,' Hester ordered angrily.

The day before she had stood on the beach, her heart pounding with fear as he had scaled the cliff face, but now she was too angry to give him credit for his bravery in rescuing Eadric. Nor had she said anything of it on the previous day. Guy had seemed to avoid her, preferring to disappear—she knew not where—rather than to spend time with her. She had been left alone, feeling feeble and exhausted after her terror on the beach, struggling to push to the back of her mind that bewildering emotion which had swept through her as she had watched, transfixed by the fear that Guy might fall to his death. Why had she cared? her mind had continued to ask, in spite of her determination to quash such awkward questions. Now, though, she knew exactly what she felt for him: fury.

'Amir, lie down,' Guy said quietly and the dog immediately sank to the floor, obedient as ever to her master, while keeping her dark brown eyes fixed on Hester in an attitude of aggressive vigilance.

'So, there you are.' He looked up at Hester with a smile. As if he'd been waiting for her! When she knew full well that he had not wanted her presence at all. The hypocrite! His pretence of friendliness disconcerted her for a moment, but she scowled back nevertheless. She would not be deterred.

'Why didn't you tell me you were coming here?' she demanded.

'To Abbascombe or to the estate room?'

Hester stamped her foot in fury and saw the corners of his mouth twitch with suppressed laughter. His amusement infuriated her all the more.

'Don't play games with me,' she snapped at him.

'I didn't think you cared much where I went, my lady wife. I thought the company of others was more to your taste. William, for instance. Would you not prefer to be in the fields with William?' He dropped his eyes back to the papers spread on the table so that his expression was hidden.

'That is besides the point…' Hester paused, waiting for a response. Maddeningly, he continued reading as if she weren't even there. Goaded by his unresponsiveness, she continued her attack.

'Don't think I don't know why,' she said, her sense

of injury making her voice harsh. He glanced up, raising his eyebrows.

'My lady, I would not presume to imagine that there is anything you do not know,' he said in a level tone, his cutting reply accompanied by another irritating smile. The smug intruder! Oh, yes, he knew very well that everything here belonged to him and that he could do as he pleased, but that was no excuse for such bad manners. Any oaf could see that it would have been only courteous to have informed her that he intended to look through the records and accounts she had kept whilst he had been away playing his war games—especially after his talk the day before of working together as a team. Instead he had come creeping in here like a spy, like the intruder that he was in her Abbascombe.

'You came here alone because you meant to check up on me behind my back. Did you tell William you wanted to look through the accounts?' she challenged him.

'If I had meant to keep it a secret from you, William would have been the last person I should have told,' Guy said coldly, his eyes fixing on hers, his brow clouding over in an instant. At least that infuriating twinkle of mirth was no longer glistening in his eyes, but Hester wasn't sure she preferred the look of glowering displeasure which had replaced it.

'So you're checking up on both of us?' she persevered indignantly.

'My lady, I am merely casting my eye over the records of my demesne.' That possessive 'my' made her flinch. She flicked back her plaits in an attempt to disguise her disquiet. 'Anyone would think from your reaction that you had something to hide.' He threw out the stinging remark casually, his eyes returning to the table to examine the papers even as he said it.

'What do you mean?' Hester burst out, burning with rage at the implied accusation. 'Explain yourself, sir!'

'Well,' he said slowly without raising his eyes, as if he were engrossed by the papers. 'You're so keen to prevent me from looking over the accounts, a man with a suspicious mind might believe you had something you wished to conceal.'

'I have nothing to conceal. How dare you suggest such a thing? I have cared for this demesne to the very best of my ability whilst you have been away, God knows where. I am proud of everything I have achieved here and I have nothing to hide at all.' Hester felt her indignation storming through her like thunder.

'Good. Then you can have no objection to my taking a look,' he replied coolly.

Instantly she realised she had been outmanoeuvred. He could read her like a book. How was it that he could predict her reactions with such ease and confidence? Damn him with his cleverness and his certainty of possession. They both knew he could do whatever he liked, look at any of her papers, go through any of her accounts, order her to leave the room if he wished. He could do anything here: he was lord of Abbascombe. But that didn't mean she was going to make it easy for him. There was no way she would let him have it all without a fight. She stood in silent vigilance.

'I thought you would be too busy to supervise my reading,' he said, glancing up at her after an awkwardly long silence, during which she had kept her eyes fixed on him, hoping he would feel uncomfortable under the heat of her gaze. 'After all, you're always telling me how much you have to do,' he continued in that annoyingly measured tone, the tone of a man who knew he had complete control.

Hester couldn't think of a sufficiently cutting reply, so she said nothing and hoped that her silent presence would at last unsettle his apparently imperturbable concentration. After a few more moments of silence, it seemed to have worked. He parted his lips to speak again.

'I can't quite read your writing here. Perhaps you could enlighten me,' was all he said, though. Adding insult to injury! With an imperious crook of his finger, he beckoned Hester over. As if I'm a blasted dog, she raged inwardly.

'There's nothing wrong with my writing,' she objected, but secretly she knew he had a point. Her script wasn't always clear. William sometimes teased her about it. But William's gentle teasing was altogether different from this.

'Your script is rather obscure,' he was saying, screwing up his eyes in what she suspected was an exaggerated attempt to read whatever lay before him.

'Perhaps the fault lies with you. Perhaps you have forgotten how to read during your long absence in the wars. Soldiers are not renowned for their literacy,' Hester countered. Why should she admit that keeping the accounts was her least favourite job at Abbascombe, that she would much rather be out in the fields doing something practical, and that consequently her writing was often slapdash, transactions recorded hastily so that she could be out in the fresh air without delay?

'On the contrary, my lady, I did a great deal of reading in the Holy Land,' he assured her. The twinkle had returned to his eye and Hester realised he was enjoying the astonishment which she had failed to hide.

'Yes,' he continued. 'I was not fighting all the time and there are many Arabic writings which are well worth the reading. Of course, their script is different from our own—and completely dissimilar to yours,' he commented, frowning again at her untidy scrawl with its blots and crossings-out.

'The Saracens can write?' Hester asked, amazed at the idea.

'Not only can they write, but they are great scholars and have much to teach us, if only we would talk to them instead of fighting,' he replied. Hester stared at him.

'Talk to them?' she repeated. 'But you went there to slaughter them.'

He didn't reply immediately. The pause hung in the air as he considered his answer.

'I was very young when I set out,' he said at last, as if he had rejected a more complicated explanation. 'If I could travel back ten years, knowing what I know now… Why, there are many things I would do differently. But enough of such fancies,' he continued, changing the subject abruptly. 'Sit yourself down, my lady, and decipher your scribble for me. If you are able.'

It was flung at her as a challenge and Hester rose to it immediately. She would show him that there was no area in which he could rout her. She could fight with as much determination as any crusader. Let him just watch and see.

Guy rose to his feet and indicated the place he had vacated. He seemed about to hand her into the heavy wooden chair.

'It's all right. I'm not helpless,' Hester snapped, managing to avoid the touch of his hand. Guy inclined his head in a bow of courteous acknowledgement. Was it courtesy, or was he mocking her?

'I don't know what you're making such a fuss about,' she chastised him with a flourish of bravado, as she pulled the chair up against the table and began to study the document which lay open before her. 'Any fool with an ounce of education can read my writing. It's as clear as day.'

'No doubt you are right, my lady.' He inclined his head again as if he were the most attentive courtier. 'Perhaps you would humour a fool such as I by telling me what it says here.'

Hester peered at the place he had indicated on the page. Of course, she could figure it out. And there was no way he was going to make her ashamed of her work. If that was his intention he could think again. If her writing were a scribble, that was because she had so much to do. Perfecting a ladylike neatness in her script had hardly been a priority! Nor had she written for any eyes other than her own.

Hester's eyes settled on the page and the words failed to arrange themselves into immediate clarity. She had hoped to have been able to read them off quickly and with obvious ease, just to prove him wrong. She squinted at her scrawl, hoping that narrowing her eyes might somehow lend order and sense to the page. She hated to admit it, and certainly would not own it to the smug man standing behind her, but the writing was not entirely clear, even to her.

'So, my lady, enlighten my darkness, if you please.' He leaned forward and breathed into her ear, his sarcasm hot against the skin of her neck. She shivered involuntarily.

'I—' she began, scanning the page for a clue.

'Yes?' he urged, leaning closer, his proximity practically unbearable. She felt suddenly as if there were no air in the room. His face was almost brushing against hers as he scrutinised the page, and the skin of her cheek prickled uncomfortably at the sensation. Her nostrils were filled with the musky masculine scent of his hair. She began searching desperately for some meaning in her scrawl. It would be too humiliating to admit defeat. She had to make sense of the document.

Suddenly the words were swimming before her eyes. She tried to concentrate, to make them stand still and be read, but the heady closeness of him filled her senses until her brain seemed to be swimming too.

'Umm…it's a record of…' she continued, playing for time.

'Don't tell me you can't read your own writing, my lady?' he whispered teasingly in her ear, his deep voice rich with amusement.

'Of course I can, but you're obscuring the light. Stand back a little, if you please, sir.'

He took half a step away from her and Hester managed to lock her eyes back on to the page. She could feel the heat of a blush in her cheeks and stared determinedly at the table to prevent him from seeing the give-away colour lighting her face. He mustn't know he had this effect on her, she mustn't allow him to see her weakness. Soon, surely in a few days' time at the most, this strange effect which his unfamiliar presence had upon her must wear off. Hester tried to reassure herself, to impose a calm which she did not feel. She grappled with the swimming words, and managed to hold one long enough to decipher it.

'It's a record of the lambing last spring,' she brought out at last, relief surging through her chest, like a gasp of fresh air after confinement.

'Yes, I managed to gather that much, but what does it say here?' he asked, stepping forward once more and leaning over her shoulder to point to the place. As he did so, the bare skin of his hand brushed against hers, sending her skin tingling with surprise at his touch. Did he know how his touch affected her? After what seemed hours, but could have been only seconds, he straightened his back so that his face was no longer on a level with hers. But now she could feel his thigh pressing against the back of her arm, the firmness of the muscle through the leather of his breeches, the hem of his jerkin brushing against her back as she sat, trapped between the table and his powerful frame.

'Umm...th—that's the number of lambs that were born,' she managed to stutter. 'And, er, this is how many survived. And here it says that we lost one ewe.'

'Only one. That was good work,' he said, seeming to be genuinely impressed.

'Yes, we were very pleased,' Hester told him, trying her best to sound as normal as possible, even though the whole room seemed to be bursting with his presence.

'And here?' he asked, pointing to another place on the page. His fingers brushed against hers once more and, without thinking, Hester pulled her hand away in a rapid reflex action.

'Umm,' she said, putting her hand to her hair in a pretence of smoothing her plaits, hoping to disguise the effect which his touch had upon her. 'Oh, er, that says, umm…' She managed to read the words aloud, stumbling and faltering over them, feeling foolish and awkward under the weight of his gaze, still patting at her hair in an attempt to look casual and unconcerned. As she finished reading she let her arm fall to her side. As she did so, the back of her hand brushed against the firm muscle of his leg, sending a bolt of panic through her body, so that she almost jumped out of her chair with the shock. 'Oh, I—I—' she stammered stupidly.

'I think I begin to comprehend your script,' he cut in, his voice seeming to vibrate around the four walls of the room as he strode to the opposite side of the table.

Amir let out a long, low growl, as if she too found the tension in the room unbearable. Hester snatched at the noise like a lifeline thrown to a drowning woman.

'Must we have that dog in the room with us?' she demanded, hoping to deflect Guy's attention away from the alarming effect he had on her. Somehow she had to disguise her weakness, otherwise how would she ever win this war for the control of Abbascombe?

'Amir seems to feel much the same way about you.' Guy laughed disconcertingly. 'Come, lady, it's time you made friends with the brach.'

'I make friends with her?' Hester protested hotly. 'I was not the one who began the hostilities. It was she who attacked me in the field. Have you forgotten?'

'She would never have brought you down if you had not behaved in so threatening a manner. My loyal brach was defending me. She at least loves me. Perhaps it is a shame that she is not Lady Beauvoisin.'

'According to your friend Sir Edward, there is little difference between your dog and your wife.'

Guy shrugged. 'Oh, but there is: the most important difference possible. Amir would do anything for me.'

'She is loyal to you because you feed her,' Hester informed him curtly.

'My lady, is the concept of love totally alien to you?' he demanded suddenly, his eyes scanning her face. This was not the way Hester had intended the conversation to develop. She had meant to use Amir as a way of distracting his attention from herself, but instead he had turned the talk back on to an extremely personal tack. She stared at him. He seemed to be awaiting a response. But how dared he ask such a question when he knew what her life had been? How dared he pry into her heart, the heart where she had locked away all the pain and loneliness of those years? Hester glared at him, her hostility prickling in the air. In her mind she flung darts of loathing across the room, into his handsome, hateful face.

He stared back at her for a few, long moments. Amir growled again and the spell cracked.

'Amir is right,' he said coolly. 'Enough of stuffy papers. The rain has held off for some time, let us seize the opportunity for some fresh air. There is one similarity between my wife and my dog…' He paused teasingly, and Hester, still with anger coursing through her veins, could not resist seizing the bait.

'What is that?' she challenged him, her voice sharp with affront.

'You are both used to taking more exercise than this paperwork affords,' he replied, his mouth breaking into a grin, the scar beneath his eye creasing with amusement. He had done it again. Held out the bait and she had taken it, like a fool. But she was only too glad of an excuse to escape the close confines of that room. Even if he did seem determined that he and his horrible hound should accompany her. Anything was better than remaining closeted within those four walls with him.

Hester grabbed her cloak from the back of the settle where she had flung it, wrapped it hurriedly around her shoulders and made her way out of the room and down the passageway. At the outside door she slipped her feet into her clogs, lying caked with mud as always, on the step where she had kicked them off in her hurry. Then she stepped out into the fresh air of the courtyard. Guy was close behind her, with Amir moving rapidly at his side.

The air smelled fresh and sharp as if the recent rain had rinsed it and hung it out to dry. Hester's spirits lifted now that she was out in the open. The sky was still grey and more dark rain clouds were hovering ominously on the horizon, but it was such a relief to be out of that room.

They were walking briskly towards the cliffs. This was always Hester's favourite direction for a walk, since the best walks always culminated in standing on the cliff-edge, looking out across the sea. She strode along the path which wound between the fields, silent except for Amir's frantic barks at the seagulls swirling overhead.

Guy paused to pick up a stick, then hurled it into the air. Amir bounded away excitedly, returning rapidly with the stick in her mouth, and dropping it into her master's open palm. With an unexpected movement, Guy caught at Hester's hand as she swung it by her side and pressed the rough stick against her skin.

'You throw it to show Amir you're her friend,' he commanded.

Hester was too surprised to protest as his hand closed around hers and lingered there a moment longer than necessary. She could feel the blood rushing into her cheeks and tried to turn away from him to hide her blush, but there were no papers here which she could pretend to examine, and no shadows in which to conceal her face.

'Windy today,' she muttered inanely, hoping he would believe that the March wind was responsible for reddening her face.

'Go on, throw the stick,' he urged. Hester flung back her arm and hurled the stick as far as she could. Amir hesitated, casting a wary glance at her unaccustomed playmate, then went bounding away undeterred. She was soon back with the stick clasped between her jaws. Hester stooped to receive it, but the dog padded straight past her and back to Guy. Hester felt suddenly snubbed.

'She doesn't like me,' she said.

'She'll get used to you. She just needs to see that we are friends.'

'But we're not,' Hester countered, stating what seemed obvious.

'We must be, Hester,' he replied suddenly, stopping in his tracks and catching hold of her arm.

The sound of her name on his lips made her jump. His voice was low and earnest. 'We must be,' he repeated, his warm breath urgent against her cheek, his eyes searching her face for a response. 'If not, what sort of future do we have?'

'Future?' Hester echoed, astounded. How dared he lecture her about the future when he was the one who…?

'Well, we are married,' he murmured, his hand still gripping tightly on her arm. Hester stared at him. Was this just his way of insinuating himself into her bed? Was he trying to tell her that it was her duty because they were married, that finally he was willing to tolerate her now that he had left behind all his mistresses in the East?

She pulled away from him sharply, shooting a look of abhorrence into his dark face, and continued walking, her feet marching ahead towards the far end of the field and the cliff's edge beyond. She would make no apology for her rudeness. At least, he ought to get the message now. If he were determined to impose his unwelcome presence upon her in Abbascombe, the least he could do was to let her walk in peace without trying to force her into agreeing to some new demand for she knew not what.

He didn't take the hint, though. She could feel his presence following behind her. She refused to look back at him. Why couldn't he just leave her alone? It was bad enough having him here at all, intruding into the safe little world she had created for herself, without having him talk of being 'friends'. *Friends!* Didn't he know he was the last person she would ever choose to be friends with? Cruel, untrustworthy, irresponsible...he represented everything that was undesirable in a friend, let alone in a husband.

Her angry steps carried her onwards with such speed that she was soon at the cliff's edge, standing looking out at the vast expanse of the fierce, stormy sea stretching to the horizon. There was nowhere else she could go to escape him if he were determined to talk to her now. She stood ready for battle as the wind off the sea whistled around her ears and the waves crashed against the rocks below. A moment later he was standing beside her, his presence suddenly blotting out all other sensations.

'I suppose I should take that as a ''no''?' he asked in a measured tone of deliberate but exhaustible patience. Hester tried to ignore him and continued staring out to sea. She found she was almost scared to look him in the face, felt she could hardly trust herself to do it, that once done, she would no longer have any control over the situation.

'I know you didn't want to marry me,' he continued after a pause. 'How could you? You were only twelve years old.'

'You didn't want to marry me, you mean,' Hester interjected bitterly, still staring stonily out at the raging waves.

'No, I didn't,' he admitted. 'But the fact is, we are married and we're going to have to learn to live with it, to live together.'

'You make it sound like a disease,' she managed to blurt out, her head suddenly reeling with thoughts of the past, her heart pounding with memories of that terrible rejection, conjured up vividly by his words. How she had lived for ten years, a rejected woman for all the world to see. 'That girl's husband would rather risk death than live with her,' the gossips would have been saying.

And now he had the nerve to speak to her of accepting their marriage, of learning to live together, as if *she* were the one who had reneged on her marriage vows, as if *she* were the one who had deserted *him*, as if *she* were the one who didn't know the meaning of duty.

He was making their marriage sound like some terrible burden to be borne. Well, if that was how he felt, why didn't he go off back to his strumpets and leave her in peace? Why had he come to force himself upon her after all these years? Why couldn't he have stayed in the East, lost to all those who knew him, presumed dead, out of sight and out of mind?

'Why should our marriage mean we have a future together any more than we had a past?' She turned on him bitterly, suddenly emboldened by her sense of outrage, the wind whipping her hair against her face.

'We must try, otherwise…'

'*We* must try!' she interrupted fiercely. 'Where were you when there was trying to be done? Where were you when we were trying to survive, slaving in the fields to try to feed the children? What do *you* know about trying?'

'It hasn't all been easy for me,' he said quietly, meeting her accusing gaze.

'Good,' she snapped back. 'I'm glad.' But inside she felt no gladness. He had returned to offer her a sham marriage of convenience, to fulfil his duty by living in the same house with her. But why should she settle for that? He had talked of love when they had argued about Judith's marriage. She had seen the way that girl's face had glowed—yes, positively glowed—with some feeling which Hester did not recognise. If he could agree to Judith's search for love, why did he come to her, to Hester, with empty proposals for a loveless union? Why should she be denied what he was willing to grant to a girl in the village?

The realisation shot through Hester like a bolt of lightning: she did believe in love, after all, she had seen proof of its existence on Judith's face. She wanted someone to share that feeling with her, she had always wanted it. But if all he could offer was a cold arrangement, an agreement to share a house and provide an heir, then she wanted nothing from him. Nothing at all. She would never agree to his terms.

'Hester,' he breathed her name. His voice seemed to vibrate in the air between them, but she refused to listen.

'How do I know you won't just up and off again

when you grow tired of Abbascombe?' she demanded, her words hard with blame. 'And now that you have made Eadric your squire I suppose you'll be taking him away with you too, away from everyone who loves him.'

'Is your opinion of me really so bad?' he demanded, grabbing both her arms and pulling her towards him, so that she could look nowhere but into his face. She could see a vein throbbing in his forehead, his furrowed brow tense with questioning as his dark eyes burned into her. 'Or am I just in the way of—?'

'Of what? What do you mean? Let go of me,' she ordered, trying to shake his hands off her. But his arms closed around her all the more tightly, locking her against his broad chest.

'You are *my* wife!' he protested, as a gust of wind buffeted their bodies and swept his words away across the fields.

'*My* wife! *My* demesne!' Hester mimicked cruelly. 'Everything is yours when it suits you!' She struggled to break away, trying to force a gap between his chest and hers.

'I should have made sure you were mine,' he breathed, the words hot and urgent against her skin as his face loomed over hers. He had pulled her so close that her head was tipped up towards the sky. She could see the grim storm clouds dark and threatening above. Then he bent his head down over hers, blotting out the sky so that she could see nothing but him, his dark hair awry in the wind, framing his strong face, the scar pale against his brown skin, his eyes, dangerous pools to drown in. In another moment

his lips were on hers, urgent and demanding as he
breathed in the sweet scent of her skin. His mouth
closed on hers, hard and desperate to find some response.

Hester wrenched her mouth away, but her body
was pinioned by his arms, enfolding her like iron
bonds on a prisoner. She tried to turn her face this
way and that to escape his searching lips, but his
mouth captured hers again, covering her with hot
kisses which seemed to burn into her.

Suddenly she realised she had stopped struggling.
She was still in his arms, letting him kiss her, allowing the tip of his tongue to touch her lips in a kiss
which had become tender and compelling after the
harsh demands of before. There was still an urgency,
but now she shared it. Her mouth was moving with
his as if she had no control over it, as if she had
wanted him to kiss her, as if she were enjoying it…
It dawned on her that she *was* enjoying it…

Her mind was blank, filled with nothing but the
sensation of his kisses. Then suddenly she remembered the words he had spoken only moments before,
words which had had no affection in them, no love,
nothing but possession.

Ownership. Taking what was his by law—that was
why he had returned to Abbascombe, and now he was
carrying out his plan. Worst of all, she was allowing
him to do it. No, it was even worse than that; she was
conniving at his seizure of property, enjoying it even.
She was his property. A stinging pang of shame shot
through her. Without pausing to think, she threw off
his arms, which were no longer hard pinions, but had
become tender and caressing. She took a step away

from him, dragging the corner of her rough cloak
across her lips to cleanse her mouth of his treacherous
kisses.

'How dare you grab me like that? How dare you
humiliate me here?' Her indignation petered out as
she tried not to remember the willingness of her
mouth under his lips.

The rain had begun to fall while she had been in
his arms, and it was heavier now: great, plump rain-
drops bursting on her cloak. She stared into his eyes
for a moment. Was there anything there but the lust
of possession?

The rain fell faster, a wet, grey mist separating her
from Guy. Hester turned on her heels and ran. The
mud flew up around her. She thought she heard his
voice in the wind, but she carried on regardless until
she reached the courtyard. She tore past the stables
and into the house.

Once inside, she slammed the door behind her and
leaned against it panting. Maud appeared in the passageway.

'My lady, you're soaked,' she gasped. 'Come in at
once and get dry. Take off those wet things. There's
a hearty fire in the kitchen.' Hester began to follow
her obediently, too breathless to say anything, and too
wet to protest. 'Sir Hugo Lacave is here. He's been
waiting. I've shown him into the hall and given him
some wine,' Maud told her.

'What does *he* want?' Hester asked, stopping in her
tracks to catch her breath, her lips curling with dis-
taste at the thought of the neighbouring landowner.

'He's come to see my lord,' Maud said, trying to
bustle Hester onwards towards the kitchen. 'Come to

welcome him back, I suppose. It's a neighbourly gesture.'

Hester hung back and scowled. She remembered
his last neighbourly gesture when he had tried to grab
her in an embrace…no, not like Guy's, for Lacave's
had been hideous, reeking of ale and sweat, his greasy
hair flicking at her eyes, his rough stubble cutting into
her skin.

He had thought her fair game, a married woman
with a missing husband. She had resisted, of course—
resisted strongly. But the stupid oaf had not seemed
able to take 'no' for an answer. She had had to knee
him in the groin, leaving him writhing in an undig-
nified heap, white in the face and winded, but not so
breathless that he hadn't been able to shout curses and
insults at her. 'Damned bitch—' she remembered his
spiteful words '—you won't have another chance of
a nobleman. There's none would have you. Everyone
knows about you and your bailiff.' She had turned
and marched away, far too proud to bother rebutting
his vicious slur.

That episode had put an end to his 'neighbourly'
visits and she could tell from his face when she had
seen him by chance at market that he had not forgiven
her. So, what did he want with Guy now? What would
he have to say to her husband?

Hester shuddered at the thought of Lacave's repulsive smell, then remembered that masculine scent of
her husband, so different, so… She shuddered again,
but it was not revulsion that she felt. What was it,
then? She tried to thrust it from her mind, didn't want
to think about it, didn't want memories of that kiss
disturbing her mind, didn't want…

She heard the door slam behind her and looked round. It was Guy, with a bedraggled Amir at his side. His hair and clothes were dripping with rain, his breeches plastered against the muscular lines of his long legs. His eyes met hers. Saying what? She couldn't read the expression.

'Oh, my lord, you're soaked to the skin too,' Maud clucked. 'Sir Hugo Lacave is waiting to see you in the hall, but I'll tell him you have to change first.'

'No, Maud, I'll dry out before the fire,' he replied sternly.

'Oh, but, my lord—' she began.

'Don't fuss over me, woman,' he snapped, and pushed past them, towards the hall, with Amir, loyal as ever, following.

Some time later, after she had changed her dress and towelled her hair dry, Hester crept along the passageway by the hall.

Sir Hugo was just leaving, somewhat the worse for drink, it seemed.

'So glad of this chat, Beauvoisin,' he was saying in his whining drawl. 'It's good to have a neighbour again at last. And don't forget I can fill you in on all that's been happening round here whilst you've been away. There is much that you should know.'

'I am sure of it,' Guy replied.

'But you can hardly guess the importance of the information I have for you…of a delicate nature. Not to be dealt with here, you understand?'

'No doubt I shall understand when you tell me. Until we meet again, Sir Hugo.'

'Aye, until then.'

Chapter Five

The penuries of Lent were over. Easter had been celebrated and now it was time for the fair. There was always a fair at Wareham immediately after Easter. People came from miles around to buy and sell and some merchants even came from overseas.

There would be livestock, and produce from all around the region, fine cloths and tapestries from Flanders, where the very best were produced, and wine from France surpassing anything that Hester could make from her vines. Hester had honey to sell. Her bees had produced plentifully the year before, far more than was needed at Abbascombe. She hoped to make a good profit on the sale, and, after prolonged nagging from Maud, had eventually promised to spend the proceeds on some new fabric to replace her threadbare old summer dresses.

She had always enjoyed the trip to Wareham in the past, being surrounded by people, buying and selling, noisy haggling and merriment. In previous years, she had gone to the fair with the old Lord Beauvoisin, Guy's father, and then, after his death, with William.

It had always been an enjoyable occasion, looking at livestock together, mulling over possible purchases in an easy, companionable way.

This year, though, Guy was her companion. There had been no argument about it; he and William had arranged it between themselves, so that by the time she had realised what had been decided, it was all settled and there had been no changing it. Her exclusion from the decision still rankled and she said not a word to Guy as they trudged down to the beach before dawn to meet the fishermen who were to take them to Wareham in their boat.

Over the past few weeks he had been studiously polite to her whenever they had met, which was usually only at meals. It was almost as if they were nothing more than two acquaintances sharing a house. Neither of them had mentioned the kiss on the cliff-top, but it continued to lurk disconcertingly in Hester's mind, so that memories of his arms around her, his closeness, his strong caresses would leap unbidden into her thoughts when they were most unwelcome.

Guy had taken to chatting to the labourers as they worked in the fields, especially when Hester was elsewhere. She would arrive in the vineyard after a morning spent discussing menus with Fritha, to find him there with a hoe in his hand, working alongside the men. Then, a few minutes after her arrival, he would be off on his horse without a word of explanation to her. When quizzed, William always said that Guy simply wanted to learn about farming the demesne, but Hester remained suspicious.

In spite of everything, she was determined not to

let his presence spoil her enjoyment of the fair. As she settled herself on to one of the wooden benches in the open hull of the wooden fishing smack, she felt a quick rush of delight. It was still very early, the sun just peeping over the horizon, puffy clouds soaking up the strong pink hue of its first rays. To be out on the sea on this bright, clear morning would be heavenly indeed, bobbing on the waves with a good, favourable wind to fill their sails and speed their journey round the headland, into the great harbour, and up the River Frome to the market town of Wareham, with its priory and bustling quayside.

The wind was in their favour; the sails filled and the boat began to move quickly as soon as they pushed away from the shore, an insistent thrumming noise vibrating down the mast as the wind pushed her along. As they cut through the water the waves jumped and splashed at the sides, sending sprays of foamy water splashing up on to Hester's cloak, wetting her blonde curls so that they stuck to her forehead.

'Here,' Guy said from his seat behind her, and suddenly his hands were on her shoulders, draping one of the sailors' leather cloaks over her shoulders. It smelled strongly of the animal grease which had been used to waterproof it.

'No,' Hester replied quickly, wrinkling her nose and pushing the garment away. 'I don't want it.'

'My lady, I insist. Else you'll be soaked by the time we reach Wareham.' At that moment another wave broke against the side, sending a spray of salty water into the boat. He wrapped the cloak firmly around her and she had little choice but to accept it.

Even the sea conspires with him, Hester thought militantly as he returned to his seat behind her. She refused to look back at him or to thank him, but after a few minutes more of cold spray she was glad of the extra protection.

Her earthenware jars of honey were stacked securely in the bottom of the boat. Amir was lying beside them, sniffing at them curiously.

'Did you have to bring that hound with you?' Hester asked, throwing her angry words over her shoulder to Guy and glancing behind to fix him with her blue eyes.

'Of course.' He grinned infuriatingly, unperturbed by her ill humour. 'You know I never go anywhere without her.'

'Well, if your dog falls overboard I shall not allow the sailors to endanger us by trying to rescue her,' she warned him sharply.

'My lady, Amir knows very well how to behave on a boat. You forget that she is better travelled than you; she has come all the way from the Holy Land.'

Hester turned away in frustration. He had an answer for everything, and, most annoying of all, he always seemed to be right. She couldn't think of any riposte sufficiently caustic, so she stared out at the water and soon became mesmerised by the way the tips of the waves caught and reflected the light of the rising sun.

Out there, surrounded by the glimmering water, it was almost as if she were adrift in a sea of diamonds all sparkling and shimmering for her delight. The sight was so beautiful, it filled her with warmth despite the cold sea breeze. It was one of her secret

feelings of joy, secret because she never told anyone
of such feelings. There was no one she felt she could
tell. She knew she shared a love of Abbascombe with
William, but she would have been embarrassed to
have spoken of such fanciful feelings to him. Theirs
was altogether a more practical relationship, in which
they spoke of practical things. Poetic notions about
the way the light shone on the waves or the beauty
of the sunrise would have seemed foolish and out of
place.

Just then she felt Guy's hand on her shoulder. She
shivered involuntarily at his touch.

'Cold?' he asked, a look of unexpected concern in
his eyes as she turned to look at him.

'No, I'm fine,' she said quickly. 'I was just watching the way the sunlight flickers on the water.' The
words had escaped before she realised what she was
saying, her thoughts spilling into her speech almost
of their own accord. She bit her lip, wishing she could
recall the words, make them unsaid, feeling she had
exposed a part of herself she didn't want him to see.
She felt sure he would mock her for such fancies.

'Yes, it's beautiful,' he said quietly, his voice deep
and soft, close to her ear, his breath warm against her
neck. 'One might almost imagine that a sea god had
sprinkled diamonds over his kingdom.'

Hester gave a start of surprise. 'I— How did
you—?' she began to say.

'I can see what you're thinking,' he broke in.
'You're far too sensible to share such whimsical notions. When you look at the water I am sure you think
only practical thoughts about the speed of the wind
and the direction of the currents. Now you can mock

me for talking like a worthless poet.' He arched his eyebrows as his eyes met hers.

'No, I—I think you're right,' Hester admitted quietly, lowering her eyes in embarrassment.

'What? You're agreeing with me? That must be the first time, my lady,' he said, and Hester found it impossible to guess whether he was mocking her or not. She turned away from him in confusion, feeling a hot blush warming her cheeks in spite of the wind. What was it about him that had this effect on her? How was it that he could charm her most secret thoughts out of her head and on to her lips? And how had he, of all people, managed to guess her thoughts, to read her mind and share her feelings about the beauty of the day?

They were approaching the Studland straits, where the currents were strongest and all the skill of the sailors would be needed to bring them safely through the harbour entrance. As they rounded the headland Hester could see where the perilous currents lay, fast-moving eddies flowing alongside the quieter streams, obvious to the observant eye from the way the water shivered and shimmered restlessly.

Guy was watching intently too. She could see him out of the corner of her eye without turning her head to flatter him with her attention. There he was, darkly calm as ever, his eyes shining with the reflections of the water, his black hair ruffled by the sea breeze, his jaw strong and determined, even in repose.

His profile as he gazed at the water suddenly sent a sharp pang of remembrance through her. It was like looking at the old lord, his father. Maud was always remarking the resemblance, but Hester had hardly no-

ticed it before, until now when it struck her almost
like a blow. There he was, the old man who had taken
the place of a parent to her, who had seemed gruff
and terrifying at first, but who had treated her with
kindness and affection, so that she had grown to love
him dearly. There was his profile, so like him, it could
almost have been his ghost. And yet it was not as she
had ever seen him, for it was a youthful picture of
him, before his hair had thinned and turned white,
before his features had grown craggy, and his shoulders hunched. It was like looking at him as he would
have been long before she had been born.

Suddenly she felt a longing for the affection she
had shared with her father-in-law. She had to suppress
an urge to reach out and touch this man who looked
so like him. But just because they looked alike didn't
mean they were the same, she had to remind herself.
A similar profile did not necessarily mean a similar
character, or a similar love. Of course it didn't, otherwise Guy would never have left, would never have
been so desperate to escape the company of his wife.

And yet, the way he had spoken of the diamonds
on the water was still sending shivers through her, the
uncanny way he had mirrored her own secret
thoughts. No one had ever done that before, not even
the old lord. No one, since her own parents had died,
had ever made her feel such a sudden, sharp connection with them.

'Dolphins!' Guy's exclamation suddenly cut into
her thoughts and she looked up to see six of the creatures swimming alongside the boat, their arching
backs dipping in and out of the water. She felt a sudden joy welling up within her.

''Tis good luck, my lady, to have them swim alongside,' called out one of the sailors. 'It don't often 'appen. Beautiful creatures, they are.'

'They are indeed,' Hester replied.

'Do they still swim off the shore in Abbascombe Bay?' Guy asked.

Hester nodded. 'I saw a shoal last week. They looked as if they were playing.'

'My mother used to take me to the shore to watch them when I was a boy. They always made it look such fun to be a dolphin. My mother's face used to light up at the sight of them. I used to think of it when I was learning to be a squire with my Lord Perigord.'

'You must have missed her,' Hester ventured.

Guy nodded. 'I suppose that's why I wished to see the solar again on the day of my return—when I wandered in while you were washing and saw far more than I had hoped. I am sure you remember, my lady,' he added with a mischievous look. Hester felt herself flush at the memory and saw his smile broaden in response.

'Even before that sight, I had happy memories of that room, of sitting with my mother by the hearth. She used to crack nuts for me and I would watch the shells burn on the fire while she told me stories. Maud was my mother's maid too—I am sure you know. It's a long time ago, but Maud seems hardly to have changed. She was always good at organising everyone. I am sure she has sent you to the fair with many commissions to be carried out.'

'Not as many as usual. But I must buy some spices

for the kitchen. And some cloth for dresses for myself.'

'You sound reluctant. Most ladies would relish the
chance of new clothes.'

Hester grimaced in reply.

'Well, take care you obey Maud's orders, else
there'll be trouble,' Guy concluded.

'I know it.'

The tide was in their favour and the sailors brought
the boat through the straits swiftly and skilfully so
that in a few moments they were in the calmer, sheltered waters of the great harbour with its tiny islands,
reeds and sea birds. Now that they were inside the
harbour, they could see other boats making their way
towards the long, winding creek which led to the town
of Wareham. They followed the little flotilla of boats
round the meandering turns and bends of the River
Frome until suddenly they had rounded the last bend
and all at once they could see the quayside, alive with
customers and tradesmen swarming over its cobbles.
Behind the brightly coloured stalls rose the high walls
of the granary, and beyond that, set back from the
water's edge, stood the stone church and its priory,
serenely majestic despite the hustle and bustle of the
fair.

The fishermen steered deftly towards the quayside
and found a mooring space close to the bridge. As
they pulled tight the ropes around the wooden mooring stakes, Guy leaped athletically on to the quayside,
his long muscular legs bridging the gap with agile
ease. Amir sprang after him eagerly, delighted to be
back on firm ground. Then Guy leant over the boat
with outstretched arms.

'My lady Hester, may I assist you?' Hester looked up at him, into those twinkling eyes. She would have preferred to have been helped on to the quay by one of the sailors, but they were all busy making fast the boat and unpacking their load. The prospect of his strong grasp upon her sent an alarum ringing through her body. Her head was tolling out a warning too: remember that day in the stormy fields, remember how it felt to be in his arms, remember how you forgot everything when he held you. She glanced around desperately for some alternative.

'Lady, I only intend to help you on to the quayside, not to carry you off as a slave-girl,' he said with a grin, reading her thoughts again, his humour ready at her expense.

There was no alternative. Reluctantly, she stretched out her arms and let him take her hands. His strong fingers closed around hers. Time seemed to hesitate for a moment. As his face looked down at her, she was back in the field where she had ordered him to leave her land, lying in the mud with him leaning over her. The memory was uppermost in his mind too.

'I hope you will not treat me as rudely as you did last time I offered you my hand in this way,' he said with a grin. 'It was bad enough landing in the mud, I have no wish to go tumbling into the river. It might mar my enjoyment of the fair if I spent the rest of the day in sopping wet clothes.'

This time Hester couldn't help smiling back.

'Don't worry, I promise not to send you for a tumble today. Ducking my husband before so many onlookers would not enhance my reputation.'

'Is that the only thing that stops you?' he asked as he lifted her lightly on to the quayside.

'To be sure. I am entirely without scruples, but even I do not like to be detected in my unmannerliness.'

The sailors were heaving their load onto the quayside. Hester's jars of honey were already awaiting her attention, packed amongst straw in wicker baskets. She quickly chose a spot on the quayside to set out her wares. Guy carried them for her without a murmur and even helped her to unpack.

Honey was a popular commodity, necessary for flavouring and preserving foodstuffs, as well as simply for the pleasure of its taste. Whilst they were setting out the jars of honey, a stout matron stopped to buy two, and before she had continued on her way a merchant had approached, short and broad-set with a balding head.

'Is that honey, my good lady?' he asked. 'I have need of a good quantity of the stuff. My wife has ordered me to bring plenty home with me. I can trade you cloth for your jars. How many have you?'

'You want all of them?' Hester asked in surprise.

'Aye, if the quality is good.'

Hester opened one of the earthenware jars to let him taste the honey. It was thick and golden and she saw appreciation in his face.

'Could you use some cloth, my lady? Come to my stall and see if I have anything you like. I am sure something among my wares will take the lady's fancy,' he said, nodding at Guy.

'Let us hope so,' Guy replied, casting a sardonic look at Hester's plain woollen dress. It was the best she had, but rather worn and dull, its reddish brown doing little to enhance her complexion.

When they reached the merchant's stall Hester was awed by the variety and rich colours of the cloth, much of it far too fine for her purposes.

'Do you see anything you could use, my lady?' asked the merchant.

Hester immediately picked out a serviceable grey-blue bolt of sturdy linen, hard-wearing, practical and good for disguising dirt—an important consideration for her when she seemed to attract it so easily.

'That's a useful cloth, my lady, a very sensible choice,' the merchant was saying, slightly surprised that she had ignored all his finer stuffs.

''Tis commendably plain, my lady,' cut in a deep voice at her side, 'but wouldn't you prefer something a little more luxurious?' Guy pointed up at a beautifully embroidered tunic hanging from the top of the stall. The pale violet cloth was a light silk gleaming enticingly in the sunlight. It was embroidered gorgeously with a winding pattern of vine leaves and tendrils sewn in rich, green silken thread.

'It is lovely,' Hester said, her eyes attracted by its delicate sheen and exquisite details. 'But I doubt my honey would buy such a tunic.'

The merchant shook his head. 'But you could put it towards the price,' he assured her. 'I have these gloves to match, too, and a silken girdle in the same design,' he said, pulling out the gorgeous things and placing them on the stall in front of her. His eyes travelled over Guy's attire, clearly recognising the richness of his clothes in contrast to the poverty of Hester's old frock.

'They are your colours, much better than this,' Guy said, indicating the dress she was wearing with a wrinkling of his nose.

'What's wrong with what I am wearing?' she demanded.

'My lady, you remember my homecoming, how I mistook you for a…' He hesitated. 'How I failed to recognise you as Lady of Abbascombe.'

'Yes,' Hester said, the edge in her voice a signal of danger.

'It wasn't only the mud which misled me. It was also the dress beneath it and, of course…' He paused.

'And?' Hester pushed him, steeling herself.

'And I had not expected the Lady of Abbascombe to be out in the fields.'

'I wonder you had not, my lord, since your absence left me little choice.'

Guy bowed his head slightly, but his eyes were burning. 'This is neither the time nor the place for such a discussion.'

'I did not begin it,' Hester retorted. Then, turning back to the merchant, she said, 'I'll take the bolt of linen in exchange for the honey.'

'I must give you more than that for your honey, my lady,' he replied. 'Would you like a length of wool for the winter?' He pulled out a thick cloth of dark green. Hester felt its weight between her fingers.

'Yes, that would be useful too,' she agreed.

'Very well. We have a bargain,' he said, beginning to fold the cloths into a bundle. As he did so, Hester could not help glancing again at the beautiful tunic as it hung on the stall, its soft edges fluttering gently in the breeze, its colours gleaming in the sunlight.

Guy was right: it was lovely and the colours were perfect. She longed to try it on and to feel its soft folds on her skin, but to wear such a tunic would be tantamount to giving up her place in the Abbascombe fields. It would mean she had become one of those soft, useless ladies imprisoned in the house, chained to embroidery instead of striding about in the open air, overseeing the crops and the animals. Was that why he had suggested buying it? Was it part of his plan to confine her to the house, to take the reins of Abbascombe into his own hands?

'What use would I have for such finery?' she said, turning from the stall. Guy had been watching her as she gazed at the tunic and was not fooled by her dismissive words.

'It would not suit your days in the fields, certainly,' he replied. She looked up at him, trying to read his expression.

'All my days are spent in the fields,' she insisted defensively.

'Surely not all, my lady.'

'What reason could there be for me to wear such finery?'

'To please those who enjoy looking at you,' he said with unexpected candour.

'I have more important considerations than how I look,' Hester replied. 'Like organising the estate, supervising in the fields,' she added, wondering whether he would contradict her, say that this was no longer her role. Her heart pounded in anticipation of his answer.

'Very well, my lady,' was all he said with a slight

bow of his head. His dark hair flopped into his eyes and he suddenly looked boyish again.

'The tunic is lovely, you are right,' she began, softening.

'I am right? Twice in one day! Can it be so?' he interrupted with a laugh.

'But I'm sure it is very expensive, and I would have no occasion to wear it.'

'But you do like it?' he asked casually.

'Yes, of course I do. But it is not for a woman such as I.'

'No?' he queried.

'No, it is for one of those ornamental ladies who does nothing but sew and sing and look pretty. If I wore it, it would be filthy in no time.'

'Mud would not enhance it, certainly,' he said in a tone of mock thoughtfulness, which left even Hester smiling. 'Let me carry this,' he offered, reaching for the parcel of material. Hester's arms were starting to ache from its weight and she was glad at the prospect of surrendering her burden until Guy added, 'It is a little heavy.'

'I can manage. I'm not a weakling,' she objected quickly, snatching it back from his grasp. He stopped in his tracks, his hands still ready to take the weight from her arms.

'My lady, did I say you were a weakling? Did I imply that you couldn't manage? I merely wish to help my wife.' His eyes were on her, exasperation glimmering in their dark depths, his expression open and cajoling. Hester hesitated, then allowed him to take the material from her. 'Let me take it to the boat,' he said.

When he returned, he found her waiting in the same spot.

'I half expected you to be gone.' He grinned. 'Like one of the will-o-the-wisps they talk about on the River Frome. I thought you might have taken your chance to escape.'

'I was waiting for you,' Hester replied matter-of-factly.

'I am glad,' he said, his eyes twinkling in the spring sunshine. 'May I accompany you round the fair?'

Hester nodded and they set off. For once their silence was companionable as they wove their way amongst the stalls and people thronging Wareham High Street, with Amir following close at Guy's heel.

The unaccustomed noise filled Hester's ears as the pedlars cried out their wares and stallholders and customers haggled over goods. Everything was for sale: meat, cheeses, spices, tools, carpentry, leather, basketry, ribbons, jewellery... There were animals in pens in the street: goats, sheep, cattle, poultry. Everywhere she turned there was noisy activity.

'This reminds me of a *souk* in the East,' Guy commented.

'A *souk*?' Hester repeated.

'Yes, it is the Saracen word for a market. And it was in a *souk* that I bought my dear Amir, when she was no more than a puppy. A little bundle of fluff, weren't you, Amir?' he said, stooping to pat the dog. 'I couldn't resist her great, brown eyes looking plaintively up at me, and she has been my constant companion ever since.'

'Is her name a Saracen word?'

'Indeed it is. Amir means a commander, a leader.

'Twas not very apt when she was a puppy, but I believe she has grown into it now,' he replied with a proud glance at his hound.

'And you walked freely through a Saracen market?' Hester asked, incredulous and longing to hear more.

'Many times. They are fascinating places.'

'You seem to have mixed with the Saracen a good deal,' Hester ventured. 'It surprises me that you should have done so. And you speak their language too, the language of heathens, people you went there to fight.'

'I know.' Guy nodded. 'Is it not strange? I went there to kill them, but I had a change of heart. And I have this to thank for it,' he said, pointing to the scar by his eye. 'I was wounded, in pain and, most of all, fearing for the sight of this eye. 'Twas not the only wound I took in that skirmish, but it was the eye which troubled me. There was nothing the Christian doctors could do to reassure me, but then I heard of a person who might help, a Saracen, very learned, who was willing to help even Christians.'

'And he healed you?'

'*She* healed me,' he corrected. 'Yes, and in more ways than one, for I was wounded in spirit as well as in body. In Fatima's house I learned to live again and to see again. And I learned the Saracen ways from her, too.'

'A woman,' Hester breathed, taken aback.

'A kind and learned woman, living a life very different from yours. Her house was in a walled city, close to the mosque, which is the Saracen place of worship. Every morning I was woken by the call to prayer. ''Prayer is better than sleep,'' is the chant each dawn, calling the men to the mosque. The women stay at home to pray.'

'What are their homes like?'

'Built to be cool with thick stone walls and tiled floors. The people sit cross-legged on cushions on the floor and eat and drink from little, low tables set before them. They have beautiful carpets woven in many colours. But in all their decorations they never depict a person or an animal for fear that such an image might become a false idol to be worshipped. So their decorations are all intricate patterns and geometrical shapes. And they are fond of using decorative writing, words from their scriptures to decorate a wall.'

'And do they dress as we do?'

'No, they wear long, loose robes, and the women cover their hair and their faces when they venture out of their houses. Their complexions are not like yours either. There are no freckles and no fair hair. The women are all dark-skinned with black hair and dark eyes.'

'They sound very beautiful,' Hester commented quietly.

'Many are,' Guy agreed.

'Was Fatima?' Hester ventured, her heart pounding in anticipation of his response.

'Yes,' he replied after a pause, and Hester's heart missed a beat. 'Yes, she was, in her way. And she had an inner beauty, a serenity which she tried to give to me, shattered warrior that I was.'

'But you left her,' Hester murmured, hardly daring to breathe.

'It was time to come back,' he said with a shrug. 'And now it is time for some lunch. What do you say to a feast such as this?' he asked lightly, indicating a stall close by, well stocked with cheeses and pies. Hester nodded, though she ached with the need to hear more of Fatima.

A few minutes later, they were sitting by the bridge, tucking into a loaf of bread flavoured with nuts and a lump of creamy goat's cheese.

'And do you think of her?' Hester asked at last.

'Of Fatima? Yes, I think of her. I have much to thank her for.'

'Do you think of returning to her land?'

'Would you like me to?'

Hester hesitated at his directness. She had not expected him to turn the question back upon her. Her wish had been to find out all she could about this woman, this paramour he had left behind in the East. Of course, she had expected that he must have known many women there, but hearing him speak of this Fatima left her feeling raw inside.

'Come, we must not dally here,' he was saying, leaping to his feet, 'Else we will not have time to make our purchases. And I know that Fritha is most eager to have some spices for the kitchen.'

'Yes, she is,' Hester agreed limply, following his lead.

They headed for a stall selling spices and chose quantities of pepper, cinnamon, nutmeg, cloves and ginger.

'These spices have travelled as far as you,' Hester said, looking up at him.

'Perhaps further.' He nodded.

'Does the air there smell as that stall does, full of the scent of spices?'

'Away from the battlefields it sometimes does. At the stalls in the *souks*, or in the kitchen of a good cook.'

'In Fatima's kitchen?'

'Sometimes. But mostly the air smells of heat and dust. And the desert smells like nothing else, nothing that I could describe to you. It is the sounds which linger with me more. The sound of the *muezzin* calling the people to prayer.'

'You listened to heathen prayers?' Hester asked aghast.

'Only from outside the mosque. I would not have been permitted to enter. If I were to repeat the words of the *muezzin*'s call, you would be surprised how much it sounds like one of your own prayers. "In the name of God, the merciful, the compassionate. God is most great," he chants. "I witness that there is no god but God." See, you might pray it too.'

'But they do not mean the true God,' Hester protested.

'Oh, but they do. They mean the same God whom you hear of in your Sunday sermons.'

Hester stared at him. 'Is that true?'

Guy nodded. 'The Saracens recognise the similarities. They call Christians "People of the Book", meaning that we share many of their teachings.'

'And did they not hate you for going there to fight them? Did they really let you walk freely in their towns?'

'Many cities were hostile to Christians, and understandably so. But some were our allies. Anyway, my lady, enough of this talk. You must be bored by my ramblings.' Hester opened her mouth to object, but before she could do so, he had continued, 'I am sure you have many important purchases to make in which a husband would be nothing but a hindrance, so I bid you farewell for a short while and I shall look forward to seeking you later.' And with that he was gone, disappearing into the throng of market-goers.

Hester felt dismissed and suddenly lonely without him. In spite of her earlier reluctance to have him as her companion, she realised now that she felt bereft without him. And she longed to hear more of his time in the East, especially of the bewitching Fatima. She felt strangely unsettled by his talk of that lady's goodness. Hester longed to know what had happened to make him leave, why he had not stayed to enjoy her company since it was obvious he had loved her. Conjectures whirled through her mind, until suddenly she found she was back close to the merchant who had taken her honey in exchange for his cloth. Automatically, she scanned his stall, searching for the gorgeous tunic. It was gone. In spite of herself she felt a pang of loss.

'Don't be ridiculous,' she muttered under her breath. 'You could never have worn it. What would have been the point of having so fine a thing?' But a little voice inside her remained unconvinced in spite of her reprimands. The tunic had been the loveliest thing she had ever seen and now it belonged to someone else. Another woman would be wearing it, feeling its soft folds draping around her body. Perhaps another woman's husband had bought it for her as a present. What did it matter now? Hester tried to push it from her mind.

As she turned away from the stall, a figure stepped into her path. Hester looked up to find herself staring into the face of Hugo Lacave, his small eyes examining her with malicious interest. He wasn't as scruffy as usual, clearly wearing his best clothes in honour of the fair, but still he repelled her.

'My lady Beauvoisin,' he addressed her with a slight bow, an insinuating whine in his voice, 'what a pleasure to see you. And here you are, the loving wife, buying things to please your husband.'

'Indeed, sir,' Hester replied, contorting her face into a false smile.

'How good that is to see. I had feared you might have grown to love your independence too much and that you might not enjoy being mastered at last.'

'Then, sir, you quite mistook the case, for I have been praying for my husband's return these many years,' she lied. 'No one could be more delighted than I to see him safely returned at last.'

'Is that so?' Lacave ground out through clenched teeth.

Hester laughed inwardly at his obvious discomfort. Her answer had been calculated to annoy and had obviously succeeded.

'And now, if you will excuse me,' she continued disingenuously, 'I have a long shopping list. It is such a joy to have my lord back in Abbascombe Manor that I wish everything to be perfect for him. I am sure you understand. Good day to you.'

Hester swung away into the crowd, grinning mischievously to herself. That had certainly told him!

That miscreant who had presumed to imagine there
was a place for him in her bed!

She turned her steps towards the livestock pens,
still gloating at the look on Lacave's spiteful face, but
her attention was caught by the cries of mummers
calling an audience to their play. A crowd of spec-
tators was gathering around a makeshift wooden stage
in the street. The play was beginning.

The troupe of travelling players were acting out the
story of Noah's Ark. Noah was played by a tall fair
man in middle years, diligently building his ark while
another actor playing God bemoaned the wickedness
of man. The crowd watched patiently through these
serious speeches, knowing that comedy was to come.
God exited solemnly, to make way for Mrs Noah, a
man ludicrously dressed in the clothes of a housewife,
with a huge, padded chest sticking out in front. A
howl of laughter went up at his appearance and the
audience settled down to be amused. They did not
have to wait long, for Mrs Noah immediately began
scolding her husband, berating him for every fault
under the sun while he attempted to explain to her
that God had visited him.

The great crowd around the stage was growing
thicker and thicker as Noah fought with his wife. She
produced a rolling pin to beat him with and refused
to listen to warnings of rain, scolding him all the
while for being a no-good hare-brain, until eventually
he had to carry her, still screeching and squawking,
on to the Ark, amidst gales of laughter from the audience. Hester laughed too—she couldn't help it, the
sight was so ridiculous.

As the theatrical floods began to rise and Noah, his

wife and sons swayed as if with the motion of the seas, she suddenly caught sight of Guy beyond the stage. His tall dark back was turned towards her, but there was no mistaking him. He was facing Hugo Lacave and they seemed to be having an animated conversation.

She saw Lacave move towards Guy and put his hand on Guy's elbow. Guy immediately shook it off as if his touch were poisoned. There was an angry exchange of words, then Guy stepped close to him, said something, then turned on his heel and strode away. He was heading towards the actors when his eyes lighted on Hester as if drawn by a magnet. He immediately seemed to pick her face out of the crowd and in a moment he had found his way to her side. His breath was fast and shallow, and his face was dark with anger. He grasped her elbow, his hand gripping like a vice.

'Time to leave, lady,' he commanded.

'Already?' Hester asked in surprise, instinctively pulling away from his stern grasp. 'But I'm watching the play.'

The audience roared with laughter as Mrs Noah acted out a contretemps with one of the animals aboard the Ark.

'Time to leave,' Guy repeated, his voice icy amid the spirited guffaws. Then he seemed to collect himself and added in a more measured voice, 'We mustn't miss the tide, else we'll be stranded here for the night.'

Hester stared at him. 'But surely there's plenty of time,' she began.

'Lady, must you argue with me in every matter? I

say it is time to leave.' Something in his voice warned her not to question him further.

'Very well,' she said and turned to follow him. The crowd had grown dense behind her and they had to push their way amongst the onlookers. A group of men at the back were drinking from great flagons, unruly and raucous. Hester could smell the miasma of cider around them. They were jostling each other in rowdy banter and, as Hester squeezed past them, one of the men fell against her. She clutched at Guy's sleeve to try to steady herself as he forged ahead of her. He swung around suddenly and looked piercingly into her face, a question in his eyes.

'The man pushed against me,' Hester stammered in explanation, disconcerted by his searching gaze and his sudden desire to leave.

'Of course. I should have noticed,' he replied, his voice softening a little as he placed a protective arm around her. 'Come.'

Once in the boat, they sped quickly through the harbour and out to sea, swept along by the tide and the following wind. Dusk was falling rapidly and the sky was turning inky black. The moon, already visible, was a luminous full circle, and a few bright stars soon began twinkling around it. The splash of the waves against the hull of the boat and the hum of the wind in its sails were the only sounds.

Hester, still puzzled by Guy's insistence on leaving the fair, sat silently in the hull of the boat, watching the dark line of the coast as they sped past. The sandy beaches close to the harbour mouth soon gave way to craggy cliffs which grew steeper and taller as they sailed further round the bay. She hardly dared address

Guy after his surliness, and even Amir seemed to forbid her to speak as she lay absolutely still by her master's feet.

'There are the Pleiades. See,' Guy said, unexpectedly breaking the silence and pointing high into the night sky. His voice had shed its harshness. Despite her surprise, Hester followed his eyes and saw the cluster of stars winking in the sky.

'How do you know?' she asked. He was constantly amazing her with his unexpected knowledge, but what she really wanted to ask was what Lacave had said to him to make him want to leave the fair so suddenly.

'I learned to read the stars in the East. The Saracens have made great studies of the heavens. As I told you, they are a race of great knowledge and civilisation. Far more civilised than many I find in England.'

'You mean Hugo Lacave?'

'What do you know of that?' Guy demanded suddenly urgent, turning those piercing eyes on her once more.

'I saw you with him. You looked angry.'

'I was angry…*am* angry. Do not ask me why. Look at the glimmering on the water,' he said, suddenly pointing to the phosphorescence shining as the boat cut through the water.

'It's beautiful,' Hester said, sharing his appreciation of the strange green light shimmering in the water, while her mind raced after an explanation for his anger. They were nearly home, entering Abbascombe Bay, the moon lighting their way, the water smooth like a vast sheet of dark velvet all around them.

As they reached the shallow water close to the beach, the sailors turned the boat windward, so that it came to a halt, and Guy leaped over the side, landing thigh-deep in the cold waves. Amir plunged after him and swam eagerly ashore. Guy held out his arms to Hester and this time she obeyed without protest, allowing him to carry her through the surf. She put her arms around his neck and felt a mutinous thrill at such proximity, the warmth of his body, the strong muscles of his arms as he held her, the musky scent of his hair as her head touched his. All too soon they were on the sand and he had dropped her lightly onto her feet. They stood for a moment in the moonlight.

'You're wet,' she said, stating the obvious.

'Yes.' He laughed, not at her, but with unexpected good humour despite his recent bad temper. 'Goodnight! Thank you!' he called to the fishermen as they sailed on to their boat's mooring.

'Oh, no! My material and the spices!' Hester cried, remembering that she had left them in the boat.

'It's all right. I asked them to bring the things up to the house tomorrow,' Guy reassured her. 'So, you did enjoy spending some money after all?'

'Yes, I did,' she admitted quietly. His arm had remained around her when he had put her down on the sand. It was still around her, lightly cradling her, and Hester realised that she did not wish to shake it off. The night was soft and still around them, a gentle breeze caressing their skin.

'Come, my lady,' he said, his arm tightening almost imperceptibly, pulling her just a little closer. 'It is late. Time for bed.'

Before she knew what she was doing, Hester had shied away instinctively. She felt herself blush, suddenly confused. Of course, he meant nothing like that, he had not meant…but then why had her mind so suddenly imagined him joining her in her bed?

'There's no need to fear, my lady,' he said, his voice suddenly sharp with understanding. 'I have no intention of forcing my way into your chamber. It was merely an unfortunate choice of words.' Hester did not know what to say. She could feel the heat in her cheeks and knew that if she opened her mouth now, whatever she said would sound wrong.

'It would have been better for you if I had never returned, if I had stayed in the East to study the stars,' Guy said quietly, looking away from her, down the dark beach.

'No,' Hester stammered suddenly, surprising herself with the word.

'No?' he asked urgently, turning to look into her face, his hands grasping her shoulders once again.

'You would have become an infidel,' she said lamely, sensing this was not what he wanted to hear.

Guy laughed. 'You shouldn't listen to what they say of the Saracens. That would not have been so terrible as some would have it.'

'Why did you return?' Hester asked suddenly, her question cutting through the night.

'I missed Abbascombe, believe it or not. When I left I never thought I'd say that.' He smiled bitterly, throwing his head back, taking in the night sky. There was a pause. 'I wondered about you too,' he said quietly, as if whispering to the stars. 'I wondered how you had grown up. What sort of woman you had become. But it was perhaps a vain, foolish wish.'

A wish? Had he wished to see her after all? Hester's mind wondered feverishly. 'And have you found what you expected?' she asked out loud.

'No,' he said slowly and in the pause which followed she could feel her heart beating a tattoo of
impatience and trepidation until he spoke again at
last. 'You are so far from what I expected. I still saw
you as a little girl. I never imagined you so…' He
paused.

'So what?' asked Hester. Suddenly his expectations
mattered a great deal.

'So womanly, so beautiful. You didn't want me to
come back, did you?' he continued.

'I used to want you to come back, when I was a
girl…' she managed to say.

'You did?'

'Yes, your father missed you so much, I—'

Guy nodded a sharp, forbidding nod, preventing
her from saying more. 'But you had long ago stopped
wishing for my return, even for his sake.'

No words formed on Hester's lips. He was right.
She had not wanted him to return. It had been the last
thing she would have wished for. But now? What did
she feel now? His intrusion at Abbascombe still made
her angry, but it no longer filled her with the rage she
had felt at first. And then there were those moments
when he touched her and her body thrilled to the sensation in a way she had never experienced or expected. But how could she let him into her heart when
he had made it clear that he regarded her as nothing
more than a part of his Abbascombe estate, a possession to be claimed after his long absence, a duty to
be maintained?

'Come then, my lady,' said Guy, formal once
again, as if he had read her thoughts. 'It is growing
cold and late. We should be getting home.'

Chapter Six

The early morning sun filled Hester's bedroom with light as she lay in bed thinking of the previous day. What had all those questions on the beach meant? Did he really care whether she had wished for his return or not? Why should he, when the land was his no matter what she felt?

Her mind kept revisiting the scene of the fair when she had seen Guy talking to Hugo Lacave: the obvious ill-will between the two men, Guy's anger, and his insistence upon their immediate departure. To be sure, she loathed their neighbour, but until yesterday it had seemed as though he had been keen for the Lord of Abbascombe's friendship, not at all likely to pick an argument with his newly returned neighbour. He had visited Guy several times and Guy had repaid the calls. She had even gathered from Guy that Lacave had suggested sharing some of the farm labour.

There was a tap at the door.

'Come in,' Hester called.

'Good morning, my lady, it's another fine day,'

clucked Maud as she bustled into the chamber. 'Sir Guy was up and off long ago, at first light.'

'So early? What reason can he have for being out with the dawn?'

Maud shrugged. 'He didn't say. But I expect he has something new to teach young Eadric. The two of them rode out together. Sir Guy is certainly spending a lot of time educating him. I only hope the boy appreciates it.'

'I'm sure he does, Maud. Eadric loves being squire, though it's certainly not what I had planned for him.'

'I should think not, my lady. I never heard of a squire that wasn't noble-born. But then Sir Guy always did have his own ideas about everything. He is so like the old lord, his father.'

'Really?' Hester asked in surprise. 'Do you really think they're alike?' Ever since noticing the physical resemblance between the sire and the son, she had been regretting that her husband's personality wasn't more like that of his father.

'My lady, they are so alike that I sometimes think I am a young girl again, waiting on the old lord instead of on his son. He was just as headstrong in his day, and he caused some heartaches to his old father too, though of course he didn't run off to the crusades. But if the old squire's father had done as he had done and ordered him to marry where he did not—' Maud stopped short, biting her tongue as she realised what she had been about to say—and to whom. Her plump old cheeks turned pink and she tried hurriedly to turn the conversation. 'I mean, if he had…'

'It's all right, Maud, you don't have to pretend with me. I am well aware that Sir Guy did not want to marry me. How could I escape the knowledge when he preferred to run off to war and risk his life rather than stay in the same house with me?'

'Oh, my lady, you mustn't see it that way. He didn't join the crusades to escape from you.'

'Did he not? It certainly looked like it,' Hester replied bitterly.

'Lord love you, you haven't been thinking that all these years, have you? You poor child. He wasn't running away from you. It was his father's rule he couldn't stick. They were too alike. They loved each other, of course, though they would never say so. But two men like that in one house: it's a recipe for trouble. Both headstrong, both wanting their own way, and one compelled to obey the other only because of his age. That's what he was running from. He had to prove himself, to go away and make his own decisions, to grow up and become a man. He couldn't do that here with his father telling him what to do.'

Hester stared at her. In the last ten years she had gone over it all so many times in her head, relived that fateful day of her marriage again and again and always she had pictured herself as the cause. She had thought herself too unlovable, too repugnant to the handsome youth who had been forced to become her husband, who was now this dark, mesmerising man casting a strange spell over her which she hardly understood. A new thought suddenly struck her.

'Do—do you think he might have gone anyway, even if it hadn't been me that his father had chosen for his bride?' she asked hesitantly, the answer strangely important to her.

'Why, bless you, my lady, of course he would have

gone, whoever the bride had been. And don't you go
thinking otherwise. He was a headstrong, wilful boy
on the lookout for adventure. And no doubt seeking
a little trouble too—I wouldn't be surprised. Don't
you ever go blaming yourself. It was the old lord who
should have consulted him a little more about the
marriage, that's all. But they were never great ones
for talking when it mattered. Of course, when Sir
Guy's mother, the lady Adela, was alive that didn't
matter so much. She was the bridge between them
and she didn't mind knocking their heads together
when they needed it. But once she was gone they
were both too mighty to concede and there was bound
to be trouble, no matter how much they cared for each
other deep down. It's just like the stags in the spring,
when they fight to be king of the herd, and often as
not it's father against son with them as well, I
reckon.'

'So you don't think it was my fault?' Hester ventured, feeling the burden of years suddenly lifting
from her shoulders.

'Of course it wasn't. He didn't leave because of
you, only to prove a point to his father, to punish him
for not treating him as an adult. They were both too
proud to back down, so instead they backed themselves into corners and it ended as it did. My lady,
he may not have wanted to be married to you when
he was twenty—after all, he was already a man and
you were still a little girl—but he certainly wants to
be married to you now.'

'No, Maud, you're wrong. He missed Abbascombe,
that's why he came back, and I'm just part of his

estate,' Hester said ruefully, her eyes prickling with the thought.

'Oh, no, my lady, you should know by now that your old maid is rarely wrong,' Maud said, shaking her head and taking Hester's hand in hers. 'I've seen the way he looks at you. If it wasn't you he returned for, it's you he'll stay for. If you let him, that is. But mind, he's proud and he's still wilful. You're a pair in that,' she said, nodding her head wisely. 'Oh, yes, never was there such a pair of headstrong creatures.'

Hester tossed back her tousled hair. She was used to being called headstrong by Maud. It was the old woman's favourite lament whenever Hester did something she disapproved.

'Come, Maud, perhaps you are right. And to prove that I bow to your judgement, I will submit to your hair-brushing this morning, no matter how painful it may be.'

'Well, thank heavens for small mercies. And if it hurts, you've no one but yourself to blame, for you will go out in the wind and let it get all tangled and knotted, and then you will refuse to let me brush it properly whenever you—'

'Ow!' Hester squealed as Maud dragged the brush through her tangled curls. 'If I must suffer the torture of your brush, at least spare me the scolding.'

She eventually escaped her chamber, hair neatly plaited, all tangles driven away by Maud's ferocious brushing. She found William on the pasture land, checking over the cows, those who were still to calf and those who had calved. Her heart felt unaccustomedly light after Maud's words and there was a spring in her step which sent her skipping into the fields like a child.

'Good morning, my lady. 'Tis a fine morning. And we have a new calf. Look.' He pointed to the spindly-legged creature suckling from his mother. 'Don't go close, though. She's pretty touchy about her calf, and I don't blame her for he's a fine young fellow. But when I came down to feed them first thing this morning, she was here and no sign of him. Of course, I could see straight away that she had calved and at first I was afraid the little thing might have been still-born. So I looked all around and couldn't see a car-cass and then I noticed that when she had finished feeding from the trough with all the others she started sidling off on her own, all quiet and cunning-like, so I followed her at a distance and she went off through the copse and up the hill and along by the meadow and there he was just lying waiting, good as gold, under a bush.

'I didn't want to go near because you know a cow can be pretty fierce when she's got a little one and doesn't want you interfering with him. But I put down some feed a few yards off, and she came to it, and the little one followed, and then I put down some more, and some more, and before she knew it they were both back here with the others and now she's fine, they both are. But I'd leave well alone if I were you.'

Hester smiled up at him. 'I never cease to be glad that you are here to manage Abbascombe.'

'Why, thank you, my lady,' William said, his rosy cheeks turning a little pinker at her praise. 'But it's only what anyone might have done.'

'No, not anyone.' Maud's words were making Hester feel at peace with the world, and she had taken to heart Maud's admonition that Guy and his father should have talked more. 'And now what else is there to be done today?'

William ran through the tasks for the day. There were thistles springing up in the meadow which had to be weeded out before they took hold and some loose thatching on one of the barns to be repaired, in addition to the normal, everyday tasks of running the farm.

'Rolf and Winn are the best hands for thatching. I'll get them on to that. And I've already sent six of the others into the meadow,' William was explaining. Just then Guthrum appeared, hurrying and out of breath, his huge frame built for strength, not for speed.

'Where are you off to, Guthrum?' Hester asked in concern.

'I'm looking for Breda. She's not in her cottage and Judith needs her to help with her father. Alured has fallen ill. He has a sickness.'

'What sort of sickness? Is it serious?'

'Can't tell, my lady. Looks serious, he's laid right low. Judith wants Breda to see him.'

'I saw Breda up in the copse this morning. I'll ride up there and look for her. Save you some time,' offered William.

'Guthrum, I'll come back with you to the village and see if there's anything I can do,' said Hester.

When she reached the little cottage where Judith and her father lived, Hester found Alured laid on the low pallet which served as his bed, shivering as if he were lying on a bed of ice, while his skin burnt to the touch. His breath was laboured and the sound of his wheezing filled the room.

'How long has he been like this?' she asked Judith, who was pale with anxiety and tiredness.

'Since yester eve, my lady. At first I thought he'd sleep it off, but it grew worse as the night drew in. I don't know what to do for the best,' said the poor girl, biting back a sob, her eyes red-rimmed and watery.

'Don't worry,' Hester reassured her, putting an arm around her skinny shoulders. 'You won't have to manage on your own now. You'll have plenty of people to help you with nursing. And Breda is bound to have some potion which will do Alured good.'

Hester sent one of the village children up to Abbascombe Manor with a message for Maud to send clean bedlinen and some broth. If Alured was too ill to eat, Judith certainly needed some nourishment after her long vigil. A few minutes later, William arrived with Breda. The old woman shuffled through the low door of the dark cottage, her hands stained with the juice of the berries she had been collecting, her wrinkled face tanned like leather by the sun.

'M'lady,' she said with a nod to Hester. 'Judith, you poor lass, don't take on. We'll see your father better yet. Now, let's have a look at 'im. Alured, can you hear me?' The sick man made no sign of acknowledgement, but just continued turning his sweating head from one side of his wet pillow to the other.

'Mmm,' Breda said to herself as she felt his brow. 'Mmm. Ol' Breda reckons she can help him,' she said at last, nodding at Judith. 'Don't you worry, girl, he can pull through this. He's a strong man, Alured, still in his prime. I'll be off to get my herbs and we'll have him right again soon.'

Hester followed Breda out of the cottage. 'Do you need some help in preparing or carrying?' she offered.

'Thank you, m'lady, another pair of hands would be of use.'

Hester walked with Breda towards her cottage, longing to speed the wise woman's gait, but Breda always walked with the same shuffling steps, her old legs tired from many years of tramping round the countryside in search of the special ingredients for her potions and ointments.

Stepping out of the spring sunlight and into the one room of Breda's low-roofed cottage, Hester found herself surrounded by unfamiliar shapes and smells looming out of the sudden darkness. As her eyes adjusted to the change in light, she could pick out bunches of leaves, grasses, roots, and seed-pods hanging from the beam which stretched above their heads, some still fresh, some dry and brittle, all with their individual odours competing to fill her unaccustomed nostrils. There were leather bags and pouches and even the carcass of a dead rabbit hanging from the beam. Hester lowered her head to avoid knocking against them. Pans, jars and jugs were clustered in one corner of the room, a pile of animal skins in another, and in a third was Breda's bench-like bed, covered with a sheepskin.

Breda put her hand into one of the bags and pulled out a handful of leaves. She threw them down on to the wooden table and began chopping at them with a

long knife, its blade so sharp it made Hester wince.
Then she gathered them up and dropped them into an
earthenware bowl, scooping out a great dollop of lard
from a jug and beginning to pound the two together
with a pestle, its wooden handle smoothed by long
years of constant use by Breda's gnarled fingers.

'See how I do it?' Breda asked, glancing up. Hester
nodded. 'You come and save my old arms then, while
I look out something else to help Alured.'

The old woman shuffled around the room, pulling
down handfuls of this and that from the bunches
hanging above them. Many were the remains of plants
which Hester could not even put a name to. Hester
carried on pounding at her mixture, knowing that
Breda's skills and knowledge were beyond her experience, but Breda seemed to sense her curiosity.

'Want to know what's in it, do you?' She tossed
the words over her shoulder as she busied herself with
her pouches and purses of seeds.

'If you don't mind telling me,' Hester said tentatively. Even though she was lady of the manor, she
was a little in awe of Breda, just like everyone else.
There was always more than a hint of mystery about
the old woman, an essence of something unknowable
and profound.

'You're making the paste for a poultice there.
You've got some sage: "He that would live for aye,
Must eat sage in May." You heard that old saying?
'Tis true, mind. That'll soothe the heat in his skin,
ease the stiffness caused by the fever. And I'm a-
making of a brew here. A bit of catmint and elderflower to cool the fever, some pokeroot and boneset
for cleansing, and burdock to ease the skin. That's for

him to drink.' Breda shuffled about, throwing the contents of pouches and jugs into the cauldron over the fire. A pungent smell emanated from the pot as the water inside it boiled the herbs.

Hester carried on pounding at the paste until her wrist ached and her arm felt too heavy to move. And all the while Breda stirred her concoction over the smoky turf fire.

'That'll do,' the old woman said at last, pouring the murky liquid into a jug. 'It can cool on the way. Best to drink it warm, but not hot for a fever. Once the fever's gone, we'll make another brew with borage to strengthen him.'

'You think he'll be all right then?' Hester asked.

'Ol' Breda reckons so, m'lady. He's a strong man with a will to live. That's ready now,' she said, glancing over Hester's shoulder at the paste. 'Time to return.' They carried their bowls carefully back to where Alured lay fitfully by the turf fire, with Judith sitting beside him, her head drooping with worry and exhaustion.

Breda produced a piece of cloth and spread Hester's paste over it, then laid it carefully on to the bare skin of Alured's chest. 'Now, lift his head a little,' she told Hester, reaching for the jug containing the infusion. Hester gently cradled the ill man's head, damp with sweat and burning with fever.

'All right, Alured, my boy,' said Breda, her rich, soft voice carrying a magic of its own, for Alured suddenly grew calm and still. 'Ol' Breda's got something to ease you. You would have been a-spitting this out when you were a boy. I remember what a scoundrel you were, but you drink it down now, my love, for Ol' Breda's sake.' She spooned a little of the liquid on to his tongue. 'Now, you swallow, there's a good lad,' she ordered, and he obeyed, swallowing that spoonful and the next and the next until the contents of half the jug were gone.

'That'll do for now,' said Breda. 'Now, young Judith, you've done your share for today. You need to rest.' Judith opened her mouth to protest, but Breda was too quick for her. 'No arguing. Wearing yourself to a frazzle won't do your father any good. He'll need you tomorrow when I reckon he'll be strong enough to eat a little. You've got your work cut out, girl. We'll sit with him today, but tomorrow it's up to you, so best get your rest now. Off you go, off to my cottage. Go and have a sleep on Ol' Breda's bed. Off with you.'

Judith went off obediently, the strain on her tired face relaxing a little with Breda's confident prediction of Alured's recovery. As soon as she had gone, Breda threw another turf on the fire and hung Judith's cauldron of water over the heat, then she threw in a handful of something and the room began to fill with a clear, sweet-smelling vapour.

'Help his chest, ease his breathing that will,' Breda muttered in explanation.

Just then Maud appeared at the door, her arms laden with linen and a jug.

'How is he?' she whispered.

'He'll do,' replied Breda.

'Where do you want these, my lady?' Maud asked, turning to Hester.

'We'll change his linen now, I think, to make him more comfortable. The linen he's on is soaked through with sweat.' Hester glanced at Breda for approval and the old woman nodded. 'But he won't be able to manage the broth today. It's Judith who needs that. She's over in Breda's cottage, getting some rest.'

'Shall I take it to her, then?' Maud asked, handing the linen to Hester.

'Yes, and Breda and I will stay here,' she replied as Maud bustled off to find Judith.

Hester and Breda had begun peeling away the damp sheets from Alured's bed when they heard Guy's voice outside. Hester felt her muscles tense at the sound.

'What's going on here, Maud?' she heard him ask. Maud's reply was only partially audible, as she explained about Alured's sickness. Then, 'What?' she heard Guy demand, his deep voice carrying clearly from outside the cottage. 'She's here? Amidst the sickness? Why didn't you stop her?'

In a moment his great figure was looming in the doorway, blocking out the light.

'Hester,' he said, his deep voice shattering the quiet of the cottage.

'Hush!' Hester whispered, vividly aware that he had used her name to address her. 'Can't you see he's ill? He needs peace and quiet, not your shouting,' she hissed, moving rapidly towards the doorway, pushing him out into the open air. He grabbed at her elbow and pulled her with him.

'Of course I can see how ill he is. Do you think I'm blind? I can also see the danger you're putting yourself in. Are you mad?' he demanded. His face was paler than usual and he looked tense and strained, his scar standing out like a gash beneath his eye, his hair sticking to his forehead with sweat. He was wearing his everyday riding clothes, but somehow there was something different about him, some subtle change which Hester sensed but could not identify. She shook off his arm.

'I'm helping Breda to nurse him. What did you expect me to do?'

'I expected you to show a little sense and stay in the house. There's any number of people who could do this work. Why tempt fate by coming here and putting yourself in contagion's reach?' he demanded, his voice urgent, his eyes heavy on hers.

'Because I care, of course. Because I wanted to come and help. Because I couldn't bear to stay away looking after myself while Alured struggled for his life in the village. What sort of woman do you think I am?'

'A very foolish one,' came his rapid answer.

'I would rather die of sickness than be the fine selfish sort of lady who sits at home in her manor house protecting her own health whilst her people die.'

'Do you imagine it will help anyone if you catch the sickness and die too?'

'I don't care. I would rather die than desert them. I would never desert them.'

'And I did, you mean,' he growled back at her, feeling a rebuke where she had not intended one, but she didn't correct him. His face, with its unaccustomed pallor, looked over her shoulder into the cottage and took in the scene. 'You must go back to the house,' he ordered.

'I shan't leave here. I don't care what you say. You can't force me to do anything.'

'The law does not agree with you there, my lady,' he told her, and Hester sensed a threat in his voice as well as in his words, but she would not submit.

'Does it not?' she asked in return, knowing full well that he was right. 'Then do you care to force me, my lord?' she challenged, injecting an insolence into his formal title, so that he widened his eyes in response.

'Do you challenge me?' he asked. 'I am thinking only of your welfare.'

'And I am thinking of Alured's welfare,' Hester countered.

'I will stay with Alured, but you must return to the house,' he said with determination.

'You!' Hester exclaimed, unable to hide her surprise.

'Why not?' he demanded.

She hesitated, looking at him in astonishment.

'If they need help, I can give it just as well as you. They're my people too,' he declared with determination. He was right, but the thought made her feel suddenly possessive of her villagers. Yet how could she argue against his wish to help when she had asserted her own so strongly?

'Very well,' she said at last, and saw the sigh of relief as he heard her acquiescence, before she added, 'But I will stay too.'

'What? What is the point of that? We cannot both be needed.'

'I have told you I will not leave until I feel sure of his recovery. You should know by now, my lord, that I do not change my mind.'

'Aye, I know that well enough.'

Guy said nothing more, but his face was grim as he followed her into the cottage.

They spent the rest of the day tending to the sick man under Breda's supervision, Hester spooning more of the brew gently into his mouth while Guy supported his head, their eyes meeting every so often in the gloom.

By sunset Alured's fevered restlessness had eased and his brow no longer burned. He was soon sleeping deeply, a calm, peaceful sleep of recovery.

'No need for you to stay now,' said Breda, 'Either of you,' she added. 'He'll sleep the night through now and Ol' Breda will sit with him.'

'Are you sure you don't need help?' Guy checked. 'I am happy to stay,' he added, avoiding Hester's eyes.

'No, my lord, there's no need now. You've both done more than your duty. 'Tis enough.'

'Very well, Breda. But if you should need anything at all, please send to the house,' Hester told her.

'Come, my lady,' Guy said, grasping Hester's hand tightly, so that she had little choice but to obey.

He led the way through the doorway and into the dusky evening. Glancing up at him surreptitiously, Hester could see that his face was still pale, with dark shadows beneath his eyes and a mist of perspiration on his forehead. His shoulders seemed hunched and tense and there was something in the way he moved, an unaccustomed stiffness, a deliberateness in every movement which suddenly alarmed Hester.

'My lord,' she ventured, 'Are you all right? You seem—'

'Fine. I am fine,' he replied sharply.

'But you seem tired or—'

'Please do not concern yourself, my lady,' he said hastily, turning to face her. As he did so, he seemed to lose his balance and suddenly he was falling. Hester saw it happen as if at half-speed, his great height and strength crumpling before her, while he still clasped her hand, his fingers so tight around hers that she fell to the ground with him, landing on her knees beside him.

'My lord, what ails thee?' she asked, turning his face towards her, but he was senseless, his eyes closed, his limbs heavy.

'Help!' she cried. 'Help!'

Breda was there in a moment, leaning over them as Hester tried to support Guy's heavy form.

'Is it the sickness?' Hester cried in alarm. 'Has he caught it too?'

'No, 'tis not the same as Alured's sickness,' Breda breathed, her brow furrowed as she felt Guy's forehead, then lifted his eyelids to look into his eyes.

Hester pulled at his tightly fastened jacket to loosen the ties. She slipped her hands inside its folds to push the heavy leather away from his chest. In an instant she snatched back her hand. Her fingertips had touched...what? She looked down at her hand. Her fingers were red with wet blood. A scream filled her throat. Breda ripped open the bloodstained cloth of his shirt and there, slashed across his chest, was a wound, the sort of wound made by a sword, and it was bleeding heavily.

Chapter Seven

Guy was lying motionless on the bed in Hester's room, his face deathly pale, as if the wound had drained away all his usual colour. With the help of some of the men from the village they had carried him up to the house and Hester had not hesitated in telling them to bring him to her own room.

'It was his mother's chamber,' she explained. 'He has happy memories of this room. Perhaps it will help him to recover.'

She and Maud had carefully stripped away his blood-soaked shirt and cleaned the wound on his chest. It had been a delicate operation, requiring all Hester's patience and tenderness. Beneath the blood, they had found a gash, long and curving across his breastbone. Thankfully, it was not as deep as Hester had at first feared, but it was deep enough to have caused him to lose a worrying amount of blood and, Hester knew, even the shallowest wound could harbour a life-threatening infection.

'But how could this have happened, my lady?'

Maud was asking. 'How did he receive such a wound?'

'I don't know, Maud, but I intend to find out. It looks as though it must be a sword cut. Could my lord have been brawling with someone?'

'Brawling, my lady? Sir Guy is no brawler. How could you imagine such a thing?'

Hester felt chastised. Maud was right: she had constantly thought the worst of him. But what other explanation was there?

While they had been cleaning the wound, Breda had been preparing an ointment. She applied the creamy paste to the wound with the flat end of a wooden spatula.

'Leaves of St John's Wort to keep it clean and draw out any poison; to keep away evil, too. Some call it Balm of the Warrior's Wound,' she muttered as she anointed the wound. 'Or Touch-and-Heal some calls it, too. Root of comfrey to staunch the bleeding, root of marshmallow to speed the healing.'

She laid a cloth lightly over the top. 'That'll need changing when the blood soaks through,' she told Hester. She moved across to the fireplace, hanging a small pot over the hearth. In a few moments, a strong scent had filled the room. 'Lavender to calm his shock—'tis a great shock to the body and the spirit, a wound like that.' She nodded at Hester. 'And here,' she said, holding out a jug. 'Give him sips of this on a spoon if he'll take it. 'Tis Moonwort to soothe him and help him heal. And a piece of St John's Wort over the door,' she added. Hester watched wide-eyed as the old woman stretched up to fix a sprig to the lintel. 'Keeps devils out of the chamber. Let him lie in peace without being bothered by any bad spirits wanting to sap his strength.'

Just then Eadric appeared at the door, his eyes red-rimmed and his face blotchy from crying.

'Will my lord be all right?' he whispered to Hester, his voice trembling.

'I don't know, Eadric. I really don't know. Breda says it could go either way. We've done all we can. We must just wait and see now. If only we knew how he came by such a wound and why he said nothing of it. He sat all the day with me, helping me to tend Alured and never said a word of it, even though it must have been giving him great pain all the while. Perchance it was that exertion which set it to bleeding so heavily.'

Hester had almost forgotten whom she was talking to. Indeed, she was thinking out loud, trying to fathom the mystery for herself as she retraced the occurrences of the day, until she saw Eadric wince with sympathy at the thought of his lord's suffering.

'My lord is so brave, my lady. Even as he took the wound he didn't cry out.'

'Eadric, you were there? You saw what happened?' Hester cried. Eadric stared up at her, realising what he had said.

'He made me promise, my lady. I swore I would tell no one. He said a squire must be able to keep a secret.'

'Eadric, you must tell me. Sir Guy would absolve you from your promise now. I must know how it happened. Eadric,' she said, taking hold of the boy's shoulders and looking imploringly into his eyes. 'You must tell me. Please, I beg you to tell me.' The boy returned her gaze. She could see that he longed to tell her everything, but his sense of honour was torn between regard for her and loyalty to Guy.

'Are you sure it would be all right after I promised my lord?' he hesitated.

Hester drew him into the passage outside the room. It felt suddenly cold and draughty after the warmth of the fire-lit chamber.

'I am certain it would be all right,' she said emphatically. 'And if he recovers—I mean, when he recovers,' she corrected herself, seeing the desperate look on the boy's face, 'if he is angry, I will take full responsibility. I will tell him that I forced you to tell me. Now, please, Eadric, tell me what happened. Maud and Breda can't hear. You can speak in confidence and I will speak of it to no one.'

'You promise you won't tell anyone I told you?'

'I promise.'

'Not even my lord? You see, I want to tell you, my lady, but you were the one he particularly said must never know,' Eadric replied, his brow furrowing with anxiety.

'Me? Why was I not to know?'

'Because he said he didn't want you to be upset. He said you would be angry…because he did it for you…' The boy ended, his words petering out as he stared past Hester and into the chamber where Guy lay on the bed, pale and still as a corpse. Maud and Breda were busily tending to their patient just a few feet away. Hester reached out and pulled the door closed behind her.

'It's all right, they won't hear. Now, what do you mean he did it for me? What did he do?'

'Fought Master Lacave in a duel.'

'Hugo Lacave?' Hester repeated the name in amazement. Had this been the conclusion of that argument she had witnessed at the fair? Had they really disagreed so violently that combat had become inevitable? Certainly Guy had been attempting to suppress some strong feelings on the way home last night, but it had never occurred to her that a duel would be the consequence. And why had these two men risked their lives in this way? What could have been so important to them?

'My lady, it was because Master Lacave insulted you,' Eadric continued. 'He said things…I'm not sure what. I wasn't sure why it made my lord so very angry, because everyone knows that you and William are good friends. But my lord said it was a thing which he couldn't allow to be said of you.'

'William and me?' Hester repeated astonished. So that was what Lacave had said, that was why Guy had dragged her away from the fair, hurried her home, and behaved so strangely on the beach. Hester blinked in amazement, trying to take it all in. Her neighbour had no doubt been peddling defamatory rumours about her all round the neighbourhood, repeating the spiteful accusations he had made when she had rejected his abhorrent advances. What a hypocrite the man was, after he had tried to bed her and been rebuffed. But accusing her of immorality with William, and telling such lies to her husband, was so despicable she had not expected it, even of Lacave. Of course, Guy would have realised immediately that such accusations were vile lies…or had he? What if he had doubted her?

'Sir Guy didn't believe what Lacave told him, did he?' Hester asked urgently.

'Yes, my lady,' Eadric replied, gazing up at her with round eyes. 'He asked me whether you were used to spending time with William and whether William used to keep you company in the house. I told him what everyone knows, that you and William are very good friends and I said that you liked each other very much. You do like William, don't you?' he checked quickly as he saw Hester's face clouding over. 'My lady, did I say the wrong thing?' asked the confused boy.

'No, Eadric,' Hester reassured him, although she felt far from reassured herself. How could she explain to this innocent child that the duel he had witnessed had not been a chivalric match of honour, but a sordid scene provoked by Lacave's wounded pride and desire for revenge? Or that her neighbour wished her evil because she had kneed him in the groin rather than submit to his odious, groping embrace?

'You're right, I do like William very much,' Hester continued, struggling to find the best way of expressing herself. 'He and I are good friends. It's just that I wouldn't want Sir Guy to think that I liked William more than I liked him.'

'Of course not, my lady. He's your husband and William is your bailiff. It's different, isn't it?'

'Yes, it is. Very.' I just hope Guy understands the difference, she was thinking. 'But Sir Guy was angry with Lacave, was he?'

'Yes. My lord challenged him to combat. They met down in the valley by Belton's Copse. My lord took me to help him with his things and Master Lacave's squire was there too, but no one else knew of it.'

'And Sir Guy lost the duel?'

'Oh, no, my lady. He was only wounded because Master Lacave wasn't fighting fair. He tripped my lord up and caught him off balance and, as he fell, Master Lacave lunged at him with his sword. My lord managed to roll away and dodge the worst of the thrust and he got back on his feet straight away and carried on.'

The door to Hester's bedchamber suddenly burst open and Eadric's mouth clamped shut in alarm. Maud emerged, carrying a bowl. Seeing them there, she paused as if to speak, but Hester sent her on her way with a slight movement of her head.

'Go on,' she said to Eadric as Maud disappeared down the corridor.

'Well, my lady, Master Lacave was no match for him. My lord is such a good swordsman. Master Lacave is good, but not good enough to beat my lord, even though he fought foul. My lord knocked the sword from his hands. Master Lacave fell with the force of it and my lord could have run him through there and then, but instead he pinned him to the ground with the point of his sword and ordered him to take back what he had said about you and to swear on his life that he would never repeat it to anyone ever again.

'Master Lacave's face went all white and he was pouring with sweat. And he said everything that my lord told him to. And then he begged my lord to spare him. And my lord said he'd never meant to kill him anyway. And then he gave Master Lacave such a look, as if he were no more than a slug on the ground and he turned his back and we rode back home.

'And all the time he was telling me that killing made no sense and that he hoped the man had learned his lesson. He said he'd seen too much bloodshed in the Holy Land and that there was nothing glorious about killing a man. I asked him about his wound and he said it wasn't too bad and that I could dress it for him when we got home. But when we reached the stables, we heard about the sickness and that you had gone to nurse Alured in the village and my lord was very worried about you and said he must ride straight there to talk some sense into you. Pardon me, my lady, for saying so, but those were his words,' said Eadric, blushing.

'Don't worry, Eadric, I'm not offended,' Hester assured him, her own cheeks blushing pink at the thought of Guy sacrificing his health in an attempt to protect her, with his wound still fresh and painful, bleeding beneath his shirt. She couldn't help remembering the way she had argued with him, behaved so gracelessly in the face of his concern, when all the while he had been suffering from this awful wound, a wound which he had incurred for her sake.

'Just tell me exactly what he said,' she begged Eadric. 'I need to know.'

'He said that if you didn't care about yourself, there were others who did. And then he told me that women were…un-fath-apple…' Eadric paused, frowning.

'Unfathomable?' offered Hester, managing a slight smile in spite of everything.

'Yes, that was the word. Women were unfathom-apple creatures. And he said that I should hold on to my heart.' Eadric brought out the words in a rush, his blush deepening at the thought of repeating such a conversation to Hester.

'Your heart? Are you sure that's what he said?' Hester asked, astonished. All this time she had been thinking the worst of him, yet he had been speaking to the boy of losing his heart. Could it be that…? She pushed the thought to the back of her mind, but it kept resurfacing…

'You've done well to tell me, Eadric. Thank you. Don't you worry about Sir Guy. We're doing everything we can to make sure he recovers. And now that I know how he came by the wound…' Hester faltered, emotion suddenly tightening in her throat. 'Well, just don't worry. He's a strong man, and Breda says there's hope. Now, you run home, I expect your mother's wondering what's happened to you,' Hester finished with an attempt at cheerful normality.

Eadric nodded obediently. 'I'm glad I told you, my lady,' he said as he turned to leave her. 'It was too much carrying such a big secret around with me now that Sir Guy is so ill.'

'Of course it was. And Sir Guy need never know that you told me. I promise I won't speak to him of it.' I may never have the chance, Hester added silently to herself as Eadric walked away from her down the staircase, his new boots, the ones Guy had given him, ringing on the stone.

How could she bear it if Guy were to die now, knowing as she did that he had received this wound while protecting her honour? Worse still, that he had failed to treat his wound because he had been more concerned for her health than for his own. And now he was lying in her chamber, gravely ill, battling for life.

Hugo Lacave had accused her of infidelity, yet Guy had not challenged her, had sought no answer from her. Judging from his conversation with Eadric, he had believed her to be enamoured of William. In spite of that, he had ridden to combat to defend her good name. It was an act of such extraordinary chivalry that it took her breath away. He had sought to gain nothing from his action, had kept it a secret even in the face of her hostility and ingratitude. Now he might be dying—and all for her sake…

As Hester entered the chamber she realised her heart felt…different. It wasn't a sudden feeling, but one that had been creeping up on her gradually, and now she understood that it had taken possession of her, and that nothing would ever feel the same again. He had spoken to Eadric of love. She hardly dared allow herself to draw a conclusion from what he had said, but Eadric's words continued to echo in her head: 'He said that if you didn't care about yourself, there were others who did…and he said that I should hold on to my heart.'

Inside the room nothing had changed. Breda was bending over the bed, peering into Guy's face, as if the outcome of his illness were written there in a secret script. A moment later, Maud returned.

'Now then, my lady, you're worn out and it's high time you went and rested,' she immediately began clucking at Hester.

'Oh, no, Maud, I can't leave now, I must stay and tend to my lord. I can't leave him,' Hester objected.

'Nonsense,' the old woman countered, hands on

her hips, a stubborn look in her eye. 'I am here to
look after him and there's any number of helpers to
tend to him. There's no need for you to wear yourself
out sitting up all night.'

'But, Maud, I want to,' Hester replied, determined
that she would not be talked out of the room. This
was one instance where Maud would not get her way.

'You need to have a good meal. Look at you,
you're fading away to nothing. I don't want to have
two invalids on my hands.'

'I couldn't possibly eat,' Hester protested earnestly.
'How can you think of such things with Guy lying
here like this?' Hester bit her lip, realising that, for
the first time, she had used his Christian name to
Maud. She drew breath and continued nevertheless,
'I can't eat. I can't. And I can't rest while he's like
this either.'

'Oh, my lady—' Maud began, but Breda broke in
with her slow, deep voice.

'Let 'er be, why don't you, Maud? The lass is
right.'

'Her ladyship, you mean,' Maud corrected, bridling
at Breda's interference.

'She wants to be with 'im,' Breda continued regardless of Maud's pique. 'I'll wager he'd rather have
'er here than either of us old 'uns too. Dost thou not?
Maybe it'll do 'im good to have his wife here showing she cares for 'im. I do believe they can still hear
often as not when they're like this. 'Tis uncanny how
some can be summoned back by the voice of one they
love.'

Hester felt her heart suddenly racing at Breda's
words. Did he love her? Could he love her after the

way she had treated him, after she had made it so clear that she wanted nothing to do with him, that he was unwelcome and unwanted?

'But my lady will wear herself out,' Maud was protesting.

'She'll wear herself out more with worrying if thou dost not let her stay with 'im. She'll lie awake and pine, then. She ain't a-going to sleep if you send 'er away. Not 'er. So don't it make more sense to let 'er do as she wishes?'

'I'm not leaving him, Maud,' Hester added, her determination fired by Breda's backing.

'Well, my lady, there never is any point in trying to oppose you when you've made up your mind,' Maud said, tutting with annoyance. 'But just promise me one thing—when you get too tired or when you need help, you won't be too stubborn to ask for it.'

'I promise,' Hester assured her, not angered by her maid's cross words, knowing that they were inspired by concern for her well-being.

'Well, at least that's something.' Maud nodded as she opened the door. 'I'll be in the kitchen if you need me,' she added as she left the chamber.

Hester turned to Breda. 'Thank you for helping me to persuade Maud.'

'Well, we all must do as our hearts tellen us. Ol' Breda knows these things. 'Tain't no good going against the heart.'

Hearts again. Hester felt as though the subject were inescapable. First Eadric, now Breda, and all the time Guy lying there, so that she felt as though his pale, wounded body were pulling at her heartstrings.

'I meant what I said about 'im hearing you, mind,'

Breda continued. ''Tis true. Maybe he's a-listening to us talking now, 'tis as like as not. So no holding back now. This is the time to speak all those things you been a-hiding of.'

'What do you mean?' Hester asked, alarmed. She always felt on edge when Breda was around, as if the wise old woman knew a little too much about her for comfort. Could it be that Breda could read her mind? Could she discern the turmoil of Hester's thoughts?

'What I means is that the power of love in a sick-room can be stronger than any ointment that Ol' Breda can make. It can pull a man through when his life hangs in the balance. I have seen it happen many and many a time. Even when it seems as if they can't a-hear nothing you say, they can still feel the tug of ties pulling them to stay in this world. If he feels your love, he'll have a reason to stay.'

'My love?' Hester echoed. 'I—I'm not sure that—'

''Course you do, lass. Aye. My lady, that's what I should be calling you, in't it? Ol' Breda keeps forgetting. It's a strange life for you high-born girls. You can't choose for yourselves; got too much money for that, see. Terrible thing to have too much money, just as bad as 'aving too little. But sometimes, now and then, a high-born girl can end up with the right man anyways. Just because you didn't choose 'im yourself, don't mean you can't love 'im.

'You thinks you hate 'im sometimes but that's just the other face of love, that is. You can be angry and bitter with 'im, but in your heart, there's love. Ol' Breda sees it,' she nodded wisely, tapping her finger against her chest.

'Your power is greater than mine here now,' she

assured Hester. 'I shall go and tend to Alured. I'll
come back later. The young lord's already growing
hot,' she said, nodding at Guy. 'Like as not the fever
may descend upon him soon, but for now 'tis better
you two should be alone. Maud thinks any hands will
do to care for him, but 'tis yours that are needed. Your
touch on his forehead. Your skin on his skin, holding
him fast in this world. He loves no one else.' Hester
felt a little gasp catch in her throat. Breda's words
seemed to loom in the air around her. Was she right?

'He loves Amir more than he loves me,' she countered, collecting herself.

'Ah, the dog. You ain't a-going to be jealous of a
dog, are you, a fine lady like you? Silly girl! It's thou
he loves. And thou lovest 'im. It don't take no wise
woman to see that. Why do you think Master Lacave
was so jealous as to lie to him?'

'You overheard what Eadric told me?' Hester
blurted out.

'Ol' Breda don't need to overhear. Ol' Breda jus'
knows. Now, don't you go fretting about some dog.
A dog can cheer him when he is weak and recovering,
but only you can work this magic now, a web to hold
him in this world. All you have to do is speak your
heart, girl. He will hear you, though he seems not to.
I'll tell the others to keep away unless they're called.
Now you must go to work, tending 'im with love.'
And with that Breda shuffled out of the room, leaving
Hester wide-eyed and wondering at the task she had
ahead.

She stared at the man on the bed, his hair matted
and soaked with sweat, plastered to his forehead. His
dark eyes shut against the firelight. She went to the

bowl of cold water at the bedside, dipped a cloth into it, then wrung it out and placed it on Guy's brow. She could feel the heat emanating from his skin.

As she moved to take the cloth away, his hand suddenly clasped round her wrist.

'Hester,' he whispered.

'Yes, I'm here,' she responded, her whole being frozen by the sound of his voice.

'Don't leave me,' he murmured, his eyelids flickering.

'I shan't,' she promised, as he subsided once more into silence.

The silence did not last long. Breda had been right that the fever was on its way. Guy's skin was soon burning to the touch, and with the fever came troubled dreams. Breda's bunch of St John's Wort above the door seemed to be no protection against the spirits of Guy's past. They floated through his mind as he lay restlessly on the bed. In the heat of his fever he seemed to be imagining that he was back in the heat of the Holy Land.

'Sandstorm!' he cried, screwing up his closed eyes. 'Stinging, can't see. Horses. Sand burying the horses. Quick, help.'

A moment later he was riding into battle, but the cry on his lips was not the traditional crusaders' cry of 'God's will', instead he was muttering strange foreign words over and over, '*Allah Akhbar. Allah Akhbar.*' He went still for a moment, then, 'Carnage,' he said simply. 'Blood on sand... Birds circling... Tearing flesh...'

'There,' Hester said, dismayed by his words, clasping his hand, trying to give him reassurance. 'Don't think about it. You're safe now. Safe here with me in Abbascombe. Think about Abbascombe.'

Guy seemed to hear her, lay quiet for a few moments, then 'Father!' he exclaimed, his voice suffused with pain. 'Never told him.'

'What didn't you tell him?' Hester asked, but Guy only repeated,

'Never told him.'

'I think he knew,' she said, trying to comfort him. 'Try to rest. Please try to rest.' His skin was burning, hotter all the time, and blood was soaking the cloth which Breda had placed over the wound. Hester peeled it away delicately and smoothed on more ointment, placing a fresh cloth over the top.

Guy began speaking in a strange tongue, gabbling unfamiliar words.

Hester guessed it must be the language of the Moors.

Suddenly she realised that one word was cropping up again and again. 'Fatima…Fatima…Fatima…' The name of the woman he had spoken of at the fair, the name of his paramour. Hearing him speak of her in his dreams made her heart thud against the wall of her chest. In extremis, it was Fatima whom he called on, Fatima whose name was on his lips and in his heart.

She thought back to how she had felt when he had first returned, how she had wished him back in the Holy Land in the arms of whichever woman he had left behind. How she had longed to be rid of him, to be alone at Abbascombe once more. But now the thought of him with another woman burned like a brand into her flesh, torturing her soul. What if Guy were now wishing himself back in Fatima's arms? If he were, it would serve her right after the way she had cursed him and wished him gone.

The click of the door opening behind her brought Hester turning sharply to see who had entered. It was Breda.

'Fever,' the old woman said simply, looking at Guy. 'I thought so. You're doing everything right, lass,' she reassured Hester. 'Nothing more you can do. Have you been a-talking to him?'

'He's been talking all the time,' Hester explained, trying to push Fatima's name to the back of her mind.

'Aye, but maybe you can give his mind some rest by talking yourself. 'Appen he'll like to listen to you. Ol' Breda thinks you have plenty to be a-telling 'im. Now, here,' she said, handing a cup to Hester, 'he needs to drink. I've made a brew of mint and elderberry. 'Twill help to calm the heat in his body. See if you can get him to take some. And this wound is still a-bleeding. Looks bad if that goes on. We must try to staunch the blood, else he'll fade away. Leaf of woad is what we need, the large, flat leaves to lay over the wound. They need to be fresh. I'll go out and find some. You want someone to help you whilst I'm away? Maud is a-fidgeting down in the hall.'

'No,' Hester replied adamantly, 'I can manage on my own.'

'Good lass,' Breda replied as she shuffled towards the door. 'I'm off for some woad leaves.'

'Will you be able to find them in the dark?' Hester asked uncertainly. The night outside was thick and heavy with cloud, the moon barely managing to peek through.

'Aye,' replied Breda, 'I don't need the light to walk hereabouts. Ol' Breda knows the way like the back of 'er hand.' She hesitated at the door, then turned back. 'We'll do our best by 'im, my lady, but 'tis not certain whether even the woad leaves will work. There's no saying whether he'll pull through or not. That's up to 'im. He's the one who's got to fight the fever. He's got to want to stay here in Abbascombe.'

With that she disappeared, and Hester was left alone with Guy once more, a lump in her throat after the old woman's parting words. Breda was right. Fatima or no Fatima, Hester was the one who had to make him want to fight for his life, she had to show him that he was wanted in Abbascombe. She was the one who had to make up to him for the recent weeks when she had gone out of her way to make him feel unwelcome and unwanted.

The idea of provoking him into disappearing on another ten-year journey had been her overriding concern since his return…until recently, that was. Hester couldn't say when the change had occurred. All she knew was that gradually she had begun to resent him less, until now the thought of his death filled her with horror and with a longing to keep him alive.

'We're going to make you better,' she declared, returning to Guy's side and clasping his hand. He stopped his feverish muttering at the sound of her voice. 'Do you like to hear me speak? Is it as Breda said?'

His stillness encouraged her to continue. Breda had told her to talk to him, to speak words of love, to tell him to cling to life for her sake. But how could she speak of such things after the way she had behaved

to him? And did she love him? Certainly she did not
wish him dead, but did that mean she wanted him to
live with her as her husband? Hester opened her
mouth, but no words came out. She took a deep
breath. As she did so, she felt his hand squeeze hers.
He whispered something, a word. Hester bent her face
close to his lips. He spoke again.

'Hester,' he whispered. 'Little girl. Poor little girl.'

Hester flinched. Was he speaking of her? Of how
she had been when he had first seen her, the memory
he had taken with him to the Holy Land? Had he
pitied her, rather than despised her as she had always
assumed?

'I'm here,' she murmured in reply, squeezing his
hand in return. 'Hester is here to look after you.'
Suddenly speech seemed ready to flow out of her,
loosed by his words. 'Dear Guy, you are so ill, and
all for my sake. You are so ill that Breda says you
may not survive. But listen to me, Guy: you must get
better. You know me well enough to realise that I
will not tolerate being disobeyed,' she said with a
quivering smile. 'You must throw off this fever and
get better. Else…else who shall I have to argue and
fight with? Or to love?' The word slipped out un-
planned, and Hester found herself biting her tongue
with shock.

Love? Did she love him, then? With a pounding
heart, she realised that there could be only one explanation for her determination to save him from the
jaws of death: she loved him, felt she could never
love anyone else but this husband of hers, unwillingly
given and unwillingly taken, yet she had grown to
love him. And the irony was that she was only just

beginning to understand her strange mixture of feelings, now that she was in danger of losing him again. And this time the loss could be forever.

'Yes, I love you,' she repeated as she bathed his burning forehead and spooned a little more of Breda's potion through his parted lips. 'Do you remember the day you arrived? How angry we both were. But even then just the sight of you made me tingle with a feeling I had never felt before. And when you kissed me on the cliff, that same feeling burned through me. If only we could start again, perhaps I could learn not to fight you all the time. Perhaps we could run Abbascombe together, perhaps we could learn to be happy.'

In her mind, Hester was imagining them walking together through the fields on a warm summer's day, the sun high above them, the crops ripe in the rich ground. Suddenly the thought of losing him, of spending another summer making that walk alone filled her with dread. Suddenly the force of her feelings hit her like a tidal wave.

'My husband, my love,' she said, kneeling beside the bed, resting her head close to his on the hot, damp pillow, 'don't leave me again. I cannot bear to lose you a second time. It has been bad enough without you these ten years. Stay here now. Stay here and love me as I love you.'

The words were suffocated in her throat as a great sob rose up and Hester suddenly realised she was crying, tears falling from her eyes on to his face. Tears which she had never once shed since the death of her parents. She loved him. She was sure of it now. But

what if it was too late? What if he should slip away
from her into death, leaving her alone and loveless
once more?

'My love!' she cried. 'My love!'

Chapter Eight

The door clicked behind her, but Hester couldn't look up, her eyes were so clouded with tears. She heard Breda's familiar shuffling footsteps, and felt the old woman's hand on her shoulder. She tried to hide her tears, but Breda saw everything immediately, as always.

'There, girl,' Breda said. 'Tears can heal too. There's nothing wrong with tears.'

Snuffling, Hester tried to halt her crying as Breda laid the freshly gathered woad leaves over the wound.

'It's easing,' Breda said with a nod. 'Less blood than there was. 'Tis a good sign, girl.'

Hester allowed herself to breathe a sigh of relief. 'You must get better,' she whispered, still clasping Guy's hand, giving up the idea of trying to hide anything from the wise woman. 'Stay with me. Please stay.'

As the night wore on, Hester never moved from Guy's side. Most of the time she clutched his hot hand and whispered encouragement into his ear. She mopped his brow with Breda's cooling lotion and changed the woad leaves on his wound until finally the bleeding had eased to a trickle.

It had been a long, dark night, but at last dawn was breaking. Through the little window in the wall, Hester could see the sun rising over the sea, pinks and oranges mixed with the pale blue of the sky, streaks of clouds reflecting the perfect colours. She turned her eyes back to Guy. He was sleeping a deep, peaceful sleep, his chest rising and falling evenly, his skin no longer livid with fever. No more blood had seeped through the leaves spread over his chest. The bleeding had stopped. He was safe.

'He's through,' Breda said with a smile. 'Could 'ave gone either way, but I reckon he'll be all right now.'

Relief coursed through Hester's veins in a rush. 'He's going to be all right?' she repeated. 'Are you sure?'

Breda nodded in reply. 'Now, my lady, you'd better go and take your rest before Maud comes a-scolding of us. There's nothing more for you to do here now. He is sleeping, a deep sleep, most likely a very long sleep. You must sleep, too, so that you can be ready when he wakes.'

Hester nodded her acquiescence. Just then, the door creaked open and Maud stood in the doorway.

'My lady?' she whispered, the two words expressing all her concern and inquiry.

'He's asleep, Maud,' Hester whispered back, her face aglow with relief and happiness. 'A real, restful sleep. Earlier he was racked by fevered nightmares, dreaming he was back in the East, but now he's calm. Breda says he's going to be all right.'

'Oh, heavens be praised,' Maud exclaimed, stepping closer to the bed and examining its occupant. 'Yes, yes, you can see it in his face. The worst is over and he's come out the other side. Now, my lady,' she said, turning to Hester. 'No more arguing from you. It's high time you had a thought for yourself. You must eat and sleep yourself now. I'll sit with him while you take your rest.'

'But I must be here when he wakes,' Hester protested, although she realised for the first time that her whole body felt heavy with exhaustion.

'It may be many hours before he wakes. The more sleep he gets the better. And it will be better for both of you if you are fresh when he wakes, not worn to a frazzle and ill yourself.'

Hester reluctantly moved towards the door, glancing back all the time at Guy's sleeping face. She felt as though she were wading through water, her limbs were so heavy with exhaustion. As she opened the door and stepped into the corridor, she almost tripped over a great obstacle in her path.

'Amir!' she exclaimed, looking down at the animal who lay before her feet, blocking her way. The loyal dog raised her head and looked up at Hester with sad, dark, inquiring eyes. 'Have you been lying here all night?' Hester murmured, as she bent to stroke her. Amir accepted the touch placidly, and Hester felt a little beat of joy in spite of her tiredness. 'Were you worried about Guy, too? Were you missing him? I think you'd better come and see for yourself that your master is all right.' She turned and led the dog back into the chamber.

'My lady, you can't bring a dog into the sick room,' Maud exclaimed.

'She's been lying outside, pining for her master,' Hester explained. 'If we don't let her stay with him now, I fear the creature may fade away with sorrow. Sir Guy would never forgive us if we allowed that to happen,' Hester added deliberately, knowing this would carry weight with Maud.

'You're right about that,' Maud agreed thoughtfully. 'He loves that dog.'

Amir was already beside the bed, wagging her tail, but absolutely silent, seeming to understand that discretion was required if she were to be allowed to stay. She licked Guy's hand, then curled up beside the bed, her head resting on her paws, her eyes fixed immovably on her beloved master.

'Let her stay,' Hester urged. 'He'll be glad to see her when he wakes.'

'Oh, very well,' Maud acquiesced with a tut.

Hester went off in search of rest, her heart light with joy, her body heavy with weariness. She stumbled her way to the neighbouring chamber where Maud had laid out her nightdress and a sumptuous breakfast. At first she felt sure she was far too tired to eat, but the sweet smell of the steaming bowl of porridge was so tempting... Suddenly she remembered that she hadn't eaten since the previous morning and instantly felt hungry. She quickly gulped down the sticky mouthfuls of porridge, tasting the flavour of her own bees' honey used to sweeten the oats and milk. Then she collapsed on to the bed.

This was the chamber where Guy had been sleeping. As her head sank into the soft feathery pillow, she caught a hint of his scent, that musky masculine aroma…she had smelled it on his leather jerkin when he had been climbing round the rock face to save Eadric, and again she had smelled it when he had held her so tightly on the cliff-top on that stormy day. The thought of that kiss filled her mind once more. She pulled the bedclothes tightly around her, as if they were his arms clasping her. She wrapped herself in his scent and fell at once into a deep, deep sleep.

In the chamber next door, Guy was dreaming. Hours before he had been inexplicably back in the East, the crushing heat and the all-pervading dust and sand prickling his skin, back amidst the horrors of war: the deafening din of battle, the mutilations, the terrible cruelties he had witnessed. His mind had been tormented by reliving such horrors once again…then in an instant the terrors had vanished, dispelled as if by magic by the touch of a gentle hand and the whisper of a soft voice.

He couldn't quite remember the words. They had floated into the recesses of his brain, but they had spoken of love, of needing, and they had brought him back from the war, until his mind had found a haven of peace. There had been cool air after the burning of the desert; an oasis, a beautiful oasis where Hester had been with him. He had seen those freckles, which still gave her the look of the little girl he remembered; those eyes, so clear and turquoise, yet capable of such fiery anger. But this was not the angry Hester, this was a wife who loved and wanted him. She wanted him to escape from the tumults of the desert and take refuge with her in the oasis.

When Guy opened his eyes, he felt an immediate, sharp disappointment that her face was not the first thing he saw. Instead, he was looking up into Maud's wrinkled visage as the old woman bent over him.

'My lord, take a sip of milk,' she was urging. He sipped obediently, then turned his eyes around the room. He could see no one else. Yet he had felt sure that Hester had been there. He tried to say her name, but Maud hushed him into silence.

'There, there,' she cooed. 'Don't you tire yourself. Time enough for talking later when you're feeling better.'

He shut his eyes again, letting the pillows take the weight of his head. His whole body felt so very heavy, and terribly stiff, aching as though he had been in battle all the night. But he hadn't been in battle. He had been listening to Hester.

My wife, he thought suddenly, the words sounding comforting in his head. *My* wife. She had told him many things. She had told him that she loved him. Her words had filled him with hope, with joy. They were the words he had longed for, yet had despaired of ever hearing. He opened his eyes again to look for her. Maud's face again was all he saw.

'Now, my lord, you've been very ill. You've been dreaming all sorts of strange things. You must go back to sleep and get better,' Maud's voice told him.

Dreaming? Had he been dreaming? It had felt so real. He had been sure he would open his eyes to see his wife's beautiful, freckled face looking down at him with love in her blue eyes, blue the colour of the rock-pools on a hot summer's day. But where was she? Had she ever been there? Or had he only wished her there in his troubled dreams?

'Don't tire yourself, my lord. Don't try to speak. Just rest and get better. Maud's by you. Would you like a drink of water?' Maud asked, holding another cup to his lips. He sipped at its contents and tasted the sweet water of Abbascombe's spring. There was something added to it, something herbal, one of Breda's concoctions. He let his weight sink into the pillows. So, Hester wasn't here after all.

'You've been asleep a long time, but you need to sleep some more,' Maud was saying.

Had it all been a dream? Imagining he was back in the desert must have been, and the oasis too, but the touch of her hands, the sound of her voice had seemed so real. If only it could have been true. If only his wife could love him as he had dreamed that she did. He longed to feel her touch, to stroke that sun-kissed skin, so soft, so beautiful, to feel her breath on his cheek. But then he remembered Hugo Lacave and the monstrous words he had spoken, insulting, outrageous in their disrespect. Yet perhaps the kernel was true.

Guy had believed the essence, even as he had raged against the man for speaking so insolently of the lady Hester, his pulse quickening again at the memory of the outrage. He would not allow anyone to speak basely of her. But who could blame her if she had found love in the arms of her bailiff? Certainly he had no right to blame her after the way he had left her to fend for herself all these years. Ten long years.

Suddenly, with a sharp pang, as painful as any wound, he felt what he had missed by leaving his child bride at Abbascombe…missed seeing her bloom and blossom into a charming, promising young girl, then into the fiery, self-possessed beauty that his wife now was.

What reason had she had to wait for him when he had deserted her, when he might have been dead? And William had been right here every day, whenever she had needed him, always bright and helpful, capable and reliable. William had provided all the support that Guy had failed to give her. William was exactly the sort of man a young woman might desire and Guy had not even been there to compete for his young wife's affections.

What right had he to claim them now? He had failed her and this was his punishment: to see his wife, the woman he loved, preferring another man. The woman who, ironically, he would now have chosen above all others to be his wife.

Suddenly he felt something moist and cool on the back of his hand. His body was painfully stiff from the fever, but he managed to turn his eyes, and saw Amir, her long graceful head resting on the edge of the bed, her nose just touching his hand. He managed to move his fingers to stroke her face, then sank back into the pillows and subsided into sleep.

As the days wore on, he gained in strength, until at last he was strong enough to get out of bed and sit by the little window, looking out over Abbascombe towards the sea.

'So you're feeling a little stronger?' Hester asked.

'Yes, thank you,' Guy replied.

Their conversations had become strangely polite

and formal since his illness, not at all like the fierce arguments which had seemed to punctuate their every meeting before.

After the intensity of nursing him through the fever, when she had bared her soul and surprised even herself with her declaration of love, Hester felt as though she had nothing left to say. She felt awkward and unsure with him. Breda had said that he could hear when he was fevered, but could he also remember what he had heard? In the cold light of day she felt exposed and foolish for having been so unguarded in her declarations to him as he had lain unconscious on his sickbed. He had said nothing of it—but did that mean he hadn't heard her words. Might it mean that he had heard them all too clearly and was embarrassed by her declarations? Might it mean that he found it impossible to return her feelings?

In spite of all that Breda and Maud had said, Hester could not help reminding herself of his real reason for returning to Abbascombe after all these years. He had not returned for her sake, but only because the war had ended. He hadn't come home to be with her— she knew that for sure, else he would have been back much sooner, or would never have left in the first place. He had never wanted her, she had been his father's choice for the sake of the wealth she had inherited. She had been foisted on him and he was just trying to make the best of it.

But she didn't want to be forced on anyone, she would far rather spend her life alone than feel that the man she loved was only putting up with her for lack of choice. It would be better to live separate lives than to live a sham. No doubt he would rather take a mistress of his own choosing. Hester's stomach churned whenever she considered the prospect: to remain at home, the spurned wife, while he escaped her company in favour of another woman. Of course he could not love her. She had not been his choice. Why should he?

Nevertheless, being close to him was so deliciously sweet. And it was almost a physical pain to feel how much she cared about him. Even now that he was out of danger she found herself wishing desperately for his complete recovery, fussing over him as though he were a baby, not an experienced warrior.

One morning she entered the chamber to find him pacing relentlessly up and down.

'What are you doing?' Hester demanded as she stormed across the room to confront him. 'Trying to wear yourself out of health and back into a fever?'

'Quite the opposite, my lady,' he returned with something of his former authority. 'I am exhausted from having lain here inactive for so long. I need to be up and about.' He spoke with determination, but as he did so, he put out his hand to steady himself against the wall.

'It is far too soon for you to be traipsing about,' Hester scolded him. 'Here,' she said, taking his arm, 'I insist that you return to bed this instant.'

'And what incentive can you offer me for returning to bed?' Guy replied, raising his eyebrows mischievously. Hester knew he was only teasing her, but she felt herself blushing fiercely at his words, and tried to hide her face by looking down at the floor. 'Ah, well, perhaps I had best do as you say,' he continued. 'I have learned to my cost that it is unwise to disobey you, my lady.'

As she guided him across the room, her arm linked closely with his, so that their hips touched as they moved, it was all she could do not to go weak-kneed herself at the dangerous closeness of his body. Although he had been weakened by his illness, the power he exerted over her seemed stronger than ever. Did he know the effect he had on her? Did he know that she longed to sink into his arms? Did he remember her foolish vows of love and longing?

'Do not chastise a poor invalid, my lady,' he continued, cultivating a submissive look. 'I miss the outdoors. I am not used to being confined to one room for so long. I wish to be out, walking with Amir, or riding along the beach.' There was no mention of Hester in Guy's description of the things he would rather be doing. She felt stung as by a dart, but she pushed the hurt away.

'It is much too soon to think of going out,' she said instead. 'You can see that for yourself. Look at you! You're a pathetic specimen, leaning on your wife for support.' The word 'wife' seemed to hang in the air.

'My wife,' he repeated, his dark eyes twinkling. 'I tell you what, my wife, I will make a deal with you. Do you remember the game of chess we played on the night of my return?'

'We?' Hester queried. '*You* played it, you mean, with your cronies.'

'Aye, you are right. We weren't very polite to you, as I recall. But then I also recall that you weren't a particularly welcoming hostess.' Hester could not argue with that. 'That night you showed an interest in the game and I believe I promised to teach you how to play.'

'I'm surprised you can remember anything of that night after the vast quantity of wine you drank,' Hester replied sharply, but beneath the surface, her pulse was racing at the idea of learning chess with him.

'My memory of that night is somewhat hazy, I admit. Are you sure that was not due to the quality of the wine?' Hester opened her mouth to protest. 'No, no. You are right,' he cut in. 'You have corrected me on that point before. Now, leaving that aside, I will promise to stay in this room for as long as you decree, on one condition.' He paused teasingly. Hester tried to contain her impatience, but couldn't help raising her eyebrows to prompt him to continue. It was the cue he had been waiting for. 'On condition that you promise to entertain me…' He paused again mischievously. Hester felt her pulse racing with suspense. 'By playing chess with me,' he concluded.

Hester could hardly wait to begin. But as Guy explained the rules, the game appeared so difficult that she wondered whether she would ever master it, or even remember how all the pieces moved.

'Think of two armies, arrayed on a battlefield,' said Guy. 'The white army is that of King Richard, the black is that of the Saracen under Saladin. Each has a vast number of foot soldiers at its fore. These are common soldiers to be sacrificed at the king's command—often sacrificed in great numbers. They are weighed down with armour and fight on foot so they move slowly, just one step at a time. Most will meet their death in a bloodbath at the centre of the battlefield.' Guy paused and frowned as if an unpleasant memory had stirred in his mind. He wiped his hand across his eyes and shook his head slightly.

Hester's mind shot back to the feverish words she had heard him speak during his illness, when he had imagined himself to be once more in the East. Clearly those terrors were still haunting his mind. She wondered whether to speak to him of them, whether to show him that she knew of his suffering, or whether he would feel affronted by her knowledge... Before she had time to decide, he had begun to talk again, his thoughts firmly back on the subject of chess.

'Behind each army stands the king,' he continued, 'surveying the scene from on high and directing the battle. As is often the way with monarchs, he seldom makes a bold manoeuvre himself, only quitting his vantage point if pressed by the enemy's forces.'

Hester again looked up at him, bemused and slightly shocked at the tone of sarcasm which had crept into his voice.

'At the king's side stands the real power of the throne, his queen. She is fast, quick-witted and can move in all directions, changing her mind on a whim—as great ladies are wont to do.' Here Guy's face broke into a broad smile and Hester wondered which great lady could have inspired such a comment. Surely not herself, no one would call her a great lady... Was it Fatìma then, was she a great lady...?

'And, as is common in the natural world, the female of the species is deadlier than the male,' Guy went on. Hester narrowed her eyes at him. She was learning not to rise to his taunts. Sensing that she was biting back a retort, Guy's smile broadened into an amused grin. His dark hair had flopped over his forehead, and he was looking almost his old self again. A little pale still, but mesmerisingly handsome none the less.

'By the monarch's side sit his bishops—or in the case of the Saracen, their holy men, the *firz*. These are warlike clerics. They are mighty in battle, and more fearsome in their religious fervour than the brave knights. The *firz* charge into the fray upon elephants from the castles at the edge of the field of battle—do you see? Perhaps camps would be a better description of these forts, because they can be moved swiftly from one end of the battlefield to the other— or across its width—as tactics demand.

'Now, let us begin,' said Guy. 'I shall be Saladin, at the head of his black Saracen army. You, my lady, may remain a Christian. When at last you win—as you will one day—your crusader will be released from his vows and will return home. However, I warn you that your victory may prove a long time in coming.'

Hester looked sharply at him. Was he mocking her or trying to tell her something? There seemed to be so many underlying meanings in his explanation of this game of chess.

Tentatively she stretched out her hand and moved one of her foot soldiers forward. The battle had begun.

Over the next few weeks Hester and Guy fought many, many battles—all of them on the beautiful, silver chessboard. At first the skirmishes were rapid, concluded all too swiftly by Hester's inexperience.

But, as the days flew by, the contests became less uneven and lasted longer. Sometimes Hester found she could give Guy pause for thought, and now and then her tactics took him by surprise. But she continued to feel frustrated, feeling that the essence of the game eluded her.

'Perhaps Sir Edward was right after all,' she said dejectedly as Guy checkmated her king once again.

'Sir Edward? Right?' he repeated in mock amazement. 'Surely such a thing is beyond belief. What could he possibly be right about?'

'About women being unable to learn chess,' Hester replied.

'Pah!' Guy exclaimed, his vehemence taking her by surprise. 'You are already a far better player than he could ever be. It just takes time to learn. 'Tis a complex game.'

'Why didn't you say that to him?' Hester asked, more than a hint of accusation in her question.

'Perhaps I should have done,' Guy replied after a moment. 'It was not very gallant of me to leave you at the mercy of his idiot tongue.' He paused, then added, 'I have not been a very gallant husband to you.'

Hester didn't know where to look or what to say. No experience had prepared her for dealing with an intimate conversation with her husband. She had been perfectly able to argue with him, to hurl insults and accusations, and she had somehow managed to speak to him when he had been unconscious. But face to face with him now, her mouth dried, her face flamed and no word that entered her head seemed fit to be spoken.

One subject they certainly never mentioned was the duel, though it seemed to hang in the air between them sometimes. Guy never spoke of the circumstances of his wound and Hester was almost afraid to—deterred by her promise to Eadric, as well as by her own trepidation.

As Guy grew stronger they began to go for walks with Amir, or rather Amir gambolled and ran rings around them, tearing off in search of amusement, while they walked slowly, enjoying the warmth of the early summer sun, the bright blue sky, the puffy white clouds, the seagulls soaring and cawing overhead.

Since Guy's illness, Amir had grown almost friendly towards Hester. She would even bring back the sticks which Hester threw for her, clutching them delicately between her sharp teeth and dropping them carefully into Hester's outstretched hand. It was as if she sensed that Hester's feelings for her master had changed.

Hester had never done so little work on the farm. She was spending so much time with Guy that she hardly even missed being out in the fields with William. She felt a little guilty about her neglect and suggested to Guy that they should direct their walk towards the vineyard, where she knew the men would be hard at work.

The vineyard was the scene of much toil at this time of year. All the new suckers which had sprung from the old wood had to be cut off one by one. Only the growth from the new wood would yield grapes and if the unproductive suckers were not removed they would sap the strength from the vine, leaving the grapes malnourished and too poor to make decent wine.

'It looks like back-breaking work,' Guy commented as he watched the men stooping down to find all the suckers.

'It is,' Hester assured him with a knowing nod.

'You haven't done this too, have you?' he asked in amazement.

'I certainly have. I'd be doing it now if I weren't keeping you company.'

'I never bothered to learn much about the vineyard,' he said, and Hester thought she detected a note of regret in his voice. 'I was always too busy out riding or honing my fighting skills,' he continued with a self-deprecating smile, which lit up his face and made his eyes sparkle in the May sunshine, leaving Hester feeling as though her heart were melting.

'Well,' she said, trying to hang on to her composure, 'There's plenty more hard work to come if you wish to try your hand at it. This is only the beginning of toil in the vineyard.'

'Have you looked at your bees today, my lady?' William called out as he walked towards them. 'They seem to be behaving a bit strangely, a bit aggressive, I thought. I wonder whether you might be in for a swarm. I don't say you are, mind,' he added, laughing and turning to Guy. 'I don't profess to be any sort of expert on bees, my lord. My lady is the one who understands them and knows how to handle them. Me, I just stand well clear. Don't like to get stung, I don't.'

Hester watched the way William spoke to Guy, so friendly, so natural. Surely Guy couldn't have sus-

pected them of being lovers when Hugo Lacave had
defamed her. The idea was too preposterous when
they were so clearly just good friends, almost fraternal
in their relationship. But then again, perhaps their
closeness might be misinterpreted. Hester wondered
from time to time whether she should brave the subject and speak of it to Guy. But every time she began
such a conversation in her head, she instantly became
embroiled in its complexities.

How to broach the subject without betraying her
promise to Eadric? How to speak of the indelicate
possibility of an affair with William without seeming
to have some guilty knowledge? Above all, the im-
possibility of knowing Guy's own thoughts and feelings? And then again, if he really suspected her,
would he not have challenged her himself? But Guy
always seemed to turn quiet when she and William
were talking, always seemed to be measuring their
demeanour, weighing them with his eyes.

'I'd better go and have a look,' Hester said, breaking the brief silence which ensued. 'Coming?' she
asked, turning to Guy.

'Yes, I'd like to see you in action as a queen of
bees,' he replied.

They strolled down to the orchard where the bee-
hives sat among the flourishing trees. The fruit was
already growing on their gnarled old branches. The
apple and pear trees must have been planted by one
of Guy's ancestors many years earlier, perhaps by his
grandfather, who had also been called Guy.

Hester couldn't help thinking what a fine thing it
was to be settled in the place of one's forebears, to
be an eldest son and to live in the knowledge that all

this would be yours to nurture and enjoy. How could Guy have thrown it all away by disappearing off to the crusades?

She glanced at him surreptitiously as they walked. His eyes were also taking in the beauties of the place, indeed he seemed to be almost caressing the old trees with his eyes, so fondly was he regarding them. Yes, she realised suddenly, he loved Abbascombe too; possibly just as much as she loved it. Perhaps what Maud had said had been true; perhaps he had needed to be away from his father.

'I used to climb these trees when I was a boy,' Guy said quietly. 'I was always scraping my knees on the bark and tearing my hose in search of the sweetest fruit. My mother must have despaired of me.'

'And your father?'

'Oh, he hadn't much time for me. He was too busy being Lord of Abbascombe. I think he just wanted me to grow up to be a good heir in his own image.'

'Maud is always saying how like him you are.'

'Is she, now? Well, she may be right. I used to think we were nothing alike. I thought he cared for nothing but his land, while I thought I had…I don't know…higher ideals, I suppose. But now…now I think I understand him more. Too late, of course. Such realisations always come too late,' he finished saying with a look at Hester which seemed to signify more than words.

'It needn't be too late,' she managed to reply, although her voice felt weak in her throat. 'You're here now.'

'I am,' he nodded. 'But I fear my absence has been too long. Too much has happened while I have been away. People have grown so used to managing without me.'

'The people were delighted by your return. You saw it yourself.'

'Not everyone, my lady. There was one who felt no joy,' he said quietly, his dark eyes seeking hers. Hester hardly had the strength to meet his gaze. She tried to formulate an answer in her head, one which would encapsulate all her complex emotions.

'Feelings can change,' she replied at last, dropping her glance to the ground. 'They are not carved in stone.'

'I am glad to hear you say so.'

'Your father felt that too. The anger he felt when you left gave way to other feelings.'

Guy nodded. 'For me also.'

'Maud says you and he were too alike to live peacefully together.'

Guy nodded again. 'She is probably right, though I like to think we might have succeeded now if he had lived. I am glad he had you here. From all I hear, you were a great comfort to him.'

'And he to me. I grew very fond of him. He was a kind father to me.'

'I'm not surprised you blamed me for causing him pain.'

'I did. But I think I see more clearly now. I see that he caused you pain too. I no longer blame you for every ill in the world,' Hester ended with a weak smile of apology.

Guy's face beamed in response. 'My lady Hester, you warm my heart with your words. But I do blame myself for leaving you to manage alone after my fa-

ther's death. You have had a hard time with too many
troubles for your years.'

'You could not have known he would die. None of
us could. He was so strong when you left. He weakened gradually, almost imperceptibly, but even
then…' Hester's voice trailed away as she remembered the old lord's lifeless body being carried up to
the house. 'None of us could have foreseen it.'

'Certainly he did not, else I am sure he would have
appointed someone to help you. He would not have
left you to manage alone so young.'

'No, but then he never gave up believing you
would return.'

'You shame me.'

'I did not mean to. After all, he was right: you did
return.'

'I wish I had learned of his death earlier, then I
would have returned home and you would not have
been left alone.'

'Did I do so badly?'

'You did magnificently,' Guy replied with a shake
of his head. 'I am in awe of your achievements, but
I should have liked… Ah, but then 'tis of no matter:
one cannot change the past.'

Hester felt herself blushing as they strolled on
through the orchard, the purpose of their walk there
forgotten until Guy broke in upon her thoughts, pointing in the direction of one of the old apple trees.
'Look, what's that?' There, hanging from a low
branch, was a huge ball of bees, the sound of their
combined buzzing filling the air around them.

'Oh, no, William was right,' Hester exclaimed.
'They have swarmed.'

'Is that bad?' Guy asked, frowning and screwing up his eyes against the sun to see the swarm more clearly. As he did so, the edge of his scar was pulled slightly, up towards his brow. Hester felt mesmerised by his face, with its sign of what he had suffered.

'Is there anything that can be done? Can I help?' he asked.

'It would be dangerous to do anything now,' Hester answered him, pulling herself back from her reverie. 'We'll have to return at dusk, when the bees will be sleepy. Or rather, I will return. You need not come.'

'But I should like to,' Guy replied, 'if you will allow me.'

Hester trembled as she felt the weight of his eyes upon her, requesting her permission. How differently she felt about him now. When he had first arrived in Abbascombe, she had spent so much time and energy either avoiding him or making him feel as unwelcome as possible. No wonder he felt he had to ask her now whether he might return to his own orchard. She looked away, unable to meet his gaze.

'Of course, they are your bees and it is your orchard,' she said. 'You may do whatever you please, my lord.'

'Hester,' he said, his face suddenly serious. 'Hester, look at me.' Hester slowly turned her eyes back to his face. 'If these bees belong to anyone, they must surely belong to you, since you are the one who has cared for them.'

'But they are yours, everything is yours,' Hester returned quietly.

'By law it may be. I cannot help the injustices of the law. But you have been more loyal to

Abbascombe than I. Do not imagine that I fail to see that, nor that I am proud of my neglect.'

Hester's heart was too full to reply. All she could manage was a slow nod in recognition of what he had said. Guy remained silent too and they walked slowly back to the house, both deep in thought.

That evening, just as dusk was falling, they returned to the orchard. Hester was wearing the wide-brimmed hat and veil which she usually wore when tending the bees. She had also donned a pair of gloves which stretched over the cuffs of her dress, so that no skin was exposed.

'You'd better stand well back,' she instructed Guy as she approached the swarm, which was still hanging from the same branch in the apple tree. She held a smoke puffer and a basket with a lid. The bees were buzzing, clinging to the tree in a great huddle. Hester deftly squirted a few puffs of smoke at them and the buzzing immediately grew quieter. Placing the puffer on the ground, she took the lid off the straw skep and held it underneath the bees. Then she reached up to shake the branch, planning that the now docile ball of bees would drop into it. She had miscalculated, though. When she reached for the branch, she found she was not quite tall enough to take hold of it firmly. Her fingertips could touch it, but what was needed was a firm grasp to shake the bees off.

As she was stretching to gain a better hold, she saw Guy's broad, brown hand taking hold of the branch. 'You need this to be shaken?' he checked with her.

'Yes, but you shouldn't be here, you mustn't stand

so close,' she whispered. 'You could be badly stung, you're wearing nothing to protect yourself.'

'Hush, do not worry about me,' he said quietly as he gave the branch a brisk shake.

Straightaway the great ball of bees fell easily into the basket and Hester covered it swiftly with the lid.

'Stand back and stay out of the way,' she warned Guy, as she carried the skep gingerly to the empty hive she had prepared. This was standing open, with the straw dome on the grass at its side so that all she had to do was place the skep inside, remove its lid and replace it with the top of the hive.

From inside the veil she was watching only the bees and did not realise that Guy was by her side.

'What next?' he asked, his voice so close, it made her jump.

'Nothing. That's it,' she replied. 'And what are you doing here? I thought I told you to stand back.'

'I'm very disobedient.' He shrugged with a winning smile. 'But you must admit I do have my uses, if only for reaching high branches.'

Hester conceded the point with a smile.

'Will the bees stay in the hive now?' he asked.

'I hope so. I've already put some honeycomb in there for them. That should keep them happy for a while. And now I'll just have to keep an eye on them, make sure they don't start feeling overcrowded again. The trouble is, I've been spending too much time with you, and neglecting them.'

'You're right,' Guy admitted, pulling a repentant face. 'I am not worth it. And then, of course, you might have a better chance of beating the bees at chess.'

'Hah!' Hester exclaimed. 'I shall beat you at chess. Just you wait and see.'

'I know it, my lady. But shall it be tonight?'

'I think you would do well to be on your guard tonight,' Hester challenged him with a laugh.

'Ah, but I am no bee, my lady. Do not expect me to do your bidding at a puff of smoke.'

Chapter Nine

Hester didn't win the game of chess that night, nor the next. But she felt sure that she was gradually improving at the game. The chess pieces no longer represented a baffling array; instead she began to recognise them as individuals, as Guy had described them.

'That was impressive play, my lady,' Guy said one evening at the end of a closely fought game.

'But I lost again,' Hester replied dejectedly.

'No matter. You had my king on the run,' Guy objected. 'I must look to my laurels. Winning against you is no easy matter these days.'

'Then maybe tomorrow your winning streak will end,' Hester said, feeling emboldened by his praise. 'Oh, but tomorrow is Judith's wedding. We shan't have time to play.'

'We shall make time. I would not miss our evening game of chess for the world,' Guy replied, the warmth of his smile making Hester's heart leap.

She had become quite reconciled to the idea that Judith's wedding was going ahead. Judith had brought her beloved Collen to meet them, and Hester had had to admit that he seemed a very pleasant young man and not at all the wife-beating sort. 'Although you never can tell,' she had added when Guy had asked her opinion afterwards.

Guy had only laughed and said, 'Indeed.'

Hester had laughed too, knowing in her heart that Collen was as kind as could be. She had noticed that he had the same beaming smile and glowing looks as Judith, that the pair of them were almost luminous with love for each other. And she had thought again of the day when she had ridden out with Guy towards the beach, when Judith had stopped them to ask Guy's permission to marry. Hester remembered with a shudder the cynical things she had said to him and the way that, even as she said them, that glowing look on Judith's face had shone disconcertingly in her mind, as if to show Hester exactly what she lacked.

Guy had waived his right to claim the hefty fine which Judith's father was liable to pay by law as compensation to the lord for his daughter's leaving the estate.

'I know it is my right,' Guy had assured Alured, 'but I would much prefer you to spend the money on Judith and Collen. We shall miss her at Abbascombe, but a fine is a poor consolation.'

It was an unusual decision, but a very popular one among the villagers, who thought well of their lord for his generosity. Alured was so delighted that he decided to make his daughter's marriage party even more splendid than he had planned and pressed Guy and Hester to attend.

'It would be a great honour to us, your lordship,'

he told Guy. 'And we would like to thank you and her ladyship for all your kindness.'

Little Nona, Eadric's sister, was to be Judith's flower-girl and Hester had given her mother some fancy cloth, which she had found in a chest, a remnant left over from some ancient Beauvoisin robe and just large enough to make a dress for the little girl.

'My lady, 'tis very fine,' Nona's mother had said, 'and Nona will have mud on it in no time. Are you sure you wouldn't rather keep it for yourself?'

'I'm afraid I'd be no less likely to get it muddy,' Hester had laughed. 'And it will be a joy to see Nona all dressed up.'

Her own clothes were more of a problem, and Hester began to wish she had not been quite so economical and abstemious at the fair. If only she had bought a length of some pretty cloth, or even that beautiful tunic. Hester tried to push the thought of the embroidered robe from her mind. There was no point pining for it, and it would have been horribly expensive, she told herself severely. Nevertheless, the image of it would keep creeping into her mind as she surveyed her worn old dresses and her serviceable new ones made of the blue linen she had taken from the merchant in exchange for her honey.

'I said you should have bought plenty of cloth, my lady,' Maud scolded, her rebuke all the more infuriating because Hester knew she was right. 'I told you your wardrobe was in sore need of new things, but did you take heed? It wasn't so bad when it was just you here at the house, but now that Sir Guy is back he'll grow tired of seeing you slopping around in the same old threadbare working clothes. It's high time you learned to dress like the lady that you are.'

Maud detected Hester's growing irritation and decided to leave hurriedly, excusing herself by saying she was needed in the kitchen. She left Hester looking dejectedly at the dresses laid out on the bed, all woefully practical and dowdy, and some exceedingly worn.

Hester resigned herself to looking as plain as usual and folded the frocks back into the heavy oak chest which stood at the foot of her bed. Of course Guy would be looking splendid, as fine and handsome as he had looked at the fair. The villagers would all be wearing their best, and little Nona would look lovely in the pink cloth which her mother had worked into a lovely dress. Hester would just have to make the best of it until the next fair gave her an opportunity of buying something pretty…but that wouldn't be until long after Judith's marriage had taken place.

The day dawned bright and clear, a perfect June day for a wedding. Hester had donned the smartest robe she had, one made from the blue linen from the fair. She was about to call Maud to ask her where she had put Lady Adela's fine old silken girdle, when there was a knock at her chamber door.

'Come in,' she called. When the door opened, it was not, as she had expected, one of the maids who stood there, but Guy. He was resplendent in a surcoat of the deepest blue, trimmed with golden braid. It was pulled in by a leather belt at his waist, so that it emphasised the broad strength of his muscular chest, his slim hips and long legs. Hester felt weak at the sight

of him, he looked so handsome, with his dark hair
flopping casually on to his forehead. And she felt
even more dowdy than she had before.

Slung over his arm was a shimmering stream of
flowing cloth, its rich, silken colours gleaming in the
light. 'Good morning, my lady, may I enter?' he
asked with a bow.

'You may,' Hester replied with a laugh at his unusual formality. 'Do you mock me, sir, with your
bow, or have you finally understood the honours
which are due to me?'

'Mock you, my lady? I would not dare,' he said
with a comic imitation of trembling which made
Hester laugh all the more. 'But I have dared to do
something else. Something which I hope you will not
take amiss,' he added in a more serious tone.

Hester raised her eyebrows and watched in silence
as he stepped towards the bed and began to spread
the cloth he carried over the counterpane. She immediately realised that they were not just lengths of
material, but clothes, already made up and beautifully
fine. There was a dress of gleaming, cream silk, its
style absolutely plain, and Hester realised why as he
laid the next item on the bed.

It was the tunic they had seen at the fair, looking
even more lovely now than it had then, its vine leaves
embroidered in rich, dark green, complemented perfectly by the pale violet of its background. Hester
couldn't help gasping with delight, but there was
more to come. Next, Guy produced the girdle embroidered in the same style and a golden net, finely
woven and exactly the colour for her strawberry
blonde hair.

'Where did you get all these things?' Hester asked, wide-eyed.

'From the fair, all of them from the merchant you bartered your honey with. Remember when I left you rather ungallantly to look around the fair on your own?' Then he looked seriously into her face. 'You are not offended?'

'Offended?' Hester repeated, almost ready to laugh at him for imagining she could be anything but delighted by such beautiful things. Then she recalled how crossly she had rejected them at the fair, when she had been convinced that he wished her to dress in finery only to keep her imprisoned in the house. 'I am not offended, they are so lovely. But you do not expect me to wear fine clothes every day?'

'I should hope not,' Guy replied with a grin. 'In fact, I beg you not to wear them everyday. I do not believe your usual adornment of mud would suit this cloth.'

Hester laughed with him. 'I was despairing about my dress for today. I was sure all the villagers would look finer than I. And Maud has hardly given me a moment's peace, she's been so busy scolding me for not buying more cloth at the fair.'

'I know,' Guy replied. 'But I am afraid Maud has been tormenting you for her own pleasure, my lady, for 'twas she who made up the dress to go under the tunic. She knew your measurements and has been sewing secretly.'

'The caitiff!' Hester exclaimed.

'I beg you not to be angry with her. I swore Maud to secrecy. I wanted it to be a surprise.'

'But how did you manage to bring them here without my knowledge?'

'They were packed in the bottom of the boat when we returned from the fair. I believe you were sitting right over them, in fact. The sailors brought them up to the house along with the other parcels the next day, but, as you know, we were not here to receive them, for we were nursing Alured in the village. When I bought them I had meant to give them to you as soon as they arrived, but my illness followed and then I formed a plan for surprising you. I had hoped to see you lost for words for once,' he added with a twinkle in his eye. 'But I see my plan has failed.'

'Why, you…' Hester exclaimed, finding herself actually at a loss for a suitable epithet. 'Sir, I must ask you to leave my chamber,' she declared with sudden severity.

'You are displeased?' Guy asked, his face falling.

'I need to change,' Hester said with a laugh, gloating at having tricked him for once.

He grinned and backed out of the chamber, bowing in mock deference.

As soon as he closed the door behind him, she pulled off her linen dress and slipped into the gleaming silk robe. It fitted perfectly: close over the bodice, flaring softly over her hips. Then she lifted the tunic delicately by its shoulders and gazed at it, entranced by its loveliness. As she did so, there was another tap at the door. Hester heard Maud's voice cooing, ''Tis only me, my lady.'

'Well, what do you think?' Maud asked archly as she entered the room. 'A bit better than what you planned to wear, isn't it?'

'It certainly is,' Hester replied. 'And you can wipe that smile off your face. I know what you've been up to behind my back. Here, come and help me, you wretched schemer.'

Maud, still chuckling with delight, helped Hester into the gorgeous tunic. It shimmered in the light, the winding leaves of its embroidery swirling around its hem, and up over Hester's shoulders, forming a rich, green garland to frame her face.

'Now, my lady, for once perhaps you'll be persuaded to wear your hair up,' Maud said as she picked up the fine, golden net which Guy had left on the bed.

Hester sat obediently while Maud twisted her plaits together, then pinned them carefully in place and covered them in the net.

'There,' she said, proudly standing back to admire her work. 'You look fit to be a queen,' she murmured, brushing a tear aside. 'There, silly me, crying already, and we're not even at the wedding yet.' Maud held up the old mirror which had belonged to Guy's mother. Its wooden frame was battered by years of use, its polished metal a little scratched and scuffed, but still serviceable.

Hester caught her breath when she saw her reflection. It was almost like looking into the face of a stranger. The figure gazing back at her was that of an elegant lady of fashion, with not a hair out of place, not at all what she was used to seeing on the few occasions when she happened to catch sight of her reflection, more often in a puddle or in the village pond than in the mirror.

When Maud asked what she thought, Hester could

only nod and murmur her thanks, then she descended the stairs feeling as if she were floating on a cloud.

Guy had bought her these clothes, had chosen them for her as a present, had gone to the trouble of having a dress made for her. It suggested such care and thoughtfulness…and all for her sake. But would he be pleased by the result? Did she look as fine as he had hoped? She stepped into the hall, her heart pounding with anticipation.

Amir was lying on the floor beside him. Guy was standing by the great fireplace with his back to her. At the sound of Hester's steps, he swung round with a rapid movement. Hester stopped in her tracks as his eyes fell upon her. There was a long silence as he gazed at her.

Disconcerted by the silence, Amir lifted her head from the ground and turned her baleful eyes on Hester, too.

'Do I not please you?' Hester stammered at last, his silence filling her with dread.

'Not please me?' he repeated, widening his eyes. 'My lady, how could anyone fail to be pleased by the sight of you?'

Hester dropped her eyes to the floor as she felt a blush of delight spreading across her cheeks. She realised she was literally glowing with his praise.

'You do not think the robes too ladylike for me?'

'No other lady could show them to such advantage,' he said, stepping towards her. 'But I believe there may be something missing.'

'What?' Hester demanded, dismayed, looking down at her dress and tunic anxiously. 'What have I forgotten?'

'It is nothing that you have forgotten,' he paused, 'But rather something that I should have…' His words petered out as he produced a silken purse from his pocket. 'This would look well with it, I think,' he continued, pulling out a necklace of the finest gold filigree. Hester stared at it, dumbstruck. She had never seen a piece of jewellery so beautiful. Every third link was the setting for a large, round pearl. In between were links of ornately wrought gold, twisted into fine, geometric patterns, each one a slightly different shape and each inlaid with tiny seed pearls.

'Oh,' she gasped. 'It is bewitching.'

'You like it?' he asked, as if relieved by her reaction. 'Then allow me to put it on for you.'

Hester stood quite still as he draped the gorgeous golden collar around her neck. It felt cold against her breastbone, but it was not that which made her shiver; it was the brush of his fingers on the back of her neck.

'I'm not very good at this,' he said apologetically, as he fastened the clasp. 'My hands are more used to handling horses and swords than fine jewellery.' As he spoke, she felt his breath caressing her skin too, the gentlest of touches. The hairs on the back of her neck tingled until she felt sure she could stand still no longer, that her legs must melt and give way beneath her. 'There, I've done it,' he said at last, just in time to save her from collapse. Then he placed his hands on her shoulders and spun her round to face him. 'No one else could wear it with such perfection,' he said simply. 'My lady, you should be known as Queen of Abbascombe from henceforth. No lesser title will suffice.'

Hester beamed back at him and raised her hand to

her neck to feel the necklace. It hung perfectly, flat and smooth against her breastbone.

'And now may I escort you to the village, Queen of Abbascombe?' he murmured.

Hester moved as if in a dream out of the house and across the courtyard. Her feet seemed to float all the way to the little timber church which lay between Abbascombe Manor and the villagers' cottages. Most of the congregation had already gathered and they oohed and aahed as Guy led Hester to the front, where they took up their places to the left of the altar.

Soon after they arrived, Judith entered with Alured and the Nuptial Mass began. As she watched, Hester couldn't help remembering her own wedding day. How different it had been from this, a freezing winter's day, and the ceremony rushed through, not even the whole Mass, just the necessary vows and the ring pushed on to her finger. It had been too large and had slipped around so that she remembered she had been scared it would drop off and roll away on the stone floor with a clatter. Afterwards, the terrible confrontation between Guy and his father. The young man striding away from his new bride, his long, athletic legs covering the width of the hall in next to no time. Then the sound of horses' hooves in the courtyard. And then the emptiness.

As the priest joined the hands of Judith and Alured, Hester felt Guy's hand brush against hers. She did not dare to look up, could not gauge whether he had meant to touch her or whether it had been an accident. Instead she kept her eyes firmly on little Nona, who was a picture of sweet prettiness in her pink frock, with her basket of petals to scatter before the bride.

The sweet scent of the flowers filled the little church as they processed out into the June sunshine. It was midday by now and the sun was high. Judith and Collen led the way to the village green, where the wedding feast was set out.

Hester had lent them the long benches and trestle tables from the hall. These were now laden with food protected by checked cloths, just waiting for the guests to arrive. It was a sumptuous spread. Hester had sent down pies and bread from her kitchens, and Alured had provided many more delicacies. There were boiled eggs and cheeses, sausages and fish, to be washed down with large quantities of ale and cider. It was a spectacular feast for the villagers, thanks to Guy's decision to waive his right to the fine for marrying out of the demesne. When the guests made toasts to the bride and bridegroom, they also made one to Guy and Hester, and Guy stood up to thank them, raising his beaker to them in return.

When the luncheon was over, the dancing began. Alured had invited a group of mummers, who struck up a lively jig which had everyone tapping their feet. The little band comprised two fiddlers, a drummer, two flautists and a man who strummed a gittern as he sang. Soon most of the guests had followed the example of Judith and Collen and were on their feet, dancing on the green.

'My lady, would you do me the honour of dancing with me?' Guy asked, turning to Hester, who was watching the revelry.

'I'm not sure I know the steps,' Hester said hesitantly.

'I don't think it matters,' Guy confided, lifting her

from her seat with a sweep of his arm. 'Come, dance with me.'

With his arm tightly around her waist and his hand grasping hers, he swept her round the green, the music growing faster and wilder as they spun. All around them was a blur as their feet flew with the jig until Hester stumbled on a hummock and fell to the ground in a heap, Guy toppling after her.

'My lady,' he said breathlessly, immediately lifting his weight off her. 'Are you all right? Have you twisted your ankle?'

'I'm fine,' Hester replied, laughing. 'I just tripped.' He was back on his feet, extending his hand to help her up. Their eyes met and at the same moment both of them remembered the scene of their meeting in the field, when Hester had tugged him down into the mud. Their faces cracked into giggles as they looked at each other, both knowing what the other was thinking.

'Am I safe to offer you my hand this time?' Guy asked, smiling back at her.

'Perfectly,' Hester replied.

'How disappointing,' he murmured as he lifted her to her feet. 'The thought of lying on the grass with you is a tempting one.' Hester felt herself flush, her cheeks hot, as he whirled her once more into the dance, her new, silken skirts twirling out around her. By the end of the jig, she was panting for breath and her sides were aching with stitch.

'I have to sit down,' she gasped. Guy led her to a bench.

'Shall I fetch you a drink?'

'Yes, please,' Hester nodded and watched as he

moved over to the table where the barrels of ale and cider stood. While she was looking away, William appeared at her side.

'My lady,' he said with a grin. 'May I?'

'Please do,' Hester replied, indicating the seat beside her.

'It's a fine marriage, don't you think? It makes me wonder whether I shouldn't think of wedding myself,' William confided, giving her a sideways look.

'Really, William?' Hester asked, pouncing on the hint. 'Do you have someone in mind?'

'Well, now you come to mention it, my lady, I do.'

'Do tell me,' Hester whispered conspiratorially, leaning close to William in order to share his secret. Just then Guy returned with beakers of cider. William sprang up when he saw him.

'A fine wedding, my lord,' William said, inclining his head respectfully.

'Indeed it is,' Guy acknowledged with the slightest of nods in return. His smile seemed to have faded and his eyes were on William. There was a tension in his body, not obvious to the general observer, but to Hester, the taut rigidity of his muscles was unmistakable. She suddenly realised how alive her senses had become to his every movement since his illness, how she constantly noticed, often almost subconsciously, the way his long, lean body moved, as if his movements stirred a chord deep within her.

'Come, my lady, you have promised this dance to me,' Guy said suddenly, grabbing Hester by the hand and pulling her to her feet.

'I have? But I've only just got my breath from the last one,' Hester objected, but Guy took no notice.

'Please excuse us,' he said quickly to William.

'Of course, my lord,' Hester heard William say as Guy whisked her back among the dancers, whirling her round in a frenzied jig, until all thoughts flew from her mind except the contours of his body as she clung to him, while the music rushed them onwards.

As the afternoon wore on, the mummers took a rest from playing while the guests took turns at singing. Then there were games of wrestling followed by the tug-o' war. Guy had been asked to lead one of the tug-o' war teams while William led the other. The village green was bathed in hot sunshine by now, so all the participants pulled off their jerkins and shirts before the start of the game. Hester watched as Guy stood there, his broad, tanned chest bare to the sunlight, clearly marked by the scar of his recent wound. He had still spoken to no one of its cause, the servants and villagers too discreet to ask him outright, while Hester, knowing the full story, felt constrained by her promise of secrecy to Eadric.

The lines of men took up their positions at the long, thick rope. It was a friendly match, but the keen sense of competition was obvious from the looks on their faces as they eyed each other before the start. A look of steely determination had settled on Guy's face, his eyes screwed up against the bright sun, the scar on his face crinkling as he regarded the opposing team, his gaze fixed on William who stood exactly opposite him, holding the same length of rope just a few feet away.

'My lady, will you drop the handkerchief to start the game?' Judith asked Hester.

'I would be honoured,' Hester replied, pulling her

handkerchief from her sleeve as she walked to the centre of the rope. She looked to her left: there stood William; and to her right was Guy. Guy took his eyes off William for a moment to look back at her as she raised her handkerchief then let it fall with a swift downward motion of her hand.

The two teams immediately began to heave with all their might, leaning back against the rope. They were strong men, accustomed to long days of heavy toil in the fields, and the teams were evenly matched, so that at first neither seemed to be gaining ground on the other. Guy, at the head of his team, was pulling with all his might, his biceps bulging with the effort, every muscle in his firm chest taut. The sweat began to gleam on his skin as he heaved against the rope.

The whole crowd was cheering them on, calling out names and unintelligible instructions in a din which filled the village green. At the back of William's team stood the biggest man in the village, Guthrum, Eadric's father. Like an anchor at their end of the rope, his great weight and strength was beginning to have the effect William had planned when he chose to place Guthrum there. Guthrum's Herculean efforts were definitely beginning to pull the other men towards him.

Hester watched as the fluttering rag tied to mark the centre of the rope began to move across the line which Alured had scratched on the ground. As soon as William's team managed to pull Guy's feet across that line, the match would be over and Guy would have been defeated.

She looked at Guy. Beads of sweat were dripping down his face, and his whole body was tense with

physical effort. She could see that he knew he was
losing ground, recognised that with a few more pulls
from William's team he would have lost the match.
A look of fierce determination had settled on his face
as his toes inched towards the line. All at once he
began a rhythmic chant, instructing his team to heave,
heave, heave. And slowly, but with increasing speed,
the rope began to move back towards his side. Heave,
heave, heave.

William's team-mates were in trouble now as their
leader's feet began to approach the line. Heave,
heave, heave. Even Guthrum couldn't hold them.
William tried to hold back with a valiant effort, but
it was too late. In another moment his feet were on
the line and an instant later the whole team had collapsed in an exhausted, sweaty heap of laughing,
panting men.

'Congratulations, my lord,' William said, dragging
himself up from the ground to shake Guy's hand.

'Thank you,' Guy nodded, his brown body glistening in the sun. 'It was a close match. You almost had
me over the line a few moments before.'

'Aye, that we did,' William nodded with a satisfied
grin. 'Next time, we'll beat you good and proper, my
lord. You wait and see.'

'I shall look forward to proving you wrong,' Guy
replied with a smile. William laughed in return, but
Hester could see that Guy's smile had touched only
his lips. His eyes remained serious as he regarded
William. For some reason winning the trial of strength
had been very important to him. The look of sheer
determination on his face set her mind racing, but her
thoughts were interrupted by Alured's voice calling

out above the din of congratulation and commisera-
tion.

'The winners are to name their prizes,' he said.

'Kisses,' called out one of the men, and with a
guffaw he and his team-mates leapt into the crowd to
catch their sweethearts in their arms. Only Guy stood
still, his eyes on Hester.

'Go on, my lord,' bellowed Guthrum, his voice almost as deep as a giant's, 'Claim your kiss.'

Hester felt herself blushing as all eyes fell upon her
and Guy. He remained where he stood, would not run
and catch her, as the other men had chased their
women. Instead he simply raised his eyebrows in a
question which seemed to ask whether she were willing to give a kiss. Hester felt her feet moving in his
direction. In a moment she was standing before him,
only inches of hot summer air between them. She
could feel the heat of his body as he stood there, bare-
chested before her. His arms stretched out to enfold
her. She leaned into the strength of his form. His lips
closed on hers.

Her eyes shut as the touch of his lips melted the
core of her being, the scent of his skin, the strength
of his arms all seemed to lift her away from the
ground so that she was floating in his embrace. She
longed to float here always, buoyed up by his love…
Then suddenly her feet were back on the grass, his
lips were no longer on hers, she was opening her eyes
and he was standing before her, watching her with
that deep, dark look of his. All around them, she realised, the villagers were cheering and shouting, delighted by this public kiss between their lord and lady.

She felt herself blushing again as Guy looked around the crowd, in acknowledgement of their delight.

'I think we have provided enough of a spectacle,' he said quietly. 'Time we let Judith and Collen take centre-stage.'

He pulled on his shirt and they walked off to one of the benches, where a great flagon of cider awaited them. Sipping at her cider, Hester watched him drain his beaker, his throat long and brown as he tipped back his head.

Afternoon became evening, and the dancing began again. Hester had been content to watch the merriment, but as the dancing became rowdier and the songs bawdier she wondered whether it might be time to leave. Judith and Collen had already crept away to be alone together. Guy seemed to read her thoughts.

'My lady, I yearn to hear the sound of the waves. Will you come to the beach with me?' he asked, whispering the words close to her ear, so that she felt his breath against her neck once more.

'I cannot think of anything I would like more,' she replied.

They slipped away quietly from the crowd without being noticed, and in a few minutes their feet were on the sandy path leading down to the sea. Dusk was beginning to fall and soon the sound of the waves had reached Hester's ears. In a few moments more her feet were on the beach, with the waves lapping gently at the sand before her. The stars were beginning to shine in the sky.

'There's Venus,' Guy said, pointing up to the bright spot twinkling with a yellow tinge, low in the sky. 'The planet of love,' he added, his eyes still on the star.

Hester felt her heart pounding with his words. How did he mean her to interpret such a comment? Could he really love her after all? What other reason could there be for all the presents, the clothes, the necklace and his attention to her all afternoon? Her heart seemed to flutter in her mouth at the thought that he might love her.

'I am longing for a swim,' he said suddenly, pulling off his shirt.

'You mustn't,' Hester protested. 'The water is cold. You will risk your health.' But Guy was already pulling off his boots. 'What if you catch another fever?' Hester persisted.

'I shan't,' Guy laughed back at her. 'It's not that cold. Why don't you see for yourself?'

'Me?'

'Yes,' he said. 'Come swimming with me.'

'But I have nothing to change into. And it would spoil my new dress,' she protested in horror.

'Your dress!' he laughed back at her. 'I wasn't suggesting that you should swim in your dress, my lady. I was suggesting you should take it off. No one will see. I used to swim here as a boy, and I never wore anything then, nor did I ever catch a chill from the water. Come, my lady, discard your finery and let us swim together as if we were two sweethearts from the village.'

Hester felt herself flush with apprehension. 'I...I... Take off my clothes?' she stammered.

'You can't keep them on. They would weigh you down, and the sea water would ruin them. What if I promise not to look?' he asked with a mischievous smile.

The moon was climbing high into the sky as Hester returned his gaze, considering. What should she do? Part of her longed to swim in the cool, salty water after this day of heat and exertion. Part of her longed to float with him, to be submerged in the waves, her body beside his, like two dolphins swimming in the sea. Another part of her was petrified by the idea, frozen with terror at the thought of such intimacy.

'Well, if you decline, I shall have to swim on my own,' he said with a sigh. Suddenly he turned his back to her and began peeling off his hose. Hester, too astonished to look away, stared as he dropped his clothes in a shadowy heap on the dark beach, the hard muscles of his sinewy body highlighted by the moonlight. A moment later he was running into the sea, his long, powerful legs striding through the waves, until he plunged with a great splash into their midst.

He disappeared from sight. Where would he surface? Hester scanned the dark waves, trying to pick out his form, at first looking close to the spot where he had disappeared, then beginning to look further and further away as he remained hidden from sight. Was he really swimming under water all this time? Could he really hold his breath for so long? Her eyes scanned the forms of the little fishing boats bobbing at moorings off the shore, but the only movement she could see in the dark was the constant motion of the water.

'Guy!' she called out in alarm. 'Guy! Where are you? Can you hear me?' There was no sound except the steady plash of the waves on the shore. 'Guy!'

she tried once more, calling at the top of her voice. What if he was caught on an anchor line? What if he had suffered a seizure and was lying helpless in the water? She couldn't afford to wait any longer, she had to take action.

Remembering his warning that her clothes would weigh her down in the water, she pulled off her tunic and dress hastily, kicking her shoes into the sand. Her chemise could stay on, it was light and thin. She ran for the water and waded in, the sudden chill making her gasp. Only one thought was in her mind. She had to find him, she had to save him. She didn't want to live without him.

Chapter Ten

As she waded in waist-deep, Hester hesitated. Now that she was in the water, it was no easier to look for him than it had been from the shore.

'Guy!' she called again in desperation. 'Guy!'

'Here I am!' She heard his voice behind her and wheeled around, but as she did so, she felt her legs pulled from under her, the sky and sea seemed to tilt before her eyes and in an instant she had fallen into the cold water, her chemise billowing out around her, her mouth gasping salty waves, her eyes enveloped by the eerie underwater darkness. She came up spluttering and seething.

'Why, you…you beast!' she spat at him. 'How could you play such a trick on me? You wretch!'

'Yes, I am, aren't I?' Guy admitted, but he was grinning from ear to ear, with no sign of contrition on his face, and every sign that he was delighted with the result of his practical joke. His dark eyes twinkled mischievously in the night as he stood before her, his wet hair sleek and thick against his head, his strong, muscular shoulders glistening with drops of water in the moonlight.

'I thought you were drowning somewhere,' Hester berated him, the fear she had felt for his safety only moments before now spilling out in angry recriminations. 'I thought you were caught on an anchor line, or injured, or that you'd collapsed, or...'

'You thought all that in such a short space of time?'

'Yes, I did. I thought you were dying somewhere in the water. How could you trick me like that?'

'You thought I was dying, and you came to save me,' he said, catching hold of her in the water, slipping his arms around her waist, but she struggled free and pushed him away sharply. He looked surprised at her strength of feeling and force.

'My lady, 'twas only a joke. I wanted you to come swimming. I knew you'd enjoy the water once you were in. 'Twas just a way of overcoming your apprehension.'

'It was an oafish, offensive way of doing so,' Hester snapped back, still furious.

'You're right. I shouldn't have made sport of you. But it has taught me one thing.'

'What's that?' Hester demanded, slightly mollified by his admission, though only slightly.

'That you were willing to risk your life to save mine. There was a time when you wished me dead.'

'As I do now,' Hester insisted, even though she knew it wasn't true. He knew, too, and this time when he put his arms around her she didn't shake them off.

'You cared enough to try to save me and for that I thank you,' he said quietly.

'Don't take it personally. I would do the same for

any husband,' she snapped back sarcastically, a little daunted by the personal turn this conversation was taking.

'Ahh,' Guy replied. What did he mean by that? She tried to gauge his reaction in the dark, but his face was inscrutable. His arms were still around her, though, and she had done nothing to shake them off. A wave washed against her back, pushing her gently towards him. The two of them floated with its motion, lifting their feet from the seabed for an instant. She scanned his face. He was at home in the night, its darkness offsetting his own, a solid shadow amidst the dark, ever-moving power of the sea.

'Oh, no!' she gasped suddenly, her hand shooting up to her neck. 'I've still got my necklace on. If it's ruined it will all be your fault.'

'I doubt whether a little salt-water will hurt it. After all, the pearls came from oysters of the Red Sea.'

'Did you bring them back from the East for me?' Hester asked, suddenly needing confirmation.

'Of course. I wanted to bring you a present.' Hester felt herself glowing at his words, but then a doubt crossed her mind.

'Why didn't you give them to me when you first returned?' she asked.

'I wasn't sure they would be welcome,' he admitted.

Hester couldn't help smiling at her own suspicion, especially when she remembered how she had seethed and cursed at his homecoming.

'Come, we must swim, else you'll be chilled by the water.'

They struck out into the dark waves. Hester had

never swum at night before and now she felt exhilarated by the way the waves pulled at her body, seeming to invite her into the dark unknown, a hint of danger lapping around her. Guy swam beside her, the power of his strokes pulling him ahead, so that every now and then, he hesitated, floating so that they would be swimming alongside each other. They swam on in silence, until, in speechless agreement, both rolled over and floated on their backs, looking up at the stars glinting in the sky above. Both silent, the magic of the moment too precious for speech.

'Come on,' Guy said at last.

'Oh, but it's so beautiful here,' Hester objected.

'Beautiful, but cold after a while. I don't want *you* catching a chill.'

They swam to the shore and found their way across the sand to where their clothes lay strewn. She dared not look as Guy pulled on his hose and his shirt over his wet skin. Now that she was out of the water, Hester was all too aware of the way the fine linen of her chemise clung to her body, revealing almost as much as if she had been naked. She longed to cover herself with something, but could not use her silken robes for fear of damaging them with water marks. Instead she folded the fine cloths carefully, holding them away from her dripping self. She felt Guy's eyes upon her.

'You're shivering,' he said, throwing his surcoat around her shoulders. 'Here. Is that better?' His voice was full of care, but she wished he would look anywhere but at her.

They picked their way back up the sandy path,

Hester's heart pounding lest they should meet someone from the village.

'Come, my lady, let's run to warm up,' Guy commanded, catching hold of her hand and setting off briskly with Hester in tow.

When they reached the manor house, they were both panting for breath but laughing at their helter-skelter run across the dark fields. Hester headed straight for her chamber, determined to escape Guy's gaze and dry off in private.

The house was deserted. She could still hear the wedding festivities, the music wafting into her room on the night breeze. It sounded fun and she guessed that everyone must still be there. She listened to their distant merriment as she tugged off her wet chemise and hastily pulled on a long, linen night-gown, throwing a woollen shawl around her shoulders for warmth. Then she put a log on the fire and tried to breathe some life into its dying embers. Her hair was hanging in cold rats' tails, dripping icy sea water down her back in a most uncomfortable way. Hester was fluffing it out in the warmth of the fire when she heard a tap at her door.

'Enter,' she called. She looked up and saw Guy standing in the doorway. He had changed out of his wet clothes too. He looked stunning, standing there in his dark, close-fitting breeches and loose linen shirt. The cloth stretched tightly over his thighs, showing the strong, lean muscles of his legs, and his shirt was unfastened so that Hester felt her eyes being drawn to the tanned skin of his neck and chest.

'Will you join me in a drink?' he asked, his voice deep and soft, seeming to fill the dark, empty house with his presence. He was holding the box containing the chess set as if it were a tray, with a jug and goblets balanced on top. He strode towards her and placed them on the low table by the fire.

'Your wine is served, my lady,' he said with a grin, filling the goblets and handing one to Hester. She took a sip. It was a rich, dark wine, syrupy in its sweetness, leaving a trail of tingling warmth as it slipped down her throat.

'Mmm,' she exclaimed in instinctive appreciation.

'You like it?' he checked, looking pleased as he set out the chess pieces on the board. 'It's an Eastern wine. I brought a little back with me. And now, my lady, let us see if tonight is to be the night of your triumph!' He looked up at her, a challenge glinting in his eyes.

'Very well, my lord, look to your laurels,' Hester replied, rising to the dare. He grinned in return, little imagining that over the last few days she had been planning the perfect strategy for a game of chess. The only question was whether he would guess her scheme. Would he thwart this cunning game of war which she had been mulling over and over in her head, constantly searching for the key to victory?

Hester pushed forward her king's pawn. This was the first step in her plan. It was so simple, it almost made her laugh out loud with excitement. She had to bite her tongue and try hard to look as puzzled as usual in order to hide her intentions from her experienced opponent. If only she could get away with it, he would be defeated in just four moves—a strategy so perfect in its simplicity that she felt sure it could work, if only she could act as if she had no plan in mind, if only she didn't alert him to her scheme.

She sipped at her wine and studied him over the rim of her goblet. He was deep in thought, his hand hovering over the pieces. She took another sip, waiting for his move, then another and another. At last he moved his king's pawn to meet hers, then looked up to find her eyes gazing steadily back at him. He smiled and the sight made Hester's heart miss a beat. Her hand trembled so much she had to put down her goblet. It was nearly empty anyway. Guy reached for the jug and filled it to the brim.

'Your turn,' he said quietly, his voice as silky and sweet as the taste of the wine, leaving Hester so flustered she almost forgot her next move.

She sipped deliberately at her goblet, doing her best to hold it steady as she tried to gather her thoughts, moving her fingers from one piece to the next, her mind forgetting everything except that smile. At last her memory cleared and she moved her queen across the board in front of the line of pawns which remained untouched.

Guy looked down at the board, idly twirling his goblet in his hand. She felt sure he could read her mind, that he knew what she was going to do. He sat motionless, deep in thought. But then he calmly took a sip of wine and moved his queen's pawn forward to lie adjacent to the first. He looked up and smiled again, but she was prepared for him this time.

Hester did her best to mirror his air of calm, sipping at the deliciously sweet liquid in her goblet with a feigned insouciance. It was stronger than the local wine, thick and fortified, and already it was beginning to work on her senses. She could feel all the tension slipping away, her shoulders relaxing as the rich liquor seeped into her, saturating her with its warmth.

'What will your reply be to that, I wonder?' he asked, his voice calm and even. 'Perhaps this will be your chance to avenge yourself for the unkind trick I played earlier. I hope my lady will not be too hard on me.'

'Perhaps,' she replied, her voice catching a little in her throat. She took another gulp of wine for courage, adding, 'I have given some thought to my revenge. It is a dish best served cold, so they say. And after this evening's adventure, I can assure you I am cold enough.'

'But beginning to warm a little, I hope.' Guy laughed as he sat back in his chair, watching her. She could feel his eyes upon her and had to force herself to concentrate on her next move. She could feel a blush spreading over her face with the sheer knowledge of how she planned to defeat him, and hoped desperately that he would think her pinkness was due to the wine and the heat of the fire, instead of to her scheming anticipation. With an effort, she managed to keep a semblance of outer calm and at last, with just enough delay to make him believe that she had no plot worked out in advance, she moved her bishop to cover her attack, as she had planned.

Guy sat up and looked puzzled. His whole posture communicated suspicion. Hester felt her limbs go tense. Guy lifted his hand to move his queen, then dropped it with a frown. Hester realised she had been holding her breath and forced herself to let it out again gently, determined not to give him any tell-tale sign of the importance of this move. She reached for the jug and topped up her goblet, hoping this gesture would mask her anxiety. Guy continued to look at the pieces on the board for what seemed like an age. At last, he sighed and shook his head. With a slight shrug he moved his knight forward to threaten Hester's queen.

'I can feel something in the air, but I cannot work it out,' he said. 'Perhaps the wine dulls my wits, but I smell danger. It is unmistakable—and my senses are usually to be trusted on such matters.' He sighed again and looked at her. 'Perhaps it's my imagination, for I cannot see any source of danger. What do you say, my lady?'

Hester smiled back at him in silence and savoured the moment.

'I hope you do not expect special favours from your opponent, sir. You must know that tactics are never discussed between opponents in games of war,' she replied archly.

'Quite right,' he admitted with a nod. 'I see I must await my fate.' He was watching her with avid eyes, longing to know the answer.

Hester took a gulp of wine in silent congratulation of herself, then, conscious that Guy was still on ten- terhooks awaiting her next move, she took another sip, a long, slow one, savouring the wine as she drew it over her tongue, just to play for time and prolong the sweet anticipation of her success. Taunting him with her slowness, she pushed her queen forward gradually, little by little, until it stood right in front of his king, taking his pawn and putting him into checkmate. Her bold attack was protected by the bishop. There could be no riposte. She imagined herself to be that small ivory piece, proud and defiant standing victorious before her lord…before Guy, her husband.

Guy stared at the board, as if unable to believe his eyes. He looked up in amazement at Hester. 'How… where…?'

Hester, unable to contain her excitement any longer, felt it bubble up within her and giggled back at him gleefully. Then, collecting herself again, she managed to calm her giggles so that now she was only grinning and squirming with delight.

'Where did you learn…?' Guy paused, a frown of suspicion crossing his face. 'Has someone else been teaching you?'

'No one else has been teaching me. I thought of it myself,' Hester retorted proudly.

'Did you now? Then you are an even cleverer pupil than I realised. It is a brilliant strategy, perfect in its simplicity. Any general would be proud of such manoeuvres. Any husband doubly so,' he said, his voice lowering as he finished. 'It is a fine revenge, my lady. Now we stand honours equal.'

A silence fell and something in the air between them seemed to change. Suddenly she felt awkward and did not know what to say to him. She grabbed her goblet from the table and drained it quickly. She felt the wine pulsing through her veins, filling her head with its warm, light exuberance.

'But you had an unfair advantage, my lady,' Guy said sternly, breaking the silence. Hester glanced up rapidly. He was looking at her. She saw an emotion flicker across his mouth.

'I did not,' she protested.

'Oh, yes, you did,' he insisted. 'For how could I possibly concentrate on the chessboard with you sitting opposite me looking like that?'

Hester glanced down at herself. She had been too busy concentrating on winning the game to consider her appearance. His arrival with the chessboard had interrupted her before she had had time to dress properly. The nightgown she had pulled on hastily for warmth was loose at the neck, revealing the necklace which she still wore and the creamy skin of her chest. Her shawl had slipped from her shoulders as her mind had become absorbed by the game and her drying hair was spread loosely over her shoulders. Her skin, warmed by the fire, was glowing in the soft light, and her eyes were still sparkling with the exaltation of victory.

She looked across the table into Guy's eyes. They seemed to be smouldering like the fire as he watched her.

'Come,' he said, and suddenly he was on his feet, the wood of his chair scraping against the wood of the floor as he pushed it back. 'They are still dancing in the village.' The notes of their music were clear on the night air, wafting into Hester's chamber. 'I like this tune. Why don't we dance?'

'Here?' Hester asked in surprise.

'Right here. I can think of nowhere better,' he replied.

She allowed him to pull her from her chair. This time he was not holding her hands to dance a jig as he had done earlier on the village green. The faint music was slower now and he clasped his arms around her, pulling her tightly against his chest until she felt she would melt into him. Her heart was racing as they swayed with the rhythm of the music. She allowed her head to rest against his chest, the skin of her cheek touching his skin where his shirt lay open, and there she was surprised to feel the rapid beat of his heart, pounding beneath his curling hair and firm muscles. Was he really as nervous as she was? Could it be possible that this moment mattered as much to him as it did to her?

She raised her head to look into his face, eager to read his expression. His dark eyes met the blue of hers. Their faces were so close she could feel his breath on her skin. Then he moved even closer, and now it wasn't just his breath that she felt, but his lips touching her mouth with the lightest of kisses, hardly more than the brush of a butterfly's wings. Their breaths mingled and it felt as though they were breathing each other's souls.

'Oh, Hester,' he whispered, his voice gruff, groaning with longing, as he buried his face in her hair and breathed in its sweet scent, still salty from the sea. 'I must take you swimming more often if this is the effect.' Then he pulled back from her, a twinkle of mischief in his eye. 'And it has the added advantage of washing away the smell of mud which you usually carry around with you.'

'The smell of mud!' Hester exclaimed. 'Well, at least I don't smell of sweaty horses.'

'*Touché.*' He laughed back. 'I did not think you cared how I smelled.'

'I don't, but sometimes it is impossible not to notice.'

Guy laughed, a deep, throaty chuckle. 'Then it is just as well we both went swimming.'

'The music has ceased,' Hester said, turning towards the window as she suddenly noticed that the night air was quiet and still.

'It ceased some time ago,' Guy whispered, still holding her in his arms, his body swaying gently against hers.

'But we are still dancing.'

'Yes. Do you think we should stop?'

He waited for her reply, but Hester's voice had dried within her throat. All she could do was shake her head. That was answer enough and in a moment his lips were on hers again, this time demanding and serious. She felt her mouth responding as if it had a life of its own, welcoming his kisses. His tongue touched her lips sending a glow of expectation through her as she parted her lips to return his kiss.

She was in his power now, surrendering to the embraces she had dreaded when he had first arrived. But how long ago that seemed. Hester realised she had been yearning for his touch for weeks now, at once frightened and fascinated by the effect he had on her. Whenever his fingers had brushed against hers she had felt a thrilling pulse shoot through her. Whenever they had stood together in the fields her mind had returned to the scene of their cliff-top embrace when the storm had broken around them.

His hands were travelling over her back, leaving trails of exquisite fire wherever his fingers touched, slipping down over the curves of her hips. He buried his face in her hair and breathed her name in a growl which seemed to come from deep within.

'Oh, Hester, Hester,' he murmured into her ear as his lips began to taste the skin of her neck, still salty from the sea.

If this was part of a wife's duties, no wonder everyone else was so keen to be married, Hester thought in awe. She had never expected to feel such pleasure, such fiery excitement from his touch. Now all she knew was that she wanted more, wanted him closer, wanted this never to stop.

He pushed the gown from her shoulders. Its loose folds fell away effortlessly. Hester felt a sudden twinge of shame at her nakedness and dropped her eyes to the floor. He sensed her hesitation immediately.

'Don't deny me,' he whispered, his hand lifting her chin so that her eyes met his. She saw the desire in his face as his lips closed on hers in a hungry kiss.

His hands were exploring the curves of her body, not harsh, yet demanding. He cupped her breast and in an instant his mouth was on her delicate skin, his tongue teasing, his teeth nipping playfully so that she yelped with mingled pleasure and surprise.

Then his hands were on her hips again, firm and sure, pulling her close against him. He pushed himself against her in an instinctive gesture of wanting. Then his hands slipped down on to her thighs and stroked her there on her soft skin until she felt she could support her own weight no longer, the tingling, tantalising pleasure was so consuming.

Her head was swimming with wine and with the heady closeness of him, the intoxication of his touch. Her skin seemed to be on fire wherever he touched her. All at once it was too much. Her legs gave way beneath her. His strong arms around her prevented her from sinking to the floor.

'Hester, are you all right?' he demanded quickly.

'Yes, I—my head's a little dizzy,' she stammered.

'You need to lie down,' he whispered in her ear.

In an instant he had lifted her effortlessly, so that she was lying against his chest, supported by his strong arms beneath her. He carried her across the room to her bed, its soft white sheets and pillows welcoming her in the firelight glow. He laid her down gently, her head sank into the pillow. His lips followed her into its softness.

'Oh, Hester, you are so beautiful. I want you so much,' he breathed and his words were like a growl of yearning.

All words had flown from Hester's head, she could only lie bathed in the sweet ecstasy of his desire. He wanted her after all. At last she knew that he wanted her. How sweet it was to be desired. She didn't care about the Saracen women he had had, the mistresses and paramours. Even his rejection of her on their wedding day mattered little when measured against this. She gave herself up to him, wanting nothing for the moment but to feel his touch, his fingers, his lips, his body.

'Do you want me?' he asked, the unexpected question jarring against her ear. Didn't he know? Couldn't he tell? The only language Hester felt she could speak now was that of the body. And her body was telling him every moment how much she longed for him.

'Mmm,' she sighed.

'Tell me, Hester, tell me,' he commanded softly.

'I'm your wife,' she said simply. They were the

only words she could find in her wine-warmed mind. They spilled on to her lips, those lips still pulsing from the demands of his kisses. She reached up to pull him back towards her. She needed to feel the weight of his body against her, his skin against her nakedness. He was to be her husband truly at last, no longer a husband in name alone. And she would know what it was to be a wife, loved and wanted at last after ten long years.

But as she reached out to pull him to her, he resisted. She opened her eyes to look up at him and saw him there, silhouetted above her, the soft firelight casting a flickering glow over the wall behind him.

'My wife?' he repeated. 'So you are, but I thought…I mean, I had hoped… No!' he said, his voice suddenly sharp and loud. 'No, of course not!' He pulled away from her and stood upright beside the bed. 'Please forgive me,' he was saying. His voice rang in her ears, so painfully hard after the softness of the words which had gone before. And it wasn't just his words: the look on his face was hard too, cold and determined. 'This was a mistake. You could not possibly… I am not…' he began saying, grasping for a meaning which evaded her. 'I shouldn't be here. This should never have happened. Please excuse me, my lady.'

My lady! Hester stared after him as he strode from the room, slamming the door behind him with such force that its heavy oak shook. Bewildered she called his name. 'Guy? Guy?' But there was no reply.

Suddenly her head felt horribly clear. Her thoughts were no longer swaddled in wine, instead they leapt into her mind with painful clarity. He didn't want her.

He had tried to fulfil his duty as her husband, but it had been too abhorrent to him. And when she had reminded him that she was his wife he had been unable to tolerate her any longer. He had left her yet again.

She burst into tears, scorching, agonising tears which racked her body with their sobs. She had offered him everything, and he had rejected her. She was humiliated not only by his rejection but, worse, by her willingness, the way she had opened to him all too readily, too stupidly, making it oh so clear to him how much she had been longing for his love all this time.

How could she have imagined that he could have wanted her? No doubt his mind was still on the paramours he had chosen in the East. He had not chosen her. He did not want her. No matter that she had offered herself to him unconditionally. He had tried to go through with it, but, at the decisive moment, he could not bear to make love to her after all.

What a sham, what a terrible mess their hollow marriage was. And the worst of it was that she adored him—and hated him now, too. How could she ever recover from this rejection? The pain of it stung so much more fiercely than the old wound inflicted by his departure ten years before. Then at least she had been a pawn in the games of others. Tonight she had been playing her own game, and she had lost.

How could she ever regain her self-respect now that he had seen her naked, felt her wanton body pressing against his, begging for more? It had been bad enough before, but how could they go on living in the same house after this?

In her anguish Hester curled like a baby into the sheets. Her hand brushed against her neck, and there she felt the necklace, like a viper clinging to her throat, its pearls and gold warmed by the heat not only of her body, but also of his. She tore it off and flung it away from her.

She buried her face in the pillow and sobbed and sobbed for her lost chance of love.

Chapter Eleven

The morning sunlight stabbed into Hester's eyes. She had cried for so long that she felt utterly drained. Her meagre sleep had come at last just before dawn when, exhausted by her misery, she had finally slipped into a shallow rest.

What was she to do? She couldn't lie in this bed any longer, with its awful memories of his body beside hers. She must get up despite her pounding head and aching body and her feeling of total emptiness.

What was there for her now, now that he had rejected her so completely, so humiliatingly, so painfully? She was doomed to live on as his unwanted wife, his presence taunting her with her failure. Doomed to live on in her beloved Abbascombe, subject to the rule of a man who found her too loathsome and repulsive to accept, even when she had offered him everything...

Or maybe not, maybe he would send her to some far-flung cottage on the very edge of the estate so that he would not have to endure her in his house. Perhaps he would bring another woman into Abbascombe, one of his choosing, one whom he could bear to look at and touch… Hester shuddered, her stomach churning at the thought. She thought she would be sick. Just the idea of another woman here, with the man she loved, in the place she loved, filled her with a desperation so intense she knew she could not bear it.

She dragged herself out of the bed, knowing that she could not remain there and also remain sane. What was to be done?

She could run away. But she had no money of her own. Everything she had inherited from her parents had become part of the Beauvoisin property when she had married Guy. Whilst she had remained at Abbascombe it had not mattered because she had been living by working the land, just like the villagers. But away from Abbascombe, how could she survive? She might ask Guy for an allowance.

No, she would never do that—the prospect of further humiliation repelled her. Go to him, plead with him to allow her a living? After last night? No, she would never stoop to that. The only reason he had married her had been for the money. He could keep it. It might act as a recompense to him for having been forced to marry such an intolerable wife.

But what else could she do? Go to a town and try to earn a living? Doing what? There were so few possibilities for a woman of her class. The only thing she knew was how to run a demesne, and no one would entrust a woman with work of that sort.

A nunnery might admit her. There was a convent near Wareham, an enclosed order where the nuns were segregated from the outside world. But to be shut up within the walls of a convent instead of out in the fresh air…no longer to feel the wind blowing off the sea, the mud clinging to her clogs, the nourishing soil sticking beneath her fingernails…how could she live like that?

And then she recollected the distant cousin who had inherited her father's title and estate, a man she had never met. Perhaps she could write to him and persuade him to take her in? Perhaps he would allow her to live in a small cottage somewhere, or work as housekeeper. Thurston was also a demesne by the sea. A different sea, to be sure, more northerly, cold and inhospitable compared to Abbascombe. It would lack Abbascombe's sweetness, but it would also lack Guy and she had to get away from him.

She went to her table immediately and pulled out parchment and ink. 'Honoured Cousin,' she began to write, then paused. How was she to continue? How to explain why she sought refuge with a man she had never even met?

'I send greetings to you, my lord,' she wrote. 'And to your lady. You do not know me except by name, but our family connection emboldens me to request your help and charity.' She crossed out 'request' and wrote in 'beg'.

'Since my husband's return from the crusades after ten years' absence I have begun to realise that it is impossible for me to remain beneath his roof. He married me against his will, fled to the Holy Land to escape me and now finds my company intolerable. Dear Sire, please, I beg of you, if you have any room to accommodate a cousin, would you think of allowing me to come to Thurston? I am willing to do any work in your house or on your demesne to pay for my keep. I have been sole lady at Abbascombe for the last ten years and have learned much of management, both within the house and on the land. I beg of you to consider my request with your honourable lady and to let me know your answer as soon as you can. With respectful obeisance, your cousin, Hester de Beauvoisin.'

The letter was finished and she felt a tiny trickle of relief seep through her veins. At least now she had something to hope for, a respite from the despair which had taken hold of her, a reason to continue living until her cousin's reply might find its way back to her.

But whom could she send with the letter? Her cousin's land was many, many leagues away. How could she ask Guy to spare her one of his men to go on such an errand? But what if…? She thought suddenly of Judith and Collen leaving for their new married home in Wareham. If they had not already gone, if she could catch them now, perhaps she could entrust the letter to them, along with some money. There were sure to be travellers passing through Wareham who might carry the letter onwards for her.

Hester pulled on the linen dress she had discarded on the previous morning. On the floor was the pile of finery which she had dropped there last night. She shuddered as she looked at it, moved towards it to collect it up and hide it from view, then found herself falter as she stretched out her hands. She could not touch it. Instead, she left it where it was. Maud would be in soon. She would pick it up with tender care, tutting all the while at Hester's dreadful carelessness with such fine clothes. Then at least it would be folded away out of sight, its tormenting presence hidden.

She crept out of the house, wary lest she might meet Guy. There was no sign of him, or of anyone else. No doubt they were all catching up on their sleep after a long night of festivities. She ran past the fields, her tangled hair wild around her head, until she reached the village. Here all was silent too. She paused at the door to Alured's house. There was the sound of voices inside: they had not yet left, she was not too late. Hester knocked at the wooden door.

'Come in,' said Alured's voice. Hester lifted the latch and entered. Judith and Collen sat at the table with Alured, their breakfast spread out before them.

'My lady!' Alured exclaimed, rising to his feet with the others. 'This is an honour. We had not expected to see you.'

'No. I… Thank you so much for such a wonderful feast yesterday, Alured. It was a wonderful day,' Hester said, remembering herself and managing to dredge up a little false brightness from some reservoir deep inside.

'I'm glad you enjoyed it,' Alured returned, beaming. 'You and his lordship certainly looked as though you were having a good time.'

'Yes,' Hester agreed non-committally.

'Thank you for your present, my lady,' Judith broke in. 'It's the most beautiful bed-linen we've ever seen. We love it.'

Hester noticed the way Judith was saying 'we', as if she and Collen really were united now, two people who thought alike and shared everything. That is what a marriage should be, she thought. How different from Guy and me. Their loving union shows our marriage for the mockery that it is, a hideous splicing, a prison for two individuals who should never have been joined.

'I've come to ask you whether you would carry a letter for me to Wareham, and whether, once there, you might find a traveller to carry it onwards?' Hester explained, plucking up courage.

'Of course,' replied Collen. 'We'll be happy to.'

'Oh, thank you,' Hester whispered, relief bringing a wan smile to her. She pressed the letter into Collen's hand, along with a purse for his expenses. 'Thank you so much. And now I will leave you to breakfast in peace. I wish you both great happiness and good fortune,' she said, turning away to hide the tear which had sprung into her eye. After so many years of not crying at all, it seemed now as if there was no holding back the tears which welled inside her. It was Guy's fault, all his fault. But why had she allowed herself to fall under his spell? Why had she ever imagined that he might love her?

As Hester walked back though the village she began to calculate how soon she might hope to receive a reply from her cousin. It must take at least a fortnight to reach Thurston, assuming that Collen were able to find a messenger quickly and that the messenger would then travel by the quickest route, stopping only when necessary. That meant she must have at least a month of misery before her, longing to know how her cousin would respond, whether he would save her from the nightmare which Abbascombe had become for her.

She dared not return to the house for fear of meet-

ing Guy. The day was growing hot already. Hester
gazed over the fields, then began to walk without a
plan. Soon she realised that her feet were leading her
automatically towards the meadow.

Only two days earlier her main concern had been
when to bring in the hay. She had stood on this very
spot, surveying the scene, judging the ripeness of her
crop. She saw now that nothing around her had
changed in those two days, except perhaps that a few
more wild flowers had come into bloom and the long
grass had grown a little taller. Yet how much things
had changed for her. Hester remembered with a pang
the optimism she had felt just a few hours before, the
feeling she had carried with her that maybe at last she
had a possibility of love. But those hopes had been
shattered, torn from her soul when Guy had slammed
the door of her chamber behind him.

Beneath her stinging sense of loss, though, something remained of her former self. She still had
Abbascombe to care for, still had the villagers relying
on her. There was still work to be done. Even though
she would not be here to share the winter supplies,
Hester still felt it was her duty to ensure that no one
would go hungry on the Abbascombe demesne.

She gazed at the long grass surrounding her. It was
swaying gently in the breeze coming off the sea, its
soft swishings whispering around her. This would become the hay to feed the animals through the winter
months. She had been holding off from cutting it,
planning to catch it at just the right moment, when it
would make the sweetest, longest-lasting hay. She
plucked a stalk and crushed it between her hands.
Yes, it was ready now. They had tended it well, root-

ing out thistles and weeds as soon as they had appeared. In amongst the grass were splashes of colour where wildflowers had grown up with it. Butterflies and insects fluttered and buzzed in the air around her.

'Make the most of it,' she said out loud to a delicate Cabbage White as it fluttered past. 'It won't be here much longer. We must make hay while the sun shines.' But when the sun stopped shining, when the winter months dawned bleak and frosty, where would she be then? In the pit of her stomach she could feel the dread beginning to mount. The future was no longer a time to be anticipated, it was a looming monster threatening to smother her.

Just then she heard the sound of a horse's hooves galloping towards her. She twisted round and saw Guy on his beautiful, black horse, charging past along the bridle path which skirted the meadow. Her heart leapt at the sight of him, his hair swept back by the speed of his movement, his face set in an expression of hard determination. He was riding as if the devil himself were behind him. Where was he going? Amir was following, running close behind as ever.

The dread within seemed to clutch at her throat, choking her. Her heart was pounding, racing at the sight of him. She felt as if she could not breathe. Hester took to her heels and ran. She did not care where, as long as it was away from him. Her feet guided her blindly onwards until she reached the orchard. She came to a halt, panting. Of course, she had to tell the bees.

Their low hum was filling the orchard. Hester's task lay heavily on her heart, but she knew she must tell them of the death of her marriage. There was no

good in putting it off; far better to get it over with. It
was no great surprise, after all. It was a marriage
which had hardly lived, a sickly thing, forced into
being in unpropitious circumstances, incapable of
thriving. For a few weeks it had seemed possible that
it might have been coaxed into health, but now, at
last, it was truly dead.

She knocked on the first hive, always the precursor
to the delivery of news, but her mind remained blank,
and no words came to her lips. She looked up at the
morning sky, the sun already warm, its bright rays
shining through the thick leaves of the apple trees.

'He doesn't want me,' she said at last, her voice
cracking with the effort of speaking the words. 'He
loathes me. I'm going to have to leave you, bees. I
shall have to leave Abbascombe. I cannot remain in
his house. I have written to my cousin. Perhaps he
will have a home for me. But if he can't have me, I
shall have to find a place for myself. I can't stay here.
There, that's my news. I've said it now.'

Although her heart was heavy with the weight of
sorrow, she felt a little better for having told the bees.
It made her feel at least that something had been decided, that there would be no more wondering. She
was to leave Abbascombe come what may and must
manage her departure as best she could.

'I shall stay until the harvest is gathered,' she assured the bees as they buzzed around her. 'We need
every pair of hands when it's time to bring in the
corn, and it will take that long before my cousin's
reply can reach me. But once the harvest's in there'll
be no reason to stay. I'm afraid someone else will
have to look after you then, my bees. I'll find some-

one good, a nice girl from the village perhaps, and I'll teach her how to keep you happy. Don't worry. It'll be all right,' she said, but there was no more conviction in her voice than she felt in her heart.

No doubt it would make little difference to the bees, but what would it mean to her? Another journey into the unknown, just as terrible and heart-rending as her journey here had been when her parents had died. Her face crumpled at the thought. Could she really cope with going through all that again? She wasn't sure that she could. But what alternative was there for her: a married woman, forced like a burden upon a man who could not stand the sight of her?

She heard footsteps behind her and turned to see Nona running towards her, her plaits bouncing on her shoulders, skirts flying around her knees.

'My lady!' she cried with a beaming smile of delight, and Hester felt her heart melt at the child's pleasure in seeing her. 'I didn't know you would be here.'

'Hello, Nona. Are you on your own?'

'Yes, everyone else is still in bed, even Eadric. He says his head is sore and I told him he drank too much cider last night at Judith's wedding. It's all his own fault for being so greedy. I've come to look at the apples. I'm watching them grow. Look,' she said, pointing up at the tree, 'they're getting quite big. Soon we'll be able to eat them.'

'I think you'll have to wait a little while yet. They won't be sweet and ripe until well after harvest.'

'I know,' Nona replied wrinkling her nose at the thought of the delay. 'I love apples. I like the little red juicy ones the best.'

'I'll make sure we keep plenty for you to eat, then,' Hester assured her, the words slipping from her lips before she realised that she wouldn't be there when the apples were picked. She would already have left for goodness-knew-where. Her heart thudded against the wall of her chest. She looked down at Nona, so bright, so perfect, so adorable, and she felt a terrible searing pain at the thought that she would never now have a daughter of her own to dote upon. The sense of loss burned into her, almost as great as the pain Guy had inflicted upon her the night before. For now she realised that his rejection meant not only the death of their marriage, but the death of her future too.

The hay harvest began the next day. Guy seemed to have forgotten his vow that he would learn about the management of the estate, for he was nowhere to be seen. Hester was glad. She did not want to see him.

Haymaking would take up most of the next fortnight, with the men scything down the long grass on the meadowland, while the women spread it out on the ground in the sunshine, turning it at intervals until it was bone-dry and ready to be gathered up into bundles to be stored for winter feed for the animals.

Hester worked with the other women, raking out the long, cut grass so that it lay open to the warmth of the sun. It would dry quickly in such hot weather; soon they would be raking it up into bundles, tossing them into the cart to go off to be stored in one of the barns, ready for the winter.

Swish, *swish*, *swish* went the scythes as the men cut down the tall swathes of grass. It was a familiar sound, beautiful to her ears. Beyond, she could hear the steady crash of the waves against the cliffs. Even on a calm, still day like today, the water was angry down there. Unbidden she saw in her mind's eye Guy climbing round the rocks, so brave, so fearless, as he approached Eadric's clinging figure. She tried to push the image away, but it hovered unwelcome before her eyes. And where was he today?

She knew he had gone out early on his horse, alone except for Amir. Where had he gone? And why hadn't he taken Eadric with him? Usually he took the young squire everywhere.

One reason leapt into her mind. He was visiting a woman. It was so painfully obvious, Hester felt she would scream with the realisation. He already had a mistress. Perhaps one he had found in England since his return. Or perhaps the mysterious Fatima. Perhaps he had arranged long ago for her to follow him to England, perhaps she had even travelled with him, to be installed secretly in a house somewhere close by, within easy riding distance. A love nest for him to retreat to, a place where he could escape from the awful wife whose presence was so abhorrent to him. Hester burned with dismay at the thought.

Well, he wouldn't have to keep Fatima hidden for much longer. Hester would be leaving Abbascombe very soon, and then he could do as he pleased. The villagers might not like his Eastern woman, but no one would dare say so to the lord of Abbascombe, and soon everyone would grow accustomed to her presence. All too soon, no doubt, they would forget all about Hester.

Perhaps Hester's name would be mentioned in fireside stories on long winter nights. Let me tell you, children, the sad story of the lady Hester who had a husband who could not love her... Hester almost wept at the thought. They might forget her, but she would never forget Abbascombe. As long as she lived her memories would live in her heart, brighter and more powerful than anything else that might happen in the future. And among those memories would be many images of Guy.

She wished she could rid herself of them, but he lurked in her heart and mind, unwelcome, yet treasured. His presence was an exquisite torture. Still she could feel the touch of his fingers burning on her skin, his lips brushing against hers, and could still see his smile in the firelight as he leaned over the chess board... It was all too much, she wished she could rip the memories from her mind, like unwanted pages from a book, but they were there, rooted like choking weeds and there was nothing she could do to rid herself of their stinging presence.

As the day grew late, the weary reapers began to pack up their things and make their way home. Hester stumbled behind them, lost in thought until she heard some of the men call out, 'Evening, my lord!'

She looked up with a start. Guy was on his horse, sitting high above them, riding homewards. He had come from the direction of Compton. Was that where Fatima was living? Hester shook her head to try to clear the stupid thought away, but it stuck. Maybe not Fatima, but someone was there, someone whose company he chose to seek, someone unlike her.

That evening she told Maud she was too tired to come down for dinner, that she would have a tray in her chamber. Maud tutted and looked stern, but said nothing. One of the girls appeared a little later with her supper and Hester ate in solitude, knowing that Guy was sitting below, alone at the great table in the hall. She hoped he would understand that she was ceding her rights as mistress, that he could do as he pleased without regard for her, that he could stay and sup in Compton if he chose. What was the point of saving face now? The truth was too painful to hide.

'Where is my lady?' Guy asked Maud in the hall.

'In her chamber, my lord. She says she's too tired to come down.'

'Thank you, Maud,' Guy nodded solemnly. His dinner lay untouched before him. Amir drooped her head onto his feet. 'That's right, my old girl,' he said quietly to the hound. 'At least I have you to care for me.'

Taking supper in her room became a habitual occurrence for Hester from then on. She would far rather do that than face Guy, impose her abhorrent presence on him. She was too proud to do that.

She counted off the days that brought her cousin's reply nearer, but the same days also speeded her departure from Abbascombe. It was a double-edged sword, both sides a sharp, cutting blade.

In the meantime she tried to fill her mind with thoughts of the farm, of which tasks should be completed. She was determined to leave it all in perfect condition for whomever would take over when she was gone. She flung herself into her work, trying to drive all memories from her head by busying herself frantically with any manual task she could find, and trying to drive all dreams from her sleeping mind with the sheer exhaustion which followed a hard day's work. The days passed somehow. The nights were more difficult.

The most important task was the harvesting of the corn, and the key to a successful harvest was, as ever, in the timing. Bring it in too early and the corn would languish unripened in the barn, making unpalatable bread when it was finally threshed and ground into flour in the winter. Leave it in the field too long and it could be as beautifully ripe as you would like, but every extra day carried the risk of rain which might ruin the whole crop.

She stood in Cliff-top Field amongst the swaying shoulder-tall corn, caught a husk in her hand and rubbed it between her palms. It released its grains, but they didn't drop out with the ready ease of a fully ripe husk. There was that slight reluctance which signalled the need for another few days of sunshine.

Hester looked up at the sky. There had been nothing but burning, dazzling sun for weeks now. Not a drop of rain, not a cloud in sight, not a single sign of a break in the reign of fierce, hot summer. But how long could it last? Every day she left the corn standing in the field was a gamble, yet every day it stood there it grew better, more wholesome, more plentiful. William wasn't willing to commit himself. As ever, this most important of decisions was left to her.

There was only one place she could go for advice, but she was reluctant. Breda knew more of her feelings for Guy than anyone else and Hester dreaded the idea of approaching her, and the possibility that the old woman might try to speak to her of Guy. What choice did she have though? She could put it off until the last possible moment, but in the end she would have to seek Breda's help in divining the weather.

Hester trudged down to the village, to Breda's low, dark cottage, her heart heavy. The old woman was inside, stirring one of her concoctions. Hester blinked as she stooped to enter the one room, her eyes adjusting to the sudden gloom. Breda's back was turned towards her, a dark shadow amongst the other shadows of twigs, herbs and pots all around. A low, constant rasping noise filled the air, and Hester realised it was the grinding of Breda's pestle against dried herbs.

'Aye, my lady, I knew you'd be a-coming today,' Breda said without looking round, her eerie second sight serving her well, as she continued with her task.

'How did you know?'

'Oh, Ol' Breda just a-feels these things. You're a-worrying about the crop. Well, you're right to be worried, there's rain on the way.'

'Rain? When?' Hester demanded in alarm.

'Not just yet. You can let it stand a day or two longer. But no more. There'll be a storm coming in off the sea, a big one. I'll tell you when I know more.'

'Are you sure it's all right to leave it another day?'

'Aye, I'm sure. And now,' she said, turning to fix Hester with her witch's eyes that pierced through the gloom, 'I reckon the corn's the least of your worries. You're carrying a great boulder of sorrows around with you. I can feel the weight of it fairly filling Ol' Breda's little house.'

Hester bit her lip to hold back her tears. She couldn't speak for fear that sobs instead of words would come gushing out. Why did this old woman always think she knew everything? Why couldn't she just stick to discussing the weather?

'Now, the village girls often come to me for love potions. "Oh, Breda, can't you give me something to make him love me?" they say. Or sometimes it's the wives when their man has got a wandering eye. I always gives them something to put in his bruet, or a little powder for his cider.'

'That won't be necessary in this case, Breda,' Hester managed to bring the words out, sounding as stern and controlled as she could.

'Exactly, my lady. That's why it's such a crying shame. It's not a potion you need. It's a good long talk with 'im and no more messing about from either of you daft ducks, behaving like I don't know what instead of getting on with the business of being married. No one said it was easy...'

At this Hester could take no more. Did the old woman think she had chosen to live in such misery? Did she imagine Hester would have let it all go on if she could have had it any other way? The truth was that her husband loathed her, could not stand her, and there was no way of overcoming such a strong feeling of dislike, even in a marriage.

She had to get away before her heart burst with the misery of hearing Breda's words, so wrong, so utterly wrong. How wrong Breda had been to encourage Hester to love him. How wrong she had been to tell Hester to declare her love when he had been fevered. How wrong Breda had been about everything. Hester could bear it no longer. She turned on her heels and fled, out of the dark little hut and into the light. She turned towards the beach, dashed down the sloping common land, slipping and stumbling through sandy dunes until she reached the shore. Here she could weep in secret. Here there would be no one to hear her sobs. Even the seagulls soaring and squawking overhead would not hear her voice, drowned out by the crash of the waves.

Breda had looked out of her door after Hester's fleeing figure. She was too old and slow to follow. And what more could she say to the lady of the manor? There was a limit to what even a wise woman would be allowed to get away with. She tutted to herself.

'Shame,' was all she said, shaking her head as she turned to resume her potion-making.

Two days later, Hester saw the old woman's shuffling figure advancing slowly towards her in the copse. Her heart sank at the prospect.

'Best get it in now,' was all Breda said though.

'The corn?' Hester asked. 'Is the storm on its way? When, Breda? How long do we have?'

'Best start first thing tomorrow and no hanging about. I reckon you'll be all right.' And with that she was gone.

Chapter Twelve

The reapers stood in a long line stretching across the whole width of the field, hovering on the edge of the great golden sea of swaying corn. Hester's eyes skimmed down the line, checking the distance between each man: too close and there would be danger from the swishing scythes, their blades specially sharpened into lethal edges which glinted in the sunlight; too far apart and some of the stalks would be missed, a little patch here and there, but little patches could add up to a valuable sum over a whole field of this size.

In the past she and William had always watched the line, guiding the men if they drifted out of step. When time was tight she had often joined in with the women and children who followed behind their men, gathering the fallen stalks into stooks, which they left behind them in the field, like a crowd of short, plump corn people standing where the sea of corn had swayed just minutes before.

This year, as ever, they were in a race against time and weather. By now everyone had heard Breda's prediction that a huge storm was on its way. The sky was still bright blue, with not a cloud in sight, the air still shimmered with the haze of heat, as it had all through the August weeks, but everyone felt Breda's prediction like a prickling on the backs of their necks, as if the storm were lurking behind them, pushing them onwards.

Everyone was in the field to help, not just the villeins who owed day labour to the manor house, but also the wealthier tenant farmers who had their own land to farm. Even the smallest children were there to gather whatever corn they could, while the babies were carefully placed in the warm shade at the edge of the field, close enough to summon their mothers with a cry when they grew hungry.

As the rhythmic swish, swish, swish of the scythes began, Hester saw with familiar pleasure the long stalks of corn falling to the ground. As they fell, they were caught up immediately by the women, who, with deft twists of a few strands, bound them into stooks and stood them upon the ground as they moved on to the next bundle.

This would be the last Abbascombe harvest she would ever witness. A shock of pain shot through her at the thought. She crushed it. Foolish to look to the emptiness of the future when she had this to enjoy now. One last harvest, heavy with sun and heat; one last delicious, nerve-racking, exhausting race to bring in the Abbascombe corn. At least she would have this to remember as she eked out the rest of her years in exile. And perhaps the villagers would remember her through the winter as they ate the bread made from this corn.

Out of the corner of her eye, Hester caught sight
of a familiar, dark horse riding towards the field. Its
rider was Guy, the last person she had expected or
wanted to see. He sped towards her, reining his horse
in sharply as he reached the edge of the field. Hester
said nothing although he was within speaking distance. Their eyes met.

'I have heard you fear a storm is looming,' he said,
turning from her to examine the bright blue sky
doubtfully.

'Breda says so,' Hester replied tersely. Why say
more? What was the point?

'I have come to help. I thought you would need
every pair of hands. Do you have a scythe I can use?'

Hester looked to the edge of the field, where a spare
scythe was lying in the grass. Guy followed her eyes.

'I'll use this one,' he said, snatching it up lightly,
as if it weighed no more than a stick. He joined the
line of men as they scythed their way down the field
and instantly fell in with their rhythmic swaying as
they cut through the stalks. But there was no village
woman to follow this new scyther and Hester saw his
corn fall and lie on the ground behind him, the
women too busy catching the bundles from their husbands and sweethearts to bind Guy's corn too.

There was no choice but to follow behind him herself. She knew well how to bind a stook. But working
with Guy, following him through the field, catching
the corn as it fell from his reach…this was more than
she had bargained for.

She quickly gathered up the corn lying on the
ground in his wake, pulling out a handful of strands
to tie the fastening. In a few minutes she had caught

up with the rest and was close behind him, catching his corn as it fell, like any other village wife.

She couldn't help admiring Guy's skill with the scythe. She had not expected such skill, had not even expected competence. But he worked as well as any of the other men, keeping up with their line, cutting the corn cleanly, not too high, leaving the stalks at just the right height for binding. His strong figure looked as formidable as ever as he moved ahead of her. The muscles of his strong thighs, hard and clear against the cloth of his breeches, his loose white shirt swaying with his body as his powerful arms swung the scythe. As the morning grew warmer, he paused to pull off his shirt, as many of the other men had done, and Hester could hardly take her eyes from the firm strength of the musculature of his back as he returned to scything.

The villagers began to sing, the rhythmic songs which had been sung by generations of Abbascombe reapers. Guy hummed along, joining with some of the choruses as he picked up the words. Hester could hear his strong, deep voice just ahead of her as she stooped to tie the corn. She felt as if every cell in her body were alert to his presence, tingling painfully with his aura. Was there no escape after all?

When they stopped for lunch, everyone made for the shade at the edge of the field and pulled out the hunks of bread and cheese which they had brought with them, wrapped in cloths. They sat eating, talking and swigging from the flagons of cider which passed from hand to hand.

Hester slunk away quietly to the cliff's edge and

gazed out at the sea. It was bad enough having to follow him through the field, catching the corn as it dropped from his scythe. She needed a little time to recover, a little time to look at something other than him. Her thoughts remained on him, though.

Guy watched as she walked away. He did not follow.

'Good to see you here, my lord,' William said, coming up beside him.

'It's the least I can do. I should have come sooner, really, but I've been a bit...' Guy faltered.

'You've been busy with other things, my lord,' William finished for him. 'It's not your job to work in the fields.'

'No, but then nor is it the lady Hester's.'

'Aye, you wouldn't see many ladies binding stooks,' William replied and Guy heard the admiration in his voice. 'But lady Hester loves the land. There's no keeping her away from it.'

Guy nodded.

'But I'm glad to see you for another reason too, my lord. Not just because we need all the help we can get with the harvest, but also because I've been wanting a moment of your time to ask your blessing for something.'

Guy raised his eyebrows. 'Go ahead.'

'Well, it's like this. I want to be wed. Gwen and me, that is.'

'You wish to marry Gwen?' Guy repeated after a moment's silence, his eyes wide with surprise.

'Yes.' William beamed. 'You can't blame me, can you?' he joked, looking over to where Gwen sat among her girlfriends, chatting and giggling as they ate their lunch. She was a plump, dark-haired girl with rosy cheeks and twinkling eyes.

'Of course not,' Guy agreed. 'She's a lovely girl. I'm just surprised, William. This seems very sudden.' Guy's heart had begun to pound. What would this news mean to Hester? Would she continue to harbour feelings for the bailiff, or might this open a chance for him to find a place in her affections after all?

'It's not really sudden at all,' William replied, calmly unaware of his lord's racing thoughts.

'But I had thought…' Guy began, his words petering out. How could he continue? How could he ask this man whether he wasn't really in love with Hester? He tried again, he must know. 'I had thought perhaps your affections lay elsewhere.'

'Really, my lord?' William asked, raising his eyebrows in amazement. 'What could have made you think that? The truth is, I have loved Gwen ever since she was a little 'un, and I a lad beside her. We used to play hoop together, and we used to scare the crows together for the old lord, your father. I can't remember a time when I did not love her. But I wanted to make something of myself before I settled anything with her, though we've had a private understanding for a while now. I wanted to have a nest-egg laid by. And now I reckon I have.'

'Well, congratulations,' Guy said, shaking William's hand enthusiastically. 'I wish you very happy.' He paused. 'And you're sure…?' He couldn't stop himself from asking, the question just slipped out.

'Aye, my lord. Never been more sure in my life,' William responded with heartfelt conviction, studying

Guy with his observant, countryman's eyes. His lord's reaction was not quite what he had expected. Perhaps he was just trying to say that marriage was a big step, or perhaps he was thinking of his own marriage. The sudden change in the relationship between the lord and lady had not escaped William's notice. They had been getting on so well, had seemed like two love-birds after the lord's fever, then suddenly the ice had reappeared between them, even worse than before. He had supposed it to have been the result of an argument, but it was taking a long time to melt.

'And you, my lord, I hope you and the lady Hester may be happy too,' William said seriously, feeling that he dared to meet Guy's eyes with a sympathetic look.

'Thank you, William. Yes, I wish it might be so,' Guy replied thoughtfully. 'Gwen is fortunate in being able to marry where she likes,' he continued slowly. 'Lady Hester did not have that choice.'

'I know, my lord, but you seemed to be getting on so well, especially after she nursed you through your fever. A lady doesn't keep vigil like that all through the night unless she cares for a man.'

'No, William, you are mistaken. It was Maud who nursed me.'

William shook his head. 'Begging your pardon, my lord, but it was lady Hester who sat up with you right through the night. Maud complained to me that lady Hester refused to budge until you were out of danger, despite all chidings.'

'Are you sure?' Guy asked quickly, his heart leaping at William's certainty. Had it not been a dream then? Had Hester been with him after all? And those soft words he thought he had dreamed, those words of love…had they truly been whispered by his wife?

'Quite sure. As sure as I can be without having seen it with my own eyes.'

'Thank you, William,' Guy said absently as he turned to wander away. 'Thank you.'

William stood watching his back as he paced through the field. His lord seemed to be paying no attention to where he was going. A group of workmen had to step aside to let him pass, and Guy continued as if he had not even noticed them. William shook his head. What a blessing it was to be a bailiff instead of a lord, to be able to claim his beloved Gwen without having to worry about estates and heirs and feudal unions.

The last stalks of corn fell beneath Guy's scythe. He straightened his back alongside the other aching, weary men and glanced back at Hester. She met his eyes, too late to turn away and pretend she had not been watching him.

His dark, tanned face looked into hers, an expression spread across it which she tried to read, but couldn't decipher. Then his handsome features softened into a warm, spontaneous smile which left her trembling inside. What did he mean by smiling at her in that way? Was he amused by her? She could not smile back at him, knowing what he thought of her. Instead she turned away just as Breda shuffled over to where the last of the corn lay at Guy's feet.

Breda was the one who always wove the corn dolly, the wise woman who could weave her magic into the corn, weave in the fertility and vitality of the corn spirit. She sat herself down with the stalks in a corner of the field whilst the others threw the stooks up into the waiting wagon, the last wagon-load of this summer to make the journey to the barn, where they would be stored in the dry ready for threshing.

The people were in high spirits, although tired. They whooped and laughed as they threw the stooks up into the arms of the men on the wagon who stacked them in piles. When the last one was in, the men jumped down and lifted the children up in their places so that they could ride to the barn with the corn.

As Hester watched, tears began to prick against her eyes. How could she leave this? How would she survive away from everything she loved in Abbascombe? She scolded herself silently, ordering herself to try to look more cheerful, to mask her misery with a pretence of happiness, lest the villagers should notice her grief.

Just then, though, all eyes fell on Breda, as she walked slowly over with the corn dolly she had just woven.

'Let me see,' Guy said eagerly, as Breda held out her work. 'She's beautiful, Breda. But she needs a touch of colour, I think. How about one of my lady's blue ribbons?' he asked. And, almost before she knew it, he was at Hester's side, plucking at the ribbon which tied her plait, a single plait hanging long and heavy down her back. Hester flinched instinctively at his touch, but Guy persisted despite the scowl she shot at him. Why did he have to torture her in this way? Why could he not just leave her alone? A painful lump in her throat prevented her from protesting.

'Aye,' Breda agreed. 'A little colour would be pretty.'

Guy began to untwist the ribbon, his fingers brushing against Hester's back. She could not help remembering the last time he had touched her, the memories seared through her like a hot blade. It was terrible to feel his touch again. How could he be so cruel? She wanted desperately to escape, but he held her firmly by her hair.

'Don't struggle, my lady,' he breathed, his breath skimming over her cheek. 'Else I shall pull your hair by mistake.' Hester longed to yank herself free, no matter what physical pain it might cost her, or how many strands of hair she might leave behind in his hands. How dared he approach her like this in front of everyone, as if they were friends, as if they were really man and wife? How dared he force her to submit to his touch in public when he knew she could not pull away, slap him, scream at him, for fear of creating a scandalous scene in front of the whole village?

'Here,' he said, handing the ribbon to Breda, who tied it around the corn dolly's neck, then threw the little figure up on to the wagon, into the eager hands of the children who each year competed to catch it. It would be stored carefully, reverentially in the manor house until the next spring, when it would be slipped back into the earth with the last handful of grain.

The wagon began to trundle back across the fields and down the hill towards Abbascombe Manor. Hester followed, still smarting from Guy's touch. He tried to walk with her, but she dodged away, determined this time to escape.

When they reached the courtyard, she saw that Maud had anticipated well. Everything was ready for the harvest supper. The tables were groaning with wooden platters of meat, cheese, bread and vegetables. The flagons of cider stood ready, and there were plenty of them.

The people sank happily on to the benches, their muscles aching, but all aches and pains were outweighed by the feeling of satisfaction that such a successful harvest had been completed in good time.

'Still no sign of the rain.' Guy's voice spoke behind her, sending a deep thrill through her body. A thrill of loathing, Hester tried to tell herself as she turned to face him.

'No,' she agreed. The sky was dusky now, night falling, the golden harvest moon already climbing through the sky. 'If you thought my decision to hurry in the corn was wrong, my lord, you should have said so. I did what I thought was best, but you are lord here, not I.'

'Did I say I disagreed? Holy blood, my lady, are you so touchy these days that even a comment about the weather fires your blood?'

Hester felt her veins seething with fury. How could he speak so after all he had done? But she would not rise to an argument here in front of all the villagers. She did not wish to argue with him at all, she just wished he would leave her alone, wished she would never have to look into his face again, wished she had never laid eyes on his handsome, rugged features.

'Hester,' his voice whispered, suddenly low and

confidential. He was using her name again. The realisation shot through her like an arrow. 'I didn't approach you to speak of the weather. I must talk to you...' He paused, then added, 'We must talk in private.'

'I have nothing to say to you, and I do not wish to hear any more of your lies,' Hester hissed back, trying to hide her anger from those around them.

'My lies?' he echoed. His hand closed on her arm, preventing her escape, pulling her closer to him until she felt she could not stand the proximity. 'I have never lied to you.'

'Unhand me, sir,' she insisted in a voice low and heavy with threat. 'Unhand me before I scream. 'Twould be embarrassing for both of us, but I will do it if you do not let go of my arm this instant.'

He hesitated, seemed about to speak again, then let her go with a sigh. Everyone else was seated; they were waiting for Hester and Guy to sit down before the feasting could begin. Eyes were beginning to turn in their direction, wondering at the delay.

'There, I have let go,' he breathed in her ear. 'But I will speak with you this night, lady. Mark my words.'

Hester flung away from him immediately and headed straight for her seat. Of course, he wished to speak to her of their farce of a marriage. He wished to call an end to it, offer her terms for leaving, so that he could bring another woman into his bed. The whole horrible future laid itself out before her mind's eye: her ignominious departure, the arrival of his mistress...

Hester lowered herself automatically into her seat

at the head of the table. It was made up to look like one great, long table, but was, in fact, many trestle tables pushed together. Her place was, as ever, at the head of one end, and Guy's, thankfully, was at the other end, the table so long that he was almost at the other side of the courtyard, far, far away from her, so far that she might almost be able to enjoy this, her last harvest supper at Abbascombe, if only she could push from her mind the prospect of this talk he was determined to inflict upon her.

If only she had heard already from her cousin, then at least she could have forestalled his speech with one of her own. But why not pretend she had heard? Why not pretend it was all arranged, and leave with a little dignity if nothing else? She would rather leave with nowhere to go than wait for Guy to eject her from Abbascombe, reject her once again, the final, most painful rejection of all.

She seated herself at the same moment that Guy sat down at the opposite end. It was as if they were distant mirror reflections of each other across the width of the courtyard.

The feasting began. The courtyard filled with chatter, laughter, jokes. The girls were giggling loudly, flashing their eyes at the boys, flirting and flouncing for their attention. Many a match was made at harvest time, a time of happiness and fulfilment before the cold weather set in. Hester watched them, many not much younger than herself, but her heart was heavy with the thought of leaving and she hardly ate a thing.

When the feasting reached a close, Guy rose to speak. It was his first speech as lord of the manor. In recent years, the task had fallen to Hester. She froze at the sound of his voice. He praised the villagers for their hard work and for the success of the harvest.

Then he continued. 'I am sure you would also wish me to thank the lady Hester.' Hester jumped at the mention of her name.

'Aye, aye,' rang out from the diners. They began to clap and cheer and a sea of faces turned to look at her. Hester felt her heart swell with their affection. They cared for her, even if he did not. The pain of leaving them was too great. She managed to smile her grateful thanks, but her heart felt as though it had finally cracked in two.

As the cheers died down, Guy continued, 'I must thank her not only on your behalf. I must thank her for myself too, for the hard work, dedication and love which she has lavished on Abbascombe, for continuing to care for the demesne when those whose job it should have been were far away.' He turned a self-deprecating smile in her direction. Hester could not meet his eyes. Instead she sat paralysed by his words. 'Now that I am back I hope to ease the burden of care which has fallen on her capable shoulders, but I must ask you all to bear with me, for a soldier's ways are not those of a farmer and I must learn anew'.

'And lastly I wish to congratulate William and Gwen, who have told me today that they intend to be wed by Michaelmas. I am very happy for them and wish them every joy.' Another cheer went up, Gwen giggled and William beamed with delight.

All eyes turned on the happy couple, except Guy's. He was watching Hester, watching her with close attention, mapping every flicker of emotion which passed across her face. And all he saw was delight.

Yes, he was sure of it. There was nothing in her face but the pleasure of seeing a friend happy. Hugo Lacave had lied after all. He realised now that only his stupid jealousy had prevented him from seeing it before.

The beakers were raised to William and Gwen, to Hester and to Guy. Then the musicians left the table, picked up their instruments, and began to play. The villagers followed their example, standing up and moving away from the tables, but no one could begin to dance before the lord and lady had taken the floor.

Hester knew it was so. She knew that Guy must ask her to dance, that it would be too shocking to everyone if he didn't. Now that Abbascombe had both a lord and lady once again, there was only one way that the merriment could begin: with the pair of them dancing together. She could see him scanning the crowd for her face, then his eyes found her and he was moving towards her.

She saw his approach. Suddenly all the noise and movement around her seemed to fade away, so that she was aware of nothing but him. The crowd parted to let him through. Must she dance with him? She hardly knew what she would do. Could she bear to feel his touch on her skin, his body pressing against hers, to smell his warm, manly scent, to look up into his eyes, all these things she had experienced the last time she had danced with him at Judith's wedding on the village green? How could she submit to such torture, the torture of being in his arms for all to see, when she knew that she was the last person in the world he wished to hold, when she knew that the very sight of her must be abhorrent to him?

There was only one thing to do. She would reject his hand, she must. How could she endure the closeness of him, knowing as she did, that he could never be hers, that she was to leave him, to cast herself into exile, rather than remain here, an unwanted, tiresome burden in his home? She screwed up her courage as he reached her. He halted before her, his hand extended in invitation.

'My lady, I believe it is customary,' he was saying, 'for the lord and lady to open the dancing.'

She hesitated, forming the words in her throat, the words which she would fling in his face. He was not the only one who could reject.

As she summoned the searing words, the night sky above her was suddenly wrenched in two, split asunder by a bolt of lightning. The night was alight all around them for an instant. A tremendous clap of thunder followed, so loud the very earth seemed to shake. Immediately everyone was dashing for cover, as the great, heavy drops of rain began exploding all around them. Everyone was running, helter skelter, into the house.

Hester's one thought was not for safety or for shelter from the rain, but just to get as far as possible away from Guy, to find some corner where she would not be discovered. After this long day of torment, she wanted only to escape him, and to hide her pain from his dark, cruel eyes.

She pushed her way against the crowd as they headed for the great hall of the house to continue the dancing there. She could hear the musicians striking up inside, undeterred. The villagers were determined to have their fun and dancing, storm or no storm. The hall would not do for her, though. Let them all go there. Hester needed quiet solitary darkness, to be alone with her sadness.

She fought her way through the pounding rain to the door of the barn and lifted the latch. Inside, as she had expected, it was dim and silent. No one else was there. She closed the door behind her and stood dripping on the corn-strewn floor. The rain had been so heavy that she was wet through, her hair plastered against her head, even her eyelashes heavy with moisture. She licked her lips and tasted the sweet rain. She smiled to herself. She had been right to hurry the reapers, to bring in the last of the corn today. Another day and it would have been ruined. At least she had ensured that Abbascombe would have bread to eat through the winter when she would be gone.

She heard the latch of the door lift with a click behind her. She froze in the darkness, hoping that whoever it was would go away without noticing her. She heard the door close again and waited hopefully, but then she heard steps advancing towards her. She wheeled around. It was him.

'Did you think I wouldn't find you?' he whispered, his voice soft and deep.

'I hoped,' Hester replied cuttingly.

'Oh, Hester,' he said, grasping her shoulders. 'Do you hate me?'

She flinched under his gaze, unable to meet his eyes in spite of the gloom.

'Yes,' she replied simply. 'Yes, I hate you.'

'Do you really?' he asked, turning her head towards him, forcing her to face him. 'Then why did you nurse me? Why did you care for me through the fever?'

She shrugged, unable to speak, the sob filling her throat again.

'I thought it was a dream. It was only today that I found out from William that you really had been there. I thought I had dreamed of you watching over me like an angel. I can't tell you how disappointed I was to wake and find only Maud in the room.'

'Disappointed?' Hester echoed, a tiny spark lighting in her heart.

'Yes, of course. I dreamed that you had spoken to me as I lay ill. I dreamed that you had said...' he paused '...had said the words I longed to hear from you.'

'What were they?' she asked, her heart beating wildly.

'I dreamed that you asked me to fight for survival, that you told me you wished me to live, that you told me...that you loved me.'

Hester shuddered at the words. Here she was in his arms again, melting again at his touch and at his voice. How could she have told herself that she hated him, when all the while her love for him had never eased?

'Was it a dream, Hester?' he demanded, his hold tightening on her arms as the tension of her silence tormented him. 'Tell me the truth. Did I dream that you said those things?'

'No,' she whispered, the word slipping from her lips so quietly she was hardly sure whether she had said it aloud or not.

'What?' he demanded again, hardly able to believe his ears. 'I didn't dream it? Was it true?'

'Yes,' Hester admitted, lifting her eyes to his. Another bolt of lightning illuminated the barn for an instant, its light bursting through the cracks in the wooden walls. Their faces shone out of the darkness for a moment, as his lips closed on hers, claiming her in a delicious kiss…

But this time she would not submit, she would not allow him to torture her once more. She struggled free, pulling herself from his grasp.

'Let go of me. I may have said those things then, but that doesn't mean I love you now,' she lied.

He looked back at her in surprise.

'And don't pretend you want me,' she continued, her long pent-up words as ferocious as the storm overhead. 'I know the truth. I know you can't bear the sight of me. I know I was forced upon you. You only married me for the sake of my money.' Guy opened his mouth to protest, but she refused to stop. 'Because your father needed the money for the estate. And now you think you're stuck with me. Well, you're not. I'm leaving. I've made arrangements and I shall leave at first light tomorrow.'

'Arrangements? What do you mean?' he demanded, grasping her tightly as a clap of thunder shook the walls around them.

'I'm returning to Thurston, to my cousin. He wants me to go and live there,' she lied, holding her head high. 'So you're free to bring whomever you like to Abbascombe. You can stop skulking around and just install her in the house. Don't imagine that I care what you do.'

'Install whom? What are you talking about?'

'Don't pretend. I can't bear it. I don't know whether it's still Fatima, or whether you've found someone new. Whomever it is, you are free to choose for yourself.'

'Fatima,' he echoed. 'What do you know of Fatima?'

'All that I need to. I know that she is the woman of your choice, unlike me.'

Hester paused, but there was no response from Guy. Her heart pounded through his silence. The rain tumbling on to the roof echoed its frantic beating. She looked at him in the dark of the barn. What was the matter with him? His shoulders seemed to be shaking. Then she realised: he was laughing.

'I had thought your humiliation of me could go no further, sir,' she wrung out the words. 'But I was wrong, for now you mock my pain with laughter.'

She turned away from him, ready to rush out into the storm to escape him, but he caught at her hand.

'Yes, my lady, I laugh. I cannot help myself. But if you knew why…' He breathed, trying to still his laughter. 'I cannot imagine why you believe Fatima to have been my mistress.'

'From your own lips. You repeated her name over and over in your delirium. It was obvious that you loved her,' Hester told him, and speaking those words felt like the final defeat.

'Aye, I loved her, but not as you imagine. Fatima was an old woman. She cared for me when I had nowhere else to go. She was like a second mother to me.'

Hester stared at him, stunned by his words. 'She is not your mistress? You have not brought her here?'

'No.'

'Then whom have you installed at Compton?'

'No one.'

'But you ride out early every day, you must be visiting someone.'

Guy shook his head. 'I knew you didn't want to see me. You wouldn't even dine with me. I decided to stay out of your way. Abbascombe seemed so much more yours than mine. But, Hester, if there is any chance that you might be able to care for me, please stay in Abbascombe and allow me to woo you as I should have done years ago,' he whispered, as he encircled her with his arms. 'I thought you could never care for me because of the way our marriage was forced upon you.'

His lips fell on hers in a kiss so sweet she could feel all the blame and harshness melting from her heart. But then she remembered the night when he had left her in her chamber. She pulled back from his embrace.

'Then why did you leave me after Judith's wedding?' she demanded.

'I couldn't stay… I…I was so ashamed of myself for trying to bed you. I kept filling and refilling your goblet, hoping that you would allow me into your bed, I desired you so much. But then, as I carried you to bed, I knew that you had drunk too much. I feared you would not have accepted me if you had been sober, and I remembered what I had said to you on our wedding day, how I had promised that I would never force you to be my wife.'

'When you rejected me and sent me back to my dolls,' Hester replied bitterly.

'Is that what you believed? That I had rejected *you*? Then I am more sorry than I can ever tell you. I never intended my words to carry that meaning. You were so young, so tiny, grieving for your parents. I was disgusted by the way my father was using you for your fortune. I thought the last thing you needed was a husband. I truly believed I was acting for the best, though now I wish with all my heart that I had stayed with you.'

Suddenly Hester saw that scene again, saw it from his point of view and recognised the honesty in his words.

'And then on the night of Judith's wedding, that promise I had made returned to haunt me. I longed for you, but I feared wretchedly that you were allowing me into your bed only through a sense of duty and because I had plied you with wine. I hated myself for taking advantage of you. And I kept thinking of you...I kept thinking that the man you would have chosen to be with was—'

'William?'

His body tensed at the name. 'Is it true then, after all? I would not blame you if it were.'

'It is not true,' Hester assured him. 'You should not listen to the lies of Hugo Lacave.'

'How do you know he told me?'

'I know about the duel too, but I cannot tell you how. I must ask permission from my source first,' she replied.

Guy sighed. 'Then at least tell me one thing. If you

were free and if I asked you to marry me, would there be any chance that you would accept?'

'You only ask me this because we are already tied.'

'No. No, I don't. Hester,' he murmured, wrapping his strong arms around her once again. 'If I had the choice of every woman in Christendom—or in the East—I would not desire a single one of them but you. I returned home to find the woman of my dreams already living in my house. But she hated me. She thought I was the very devil. Do you still think me so?'

Hester shook her head slowly.

'And would you ever have married me if you had had the choice?'

'You must ask me to discover that.'

'Lady Hester, will you be my wife?'

Hester's hesitation hung in the air between them, as Guy's tortured heart pounded in anticipation of her reply.

'Yes.' Hester breathed at last. 'Yes, I will.'

With a cry of delight, he swept her up into his arms. 'Then let us be happy together at last,' he whispered as his lips met hers. 'I wasted ten years when I could have been with you. Let us not waste another moment.' She felt his warmth and his strength through her rain-drenched clothes, and she felt his love too. At last she was sure that he loved her.

Outside, the storm was raging through the night, but here in the barn she was basking in the warmth of his love. He laid her gently on the bed of corn, and as his body touched hers, she murmured, 'My husband.'

*   *   *   *   *

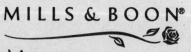

MILLS & BOON®

Makes any time special™

Mills & Boon publish 29 new titles every month. Select from...

Modern Romance™   Tender Romance™

Sensual Romance™

Medical Romance™   Historical Romance™

MAT2

2 FREE
books and a surprise gift!

We would like to take this opportunity to thank you for reading this Mills & Boon® book by offering you the chance to take TWO more specially selected titles from the Historical Romance™ series absolutely FREE! We're also making this offer to introduce you to the benefits of the Reader Service™—

- ★ FREE home delivery
- ★ FREE gifts and competitions
- ★ FREE monthly Newsletter
- ★ Exclusive Reader Service discounts
- ★ Books available before they're in the shops

Accepting these FREE books and gift places you under no obligation to buy, you may cancel at any time, even after receiving your free shipment. Simply complete your details below and return the entire page to the address below. *You don't even need a stamp!*

YES! Please send me 2 free Historical Romance books and a surprise gift. I understand that unless you hear from me, I will receive 4 superb new titles every month for just £2.99 each, postage and packing free. I am under no obligation to purchase any books and may cancel my subscription at any time. The free books and gift will be mine to keep in any case.

H0ZEA

Ms/Mrs/Miss/Mr ....Initials.....................................
BLOCK CAPITALS PLEASE

Surname ....

Address ....

....

....Postcode..................................

Send this whole page to:
UK: FREEPOST CN81, Croydon, CR9 3WZ
EIRE: PO Box 4546, Kilcock, County Kildare (stamp required)